# MOTHER'S NOT DEAD

*DCI Greg Allison Crime Thriller Book 7*

# MOTHER'S NOT DEAD

*DCI Greg Allison Crime Thriller Book 7*

BY

# ELIZABETH REVILL

# DEDICATION

For my good friend, Hayley Raistrick-Episkopos. There is no one kinder, supportive or more generous than her.

# 1

THE AFTERNOON SUN FILTERED THROUGH the kitchen window, bathing the room in golden nuggets of light. The air inside was surprisingly cool for such a warm day. Paul watched Holly as she washed dishes in the sink and wondered why she wasn't putting them in the dishwasher? He knew Holly hated all types of housework, yet lately she had been happy to scrub the front door step, polish the brass letterbox, dust and clean. They were jobs they had always shared but now she was insistent that she would do it best. This was a complete change from her reluctance to run around with the duster or push their discussions on whether they could afford getting a cleaner. And, she was singing a hymn.

Paul was more than puzzled, he was worried. These fits of cleaning were not only unusual, but they weren't constant. Her usual apathetic desire for domesticity would resurface, and she would announce that she had surprised herself and didn't know what had got into her.

She had also become incredibly amorous and demanding sexually in the bedroom and although he enjoyed this new found wildness between the sheets. It just wasn't Holly. Paul made up his mind. At the first opportunity he would speak to the chief.

Holly finished her rendition of 'He who would valiant be' and wiped her hands down her apron. That was another thing. Holly never wore an apron. She spun around from the sink and caught Paul's eye as he observed her. She smiled beguilingly. "Don't tell me, you want to go to bed?" and she giggled girlishly.

"No, no," he said just too quickly.

Holly frowned and pouted, "Why not?"

"I still have to finish the revised plans for the Mall. I've promised the developer he will have them by tomorrow. And … we need to eat!"

"Hmm, remember I can make something from nothing. Surely you can just spare an hour?" she wheedled.

Holly walked over to him seductively and traced her fingers through his golden chest hair, revealed through his open-necked shirt and giggling deliciously, she began to undo his shirt buttons.

Paul stopped her with his hands and removed them. He tried not to upset her. "Holly, it's important. Much as I'd love to take the rest of the afternoon off and spend it with you, I have to work. We have bills to pay."

"Pooh! You're just being a spoilsport." She sighed heavily and said, "All right. We'll pick this up later, won't we?" She flounced off into the sitting room, singing 'Rock of Ages', leaving Paul staring after her.


Meredith Probert sat in the dark at her bedroom window with a cup of decaffeinated coffee and two chocolate digestives. She dunked a biscuit into her drink and pulled it out before it disintegrated, and she made an appreciative sound at its sumptuous taste.

The streetlamp outside lit the road at the bottom of the drive and the two houses opposite. Meredith enjoyed looking out into the dark, through the gap in her net curtains. She would see, the feisty ginger Tom, from next door, prowling around his territory and chasing away any strange cats from his domain.

Old Mr Butterworth was at his window again. This time he had a feather duster and was swatting at something in the window. He didn't have net curtains. It amused her to watch the old man. He never disappointed, whether he was dancing to some memory of a time gone by or whether he would be practising a trick from his collection. Mr Butterworth used to be a magician. Before that he had been in the circus as a stunt rider of motorcycles and graduated to the Wall of Death and travelled with the fair. After a brush with real death he perfected his skills in magic, performing at children's parties, end of the pier, and in old people's homes. He made a good career out of it, too, by all accounts. Since he'd retired, Meredith had even had him across for some of her MacMillan coffee mornings and she had to admit he had been pretty good. He had a fine head of hair for a man his age. He'd not lost any of his dexterity or sleight of hand, but sadly of late he was becoming forgetful. It certainly put a stop to his entertaining as he would sometimes forget how a trick was supposed to go. People forgave him that. It added to his charm and character, made it a bit of a comedy show. But, Meredith wouldn't put him through the embarrassment, so she stopped asking him to perform. Instead, he would attend and help her lay out her front room with seating, occasional tables and the coffee and teacups.

Meredith sighed and dunked her second biscuit into her drink. On this occasion she didn't remove it in time and the whole thing collapsed into her coffee because she was mesmerised and stunned by what she could see. She rose and lay her cup down on the table and opened her nets a little bit more and studied what was happening in Mr Butterworth's house.

Across the road, a man and woman had entered her neighbour's bedroom. It was no one she recognised. The woman was short, about five foot two, slim with a mass of chocolate brown curly hair that hung down like a King Charles spaniel and she wore dark heavy framed spectacles. The man was slightly taller, with a good head of wavy mousey grey coloured hair. He appeared to be wearing glasses, which had either thin wire frames or no noticeable frames at all. Meredith couldn't see their features clearly but there seemed to be some sort of argument going on. Mr Butterworth was standing there in his pyjamas and dressing gown. The woman was waving her hands about gesticulating wildly and then the man shoved Mr Butterworth hard. Mr Butterworth fell to the ground and the man appeared to throw himself on top of him. Meredith couldn't see anything else.

The woman was pacing up and down, going red in the face and seemed to be shouting. A few minutes later, the man stood up. He was holding something in his hand. Of Mr Butterworth there was no sign. Meredith bit her lip anxiously. She let the net fall back, but there was still a sizeable gap in her curtains that she could look through. The man and woman seemed to be searching for something. Meredith knew something was very wrong and she needed to call the police. Meredith scrambled to her feet, grabbed the phone by her bed and dialled.


Martyn Kelland sat outside a busy taverna on the cliffs, which had spectacular views overlooking the Aegean sea. The cloudless cerulean sky held the flaming orb of the sun whose heat embraced the chair where he sat. He looked at his watch, again. Paulson was late. Kelland had taken a gamble coming here and leaving the relative safety of the Dominican Republic. His eyes swept through the people sitting outside the taverna and he narrowed his gaze.

There was a man in a straw hat and sunglasses wearing shorts and the typical garb of a holidaymaker but there was just something about him. Maybe it was his military bearing? He sat upright, every muscle seemed poised and ready for action. He looked alert, intense and was clearly watching for someone. Was it for him, or was he just being paranoid?

Martyn continued to observe him and then visibly relaxed as a young woman came and joined the man at his table. He reprimanded himself; he was seeing coppers and bogey men everywhere. The couple appeared to scour the menu and called a waiter across.

Another powerful looking man entered the bar and scanned the restaurant. He spotted Kelland and his eyes locked on Kelland, who visibly shivered. The man tipped his hat to him and then sat to peruse the specials' board.

'*Where was Paulson?*'

A motorcycle thrummed towards the taverna and pulled up outside. The restaurant owner's dog, a big brindle coloured mutt, padded across and sniffed the legs of the motorcyclist. The rider ignored the friendly dog and crossed to Kelland, He turned the chair around and straddled it before removing his helmet. The man had short, cropped iron-grey hair. Kelland heaved a sigh of relief.

"You're late!"

"Couldn't be helped. I got caught up behind a funeral procession. No room to overtake and it was moving slowly."

Kelland snorted. "Never mind. You're here now."

"What is it, boss?"

"My inside man tells me we are both on the most wanted list. Alerts have been put out for me and you, internationally."

"There's nothing we can do about that."

"But, I intend to try," said Kelland grimly.

"How?"

"We need to fit someone else up with the blame."

"That won't be easy. Remember I ran from a lorry containing a consignment of women. I can hardly plead innocent to that if I am caught and charged."

"You won't be charged. You'll be dead."

"What?"

"We find someone who resembles you in height and stature. Make sure the body is damaged enough not to reveal fingerprints or dental records. To all intents and purposes, you'll be dead. We've done it before we can do it again."

"I have questions about that. The same M.O. will arouse suspicion. It's too dangerous."

"We can find another way… For the sake of argument let's say we can do it without alerting scrutiny from the authorities. No dismemberment, burn off fingerprints, lose the teeth, make sure the face is unrecognisable."

Paulson paused and then murmured thoughtfully, "Okay. And then?"

"We get you a new identity. Shouldn't be too difficult and if the guy we off, closely resembles you, you can adopt his."

Paulson whistled through his teeth. "That'll take some doing. Where are we going to find my doppelganger?"

"I think I may have found him," said Kelland with a smirk.

"Where?"

"Here, in Rhodes. It's what gave me the idea."

"I'm listening."

"There's one more thing. If I'm to get my life back, like I said, we need someone else to blame, to take the rap for my misdeeds."

"And if Marcus Paulson is dead, he'd be the perfect patsy," mused Marcus.

"Got it in one."

"You're forgetting one thing…"

"What's that?"

"Bernie Carter and Dr Charles."

"They won't talk. They know what's good for them. I've heard they have not squeaked a word and won't."

"Then, it could work?"

"It could. But, we have a problem with Kira," said Kelland with a hint of wistfulness in his voice.

"Kira? She doesn't know anything."

"That's what I thought. My inside man tells me different. She has implicated me and you. She needs to go. No witness, no case. Comprendez?"

"And Nesbitt?"

"Gone to ground. There's a warrant out for his arrest, too. But he seems to have disappeared. No worries about him at the present."

"Then you had better tell me where my twin is," said Paulson with a laugh. "Would be good to meet him."


Meredith waited anxiously for the arrival of the police. It was sometime later, when a patrol car pulled up and two uniformed coppers got out of the vehicle, marched up Mr Butterworth's drive and hammered on his door. There was no answer. One of them went around the back and must have found a way in as she saw one officer open the front door to admit the other.

Meredith continued to watch as an ambulance drew up and she saw Mr Butterworth being stretchered out into the ambulance. The two policemen crossed the road and walked up the drive to her house and rang the bell. She hurried down to meet them.


Allison bit into his third Mars Bar of the day. He was finding it tough to limit himself, but he was succeeding… just. The sun streamed in through the window and spilled across the floor. Allison rose and walked to the window and stared out into the street busy with traffic. He took another chunk out of his chocolate treat when there was a knock on the door. Determined not to spoil his enjoyment, he carefully wrapped up the other half of his bar and put it in his drawer. He would savour the remains later.

"Come in," he called, chewing vigorously as the toffee and nougat seemed to dissolve and stick over his teeth.

"Sorry to disturb you, but I really need to speak to you," said Paul. "It's about Holly."

Allison gestured him to sit, "What is it?" But Allison seemed almost to have expected him.

"You'll think I'm insane." Paul hesitated. "Holly is not like Holly. Well, she is some of the time but at others… She acts totally out of character. How can I explain it?"

"I suggest in the words of Lewis Carroll, that you begin at the beginning and go on till you come to the end; then stop."

Paul's expression was strained and worried, "Good advice. Alice in Wonderland, isn't it?"

Allison nodded. "The King to the white rabbit as I recall."

He listened carefully as Paul began to recount events as he had experienced and saw them. "She's like a different person, Chief. All this house-proud stuff is so unlike her. Not only that, these Bible sayings… it's doing my head in."

Allison nodded again, "It doesn't stop there, does it?"

Paul shook his head, "No… in the bedroom…" He swallowed hard. "It's so unlike her. Her appetite is quite voracious. Don't get me wrong. I enjoy all the attention but… it's just not her. It's quite bizarre."

Allison said nothing but studied his fingers, still somewhat sticky with chocolate. He licked his fingertips and switched on the intercom, "Maddie? Two teas please and hold all my calls."

"Sir."

Paul studied Allison's face, "You don't seem surprised? You're not freaked out by this? Going to tell me I'm off my head?"

"No. I'm not."

"Why?"

"Because I've seen something, too."

Paul raised his eyebrows. "I'm listening."

Allison began to recount what he had seen in his office. How her eyes had rolled back in her head, and she spoke in a different voice using Biblical terms before passing out. By the time he'd finished Paul was speechless. "I wanted to tell you, Paul. I've only told my wife, Mary. I haven't said anything to anyone else. They would think I was mad. How can it be explained?"

Paul pondered a moment. "I've been thinking back …"

"Yes?"

"We've had a few signs of something otherworldly going on from years ago."

"Such as?"

"It all sounds so silly now."

"I assure you I won't think it silly, not at all. Remember, I didn't believe in psychics, psychometry or anything. Thought it was all a load of rubbish. It was Holly that convinced me. She gets too many things right, things she couldn't possibly know."

There was another tentative pause before Paul spoke again. Allison didn't urge him on or question him. He just waited until Paul was ready to speak. "I've always been used to a certain weirdness, cold spots, her telling me things before they happened but when we visited my dad… There were a number of odd instances. Cold breezes coming from nowhere and lifting the ends of the drapes. Worst of all was when I found her stuck fast against the wall quite high up, with her arms outstretched as if she was being crucified and even more terrifying, her palms were bleeding."

Allison's usually impassive expression, whenever he was told anything disturbing, changed dramatically to one of shock. "I didn't know this."

"No, we just rang to tell you Grace Clifton was in our house. We didn't tell you all the details. No one would have believed us anyway. I've only ever seen things like this on film in The Exorcist or The Omen and such-like. And there's more."

"What, more?"

"We didn't tell you everything but when Holly had a psychic showdown with Grace Clifton, dreadful things happened, objects moving on their own.

Doors slammed shut that I couldn't open…" Paul trailed off as he remembered the terrifying events from the past.

Allison digested what Paul had to say before he spoke, "So, what do you think?"

"It sounds ridiculous, but I believe Grace Clifton's spirit has come back from the grave and somehow attached herself to Holly. The point is, how do we get rid of her?"

Allison sighed. "First thing, I feel we should call in Colin. Get his take on it and his advice."

Paul nodded sagely. "I'll fix it. Do you want to be there?"

"If Holly agrees. Do you think she will?"

Paul hesitated. "I don't know. I really don't know."

As they spoke there was a rush of wind through the open window that ruffled the papers on Allison's desk. Paul and Allison just looked at each other.

# 2

ANGUS MACKAY HAD RECENTLY TRANSFERRED from the London Met. He had a big personality, Allison thought. Too big. It seemed the man in his thirties was trying either to better everyone else or ingratiate himself with those higher up the ladder. Allison took a dislike to him but no one else in the squad room seemed to mind except for Gurdip, who felt that the Scot had an intolerance to people of colour and said so to Ronnie in private.

"Give him a chance, Gurdip," Ronnie advised. "He's been chucked in at the deep end, doesn't know anyone and is trying to find his feet. I'm sure it's not personal."

"He's a grade above us and there is just something about him. All this trying to impress. Mark my words, we will all get sick of it. And why leave the Met to come to Brum? It doesn't make sense."

Ronnie shrugged, "Maybe. But at least give him the benefit of the doubt."

Mackay was around five ten and quite muscular. He had dark brown hair and blue eyes. Above his top lip was a small scar that was straight and leaned towards his right nostril. He had another one above his left eyebrow.

Gurdip stood back from the crowd in the squad room and watched as Mackay pandered to his new mates, when Pooley asked how he got his scar above his lip.

"There was a nasty scene in a bar in Balham. I got bottled by some drunken black yob. Fortunately, he only caught me above my lip. If I'd copped the whole thing my face would have been mincemeat."

There were murmurs of sympathy. Spurred on by this he continued to boast. "It was more than a bar room brawl. We had gone in to arrest a known drug dealer who'd sold some bad smack, cut with rat poison. We'd had several deaths. One victim was just thirteen. A real pretty lass. I swore we'd get him. And we did."

Again, there were grunts of approval.

Allison poked his head around the squad room door. "Have you lot got nothing better to do than stand there jawing? Get back to work. Gurdip, Ronnie!"

They stood to attention. "Sir?"

"In here with me, now."

The young detectives left the others and hurried to Allison's office, where they were invited to sit.

"This has just come in. I want you two, to follow it up. An old gent, Stanley Butterworth, 86, was found unconscious in his bedroom suffering a bad head wound. His house had been ransacked. Whether it was a burglary gone wrong or something else, we don't know. The old boy is in hospital. He hasn't come round yet. Firstly, get across to Mrs Meredith Probert, who lives opposite, him at number 55. Get her statement. She saw something and reported it to the police. By the time we got there the perpetrators had vanished." He tossed Ronnie a file. "This is what we have so far. It's not much but I'm sure you will be able to glean more when you question Mrs Probert and then get across to the hospital and wait for him to wake up. See what he can tell you."

Ronnie and Gurdip stood up and were on the point of leaving when Allison stopped them. "Wait! The new man, Mackay. What do you make of him?"

Gurdip hesitated and Ronnie jumped in. "Not formed any opinion yet, sir. Too soon to tell. He seems okay."

Allison looked at Gurdip. "Gurdip?"

"I don't know. As Ronnie says, too soon to tell, yet."

"Why do I get the feeling you don't like him? You don't join in with the others."

"Reserving my opinion, sir."

"Hmm. Okay, off you go."

Ronnie and Gurdip left Allison's office and began to browse through the file. Ronnie found the address and they went to get a car.

Allison checked his watch. He retrieved his hat and coat from the back of his door and left his office, calling to Maddie as he passed. "Take all messages and get Mark to hold the fort until I get back. I'm not to be disturbed unless it's a matter of life and death." Maddie looked at him curiously but said nothing, just acknowledged him with a nod. So, with that he left the office, walked through the squad room, where his officers had returned to their desks and appeared to be working. He gave a grunt of satisfaction but as he entered the corridor a gale of laughter reached his ears. It sounded like Angus Mackay was entertaining everyone, again. Allison's chin jutted forward into his famous bulldog expression, and he thought he'd deal with that frivolity later. He left the station, grabbed his car and headed out towards Holly and Paul's house near Worcester. He knew Paul had persuaded Holly to let Allison sit in on the first session with her and he prayed that Colin would find some answers.

Thankfully, the good weather was still holding. Ronnie felt that they had been so lucky with all the glorious sunshine of late. It was a delight to get out from the station and outside. Ronnie and Gurdip had pushed through the busy traffic and finally arrived at Meredith Probert's house.. They decided to speak to her first before looking around Mr Butterworth's home. They rang the bell. The door was opened almost immediately.

Meredith was a small woman in her fifties with an efficient air. She was smartly dressed, and her hair was neatly combed up into a French pleat. She had particularly bright eyes, which swept up and down them both as if assessing them. They showed her their warrant cards. A second or two later, she graciously invited them inside and asked if they would prefer tea or coffee. Ronnie assented that a cup of tea would be most welcome, and Meredith ushered them into her sitting room, gesturing they sit, before scurrying away to her kitchen.

Ronnie and Gurdip looked around the clean and tidy room with the cushions on the seats plumped up, the coffee table laid out with place mats and coasters. Pictures on the walls were of seascapes and the mint walls gave a feeling of tranquillity. Ronnie stood up and walked to the big bay window and stared at the house belonging to Stan Butterworth. "Can't see much of the house opposite, from here. The downstairs' windows are blocked by the hedge and that monkey puzzle tree."

"Lethal vegetation that," murmured Gurdip. "Downright dangerous. A person could get seriously injured on one of those. So prickly."

"Yes, but a great deterrent for burglars," said Ronnie.

"Think I'd prefer a bank of roses or holly bushes. Not so damaging but thorny enough to put someone off."

"Well, it didn't put Mr Butterworth's visitors off."

"No. Had to be someone he knew. Otherwise why would he let them in?"

"Maybe he didn't."

At that moment, Meredith returned with the tea, napkins and a plate of chocolate Hob Nobs and custard creams. She laid the tea cups out and began to pour as per the young men's instructions. Once they were settled, Ronnie began to ask her some questions.

"I note you can't see too much of your neighbour's house from here."

Meredith blushed. "No, I don't watch from here. I sit upstairs. You can see a lot from there."

"We'd like to take a look after our tea, if that's all right?"

"But, of course. How is Mr Butterworth?"

"He hasn't regained consciousness, yet. But when he does, we'll let you know. Can you tell us in your own words, what you saw?"

"I said it all before. It's in my statement."

"Yes, but we'd like to hear it again, please. If you don't mind?"

Meredith launched into the events of that night and what she saw. "Of course, I rang the police straight away. I knew something was very wrong." She then detailed events as she had witnessed them up to when the police arrived.

"You say you have never seen these people before?"

"No, never. He doesn't have much family. The few he does have are scattered; a brother in London, a sister in Chichester, who has two daughters, someone in America and a nephew and niece I'm not sure where."

"We will have to speak to them. Has anyone informed them?"

Meredith shrugged. "I wouldn't have a clue how to get in touch." She thought for a moment. "He kept an address book; their names will be in there. I'm sorry I can't be of more help. He's a dear old boy."

"Do you know their actual names?" pressed Ronnie.

"Um… His brother is Fred, and his sister is Sadie. Not sure about the nephew and niece but one of them should be able to help."

"Do you know where he kept this address book?"

Meredith closed her eyes as if trying to recall something, "It's either in the drawer of the telephone table or…" She screwed up her eyes again. "In one of the sideboard drawers… in the living room. Yes, top right-hand side."

"Thank you, Mrs Probert. If you happen to remember anything else, anything at all, please give us a call." Ronnie passed her a card and finished his tea. "Firstly, if we could see where you watched the events unfold."

"Of course, this way." Meredith led them up the stairs to her bedroom. "In here. I take the bedroom chair and sit by the window."

Ronnie and Gurdip crossed to the window and peered out. "You are right," said Gurdip. "It's a perfect view from here."

"I'll say," said Ronnie. "I'm not surprised you saw so much. Thank you. We'll be off now. They bade her goodbye. She smiled and tucked Ronnie's card into her pocket. "We'll see ourselves out. Thank you. And thanks for the tea."

Ronnie and Gurdip went downstairs and headed for the door. They were soon out on the street. They crossed the road to Stanley Butterworth's house, stepped under the yellow scene of crime tape, showed their cards to the policeman on duty and went into the house. From the hallway to the living room, it had been ransacked. Cushions ripped from seats, furniture overturned, drawers emptied onto the floor. It was much the same in the dining room and kitchen, and upstairs in Mr Butterworth's bedroom. The two spare bedrooms hadn't been touched, probably when the police sirens had been heard and interrupted the intruders.

Gurdip went back downstairs to the hall and the broken telephone stand. He picked up the local directories from the floor and hunted around for an address book. It wasn't there. He moved into the living room and searched through the debris on the floor and eventually found a brown leather covered address book amidst, old bills and invoices. He picked it up and flicked through it. This had to be it. He found an entry for Fred Butterworth and Sadie Baker.

He shouted up the stairs to Ronnie, "Found it! I think."

Ronnie came running down and took a look at the book. "Yes, you're right. This has to be it. One or two more places to check before we go off to the hospital."

Gurdip looked quizzically, "Where?"

"Garage and garden shed. We've looked everywhere else."

"What are we looking for?"

"I don't know. Think we'll know when we see it."

Gurdip shrugged and they went into the kitchen and utility and through the door into the garage. Ronnie whistled long and low between his lips, "Wow! Look at this place."

The young men gazed around the garage with all the tools placed strategically in size and type on one wall. They were spotlessly clean and didn't look as if they had ever been used. There was a workbench and a metal tool station full of drawers, in which were nails and screws all sorted perfectly into size and type.

Ronnie ran to the back of the garage where there was something hidden under a dust sheet. He whipped it off to reveal two vintage Indian Scout motorcycles in immaculate condition. They each had a beautiful gold emblem of an Indian chief on their fuel tanks. "Whoa! Look at these."

Gurdip looked, "They're just motorcycles."

"Not just any old motorcycles."

"What's so special about them?"

"These little beauties are imported from America. They are the type used in Wall of Death side shows."

"What are you talking about?"

"Wall of Death."

"What's that?"

Ronnie rolled his eyes, "A twenty-foot-high cylindrical barrel, drum-like structure, where the riders get up to a fantastic speed and ride around the walls on the side. The centrifugal force is such they stay there and don't come off. They travelled with fairs and motorcycle stunt shows, performing all kinds of tricks. Fantastic. Bet they're worth a quid or two. Usually pre-1929. But, could be from 1928 to 1931. Wow." Ronnie stroked his hand reverently over the bike's aluminium frame, its gold handlebars encased in black rubber and the gold starter pedal.

"Bit fancy for a fairground stunt," murmured Gurdip.

"All part of the razzmatazz, I expect, to make it showbizzy and flash."

"How come you know so much about it?"

"I used to love it as a kid. My dad introduced me to it. I carried on that interest. When I could, I'd go to watch the Ken Fox Wall of Death thrill stunt shows. They've been going since the 1920s. Still going strong now. Tell you what, when I hear of a show coming around on tour, we'll all go. It's a fantastic spectacle."

Gurdip looked bemused. He'd never seen his friend so animated about anything like this before and nodded, "Sure thing. If it's that exciting, we'll all go. You, me, Siri and Ayesha."

Gurdip's phone pinged with a text. He quickly glanced at it. "It's the station. Mr Butterworth has come to. Cover that lot over and we'll go there now. Forget the shed for a minute."


Allison arrived at Paul and Holly's house and was welcomed in by Paul. "How is she?" asked Allison.

"Holly is Holly at the moment. Her usual self and she agreed for you to sit in on Colin's session with her. We are waiting for him now. I believe Marcie is coming as well."

"Full house then," grunted Allison as he stepped into the kitchen, where Holly was making a brew.

She turned her soulful dark eyes on Allison. "Hello, Chief. Come to see the mad woman exorcised?"

"Don't say that, Holly," admonished Paul.

"Well, it's true. I know that sometimes I am not myself and I can't remember, what I do and say in those instances. So, something must be wrong. Let's hope Colin can get to the bottom of it. Cuppa?"

"Please. It's been a bit of a drive and the traffic wasn't good."

"Coming up," said Holly with a smile.

Gurdip and Ronnie had arrived at the hospital and entered Mr Butterworth's room. The old boy was sitting propped up on a bank of pillows. A drip was in his arm, and he was wired to a heart monitor. He had a nasal canula delivering oxygen to both nostrils. The man's face was battered and bruised. He looked exhausted.

The staff nurse ordered them, "Don't tire him out. He's been through one heck of an ordeal."

"Don't worry. We won't. We just need to discover what he remembers," said Gurdip with a smile.

The nurse looked unconvinced but left them anyway. Stan Butterworth opened his eyes. "Here, who are you?" he said studying Gurdip's turban.

"DC Singh and DC Soper, sir."

"What do you want with me? I've done nothing."

"No, sir," said Gurdip quietly. "You were attacked, and your house ransacked. We are here to ask you what you remember."

"Yes, if you could tell us what happened that night. It will help us catch whoever is responsible."

"I don't know," he said plaintively. "Don't know why someone would ransack my house. I've got nothing of value except my memories in my photo albums. Nobody would want those except me."

"Can you tell us anything about the people that came into your house? Did you know them?"

"I don't remember anyone coming in my house," said Mr Butterworth looking bewildered. "Who told you I was attacked?"

"Your neighbour Mrs Probert."

"Who?"

"Meredith Probert. She saw the whole thing."

"Meredith?" A light dawned in his eye. "Meredith… What did she say?"

"That two people, a man and a woman came into your bedroom. There seemed to be some sort of argument and the man pushed you to the floor. She called the police and an ambulance, and you ended up in here," explained Ronnie.

"Don't know nothing about that," he muttered.

"It's likely you have a concussion," said Gurdip kindly. "Perhaps we should come back when you can remember something?"

"I hope to be up and about. I got a show to do."

"A show?" asked Ronnie.

"With the fair. We're off to Blackpool tomorrow. I need to pack."

"Blackpool?"

"Yes. Stunt riding on the Wall of Death. Say, they didn't take my bikes, did they?"

Gurdip and Ronnie exchanged a glance. "No. We saw your lovely Indian Scout motorbikes," said Ronnie enthusiastically. "Beautiful pieces."

"That they are. Quite unique. Thank God they've not been nicked."

"No, they are quite safe," reassured Ronnie. "Still covered by the dust sheet."

"There's no bikes like those two. Worth a fortune they are."

Ronnie smiled and added, "I'm sure they are. I know how rare they are… Well, Mr Butterworth, we'll get off and come back when you've fully recovered. If you do remember anything, please call us." Ronnie handed him a card with his name and the station's number. The two DCs left leaving Mr Butterworth who was now looking agitated.


Colin had relaxed Holly enough with deep breathing exercises that could lead to meditation or hypnosis. She had stretched out full-length on the couch. Her eyes were closed, and she was breathing evenly. Paul sat at her feet, Colin sat next to her head and Allison was in an easy chair a few feet away; he could see everyone and was watching the whole of the proceedings.

Colin began leading her through a list of instructions, imagining herself in a green field filled with wild flowers. Holly walked through it trailing her hands through the grass until she reached a wooden lodge and stepped onto the veranda. There was a door leading inside, which she opened. She went inside and described her surroundings before walking towards another door that was ajar. She opened it wide and saw stairs going down into a basement or cellar. She put her foot tentatively onto the first step and slowly descended, pausing every now and then to describe how she felt and what she saw. Throughout this process, she was calm, and her voice was even and controlled until she reached the very last step and Colin asked her to look down. It was then her voice changed to a thin nasal Brummy twang.

"Can you tell me what you are wearing on your feet?"

Holly's eyes began to move rapidly. "My slippers."

"Describe them."

"Brown check fabric with a brown fluffy pom-pom." She laughed when she said the word, 'Fluffy'.

"Anything else?"

"Little fawn woollen socks to help keep my feet warm. I hate cold feet."

Paul's mouth dropped open and Allison took a sharp intake of breath.

"What else are you wearing?" continued Colin warning the others with his eyes to keep quiet.

Holly frowned and her eyes beetled together. There had been a subtle change in her features. Her face seemed fuller, almost as if another was being subtly imprinted over her own. "My serge wool skirt, a fawn lambs-wool jumper and my wrap-a-round apron overall."

"Anything else?"

"Are you being saucy?" came the reedy tones and she chuckled. It was an unpleasant sound. "I am wearing my boned corset, pink knickers, and lisle stockings. My bra is white nylon. Is that enough detail for you?"

"What else?"

"My maroon pom-pom hat. I like pom-poms. I make them for the church along with my squares."

"Can you tell me who is with you?"

There was a crafty cackle that was as dry as parchment. "Now, why do you want to know that?"

"Just interested in who you enjoy being with. Where are you?"

"Why, I am in the vestry, of course."

"Can you describe it?"

Holly appeared to be looking around her. Her head was moving from side to side. "Purple cassocks hanging on the hooks all around the wood panelled walls; white surpluses, too. Wooden benches underneath the hooks. The floor is always cold; charcoal slate but Father Barrett has already placed a thick woollen rug on the floor."

"Father Barrett? Is that who you're with?"

"I'm waiting for him."

"Why?"

"He's going to cleanse me, fill me with rapture. But…"

"But?"

"But, that happened years ago. He wouldn't like me now. Oh, wait a minute." She shivered with excitement. "There is someone else… but not here, not now."

"Then where?"

She laughed, "I'll surprise you when you least expect it."

Holly's head lolled and her eyes rolled back in her head. She suddenly coughed, sat upright and looked around. "What? What's happening?" She looked dazed. "What's going on? What did I say?"

"You don't remember?"

"No."

"What do you recall?"

"I was imagining I was walking through a meadow enjoying the feel of tall grasses under my fingertips then onto a wooden veranda, into the structure, through a door and down some stairs… That's it."

"Nothing more?"

"No. What? Why are you looking at me like that?"

Colin looked at the others, "I've never seen anything like this before. I think we need specialist help."

# 3

KELLAND AND PAULSON HAD TRAVELLED to Faliraki from Rhodes Old Town. They had stopped off at a roadside bar and studios on the edge of the town. They settled themselves at an available table and ordered two beers. The waiter nodded and went to the counter.

"Not seen anyone yet," muttered Paulson looking around.

"Patience, my friend. Patience."

The waiter returned with two drinks and the food menu, which they studied as they waited. "I'm hungry," said Paulson. "Think I'll have the chicken souvlaki and some fries."

"Doesn't that come with rice?"

"Yes. But I fancy some chips, too."

"Fair enough," said Kelland as he continued to read through the menu.

Soon the waiter returned, and they gave their orders. Paulson continued to examine everyone in the taverna and the new arrivals. He was ever wary and on his guard. So far, he had seen no one to alarm him.

The warm sun beat down and Paulson was compelled to remove his motorcycle jacket; he was beginning to sweat. Paulson mopped his brow with his handkerchief and undid his shirt just as a pumped middle-aged, grey-haired man emerged from the kitchen with a tray of food.

"Over there. Look," hissed Kelland with a jerk of his head.

Paulson turned to look at the man. "You think?"

"Look again, same height, same build, same colour hair and it's tied back. His face is the same shape."

"That's about it. He looks nothing like me."

"Maybe not facially but pretty damn close with everything else."

Paulson scratched his chin, "You know it might just work. So, how do we go about this?"

Gurdip and Ronnie were sitting at their shared desk browsing through Mr Butterworth's address book. They made a note of his sister, Sadie Baker's phone number and his brother Fred Butterworth. They looked to see if there were any more entries with surnames of Butterworth and Baker.

Ronnie chirped brightly, "Any names that are just a first name. They may be a possibility, a close friend or relative."

Gurdip nodded, "Agreed. Think we ought to run the names through our database. See if any of them have a record."

"Good idea. Although, I can't see Stan Butterworth popping up."

"Maybe, maybe not. But, you never know. We've had trouble with fairground people before and if he worked with them, he might not be as squeaky clean as we think."

"Yes, you're right! Okay, we'll give it a go."

"Course I'm right," said Gurdip with a grin. That's why I'm a detective." And he wiggled his eyebrows at him.

"Okay, I'll make a start on the phone calls, and you can check the names out," said Ronnie.

"Deal." Gurdip got up from the desk and moved onto a free computer whilst Ronnie started on the calls.

Mary was all of a dither with delight. She couldn't wait to tell Greg as soon as he got in that Cally was coming home from London for a week and she had further news that she knew would thrill him to bits. She glanced at the clock. Would he be home at a reasonable time? If not, could she contain herself until she saw him? She thought not. But to her immense relief she heard the front door bang and rushed into the hall to greet him.

"Greg! Greg! Oh, I'm so glad you're home. I've heaps to tell you."

"For heaven's sake, Mary let me get in through the door..." He trailed off as he saw her hurt expression. "Sorry, I didn't mean to snap. Just been one of those days. I didn't mean to be grumpy."

Mary's face broke into a smile. "That's all right. I know you didn't mean it. If you've had a rough day then what I have to tell you will really lift your spirits. Come on into the kitchen. Sit yourself down and I'll get us both a drink. It's a special day."

Bemused Greg couldn't help but reproach himself for his gruff manner but seeing Mary so animated he just had to smile. He pulled back his bulldog jaw and grinned at Mary's effervescence; it reminded him of their younger days together when she used to sing with the band. He sighed, what memories he had.

Greg followed Mary into the kitchen and settled at the table as Mary opened a small bottle of Prosecco for herself and poured a glass of Bombay gin with Fever tree tonic for him.

"Must be something special," grunted Allison. "Come on, Mary don't keep me in suspense. What's the big news?"

"I have lots of it," she said mischievously. "Firstly, Cally is coming home for a week to talk wedding preparations, I expect. She's getting the train from Euston and I'm picking her up on Friday."

Greg smiled. "That will be lovely for you. It will keep you busy, shopping for outfits and all the other things that need planning. It will be lovely for me, too. We don't see enough of her now she's moved to London. Let's just hope she doesn't move even further away when she's married like the other two who we never see."

"That's just it, Greg. We will!"

"What?"

"That's the big surprise. Diana is coming from America and arriving on the Saturday."

"Diana?" The chief perked up. "We haven't seen her for five years."

"Too much of a career lass. She's across for a big wine convention in London but is coming a week early to stay and she's taking enough time off to come back afterwards for a further couple of weeks. Not sure yet, how long."

Greg was now beaming, "Diana, well, well, well." It seemed he was stuck for words. He was never stuck for words.

"And what's more, Rosemary and Andrew are coming across from Australia for a three-month visit. I don't know the details and I'm not sure when. Isn't it wonderful?"

Greg's jaw dropped. "Well, I'm blowed! What about the children? Are they coming, too? Where are we going to put them all?"

"No worries there. Rosemary says they are booking hotels as we speak and yes, they are bringing Amy and Luke with them. Isn't that good news?"

Greg was delighted, his daughter Rosemary, she was the eldest, had fallen in love with an Aussie when she did her gap year backpacking around Australia. They had married and set down roots there. Diana was head of a prestigious firm of wine makers in the Nappa Valley and travelled world-wide. He grabbed his drink and made a toast with Mary. "To the girls. And safe journeys to them all."

Mary's eyes were shining, and stray tears of joy escaped. Greg stood up and wrapped his arms around his wife and she sobbed with happiness into his shoulder.


Ronnie was stunned at the information Gurdip had discovered. It seemed Fred Butterworth was serving time for multiple robberies; in particular, a heist from an armoured van, from which the gold was never recovered. It seems that Stan had been implicated in one or two minor robberies but there was never enough evidence to convict him, and he had gone on with his life. Fred, the older brother, was, at present, in Belmarsh Prison south east London serving twenty-five years to life. Stan his younger brother had a clean record except for those rumours of his involvement in a couple of robberies.

Gurdip was now on the phone to the Governor of Belmarsh Prison requesting information on Fred Butterworth. This was promised to be emailed through. Gurdip was advised that Fred was suffering ill health and had stage four lung cancer. An appeal was in progress for his release on humanitarian grounds petitioned by Fred's son and daughter. Gurdip pounced on this and asked for additional details. Could they also have a record of Fred's visitors, names and addresses? The Governor agreed.

Gurdip rubbed his hands together. Now, they were getting somewhere. He moved back to his desk, where Ronnie was still on the phone. He looked up expectantly at Gurdip as he wound up his conversation. "Thank you, you have been most helpful. I appreciate it."

Gurdip sat on the edge of the desk, "Anything?"

"Sadie Baker, Stan's sister, visits Stan as often as she can. Apparently, his Alzheimer's is progressing, and she hates to see him deteriorate like that. Also, she usually goes to Belmarsh once a month to see Fred. She's given me the lowdown on other family members."

"And?"

"Stan doesn't have any children and his wife passed away a couple of years ago. He has his nephew and niece on his brother's side and two nieces, which are her daughters. There's some maiden aunt in USA who is in a care home in Vermont. There isn't anyone else. They are a very small family."

"That makes it easier. Fewer people to interview. Think we can cross the old aunt off the list."

"Agreed. Mrs Baker gave me her address and those of her daughters'. She said he had a close circle of friends that has got smaller. There's been a few deaths among his peers, and some have dropped off because of his illness. She's promised to get me a list. So, what now?"

"We'll wait for the stuff to come through from Belmarsh and do the footwork."

"Good old fashioned police work."

"If you say so."

"So, what about you and Siri?"

Ronnie looked surprised at the sudden change of subject, but said seriously, "Gurdip, I am not rushing things out of respect for your family, but I can tell you. She is the best thing that has ever happened to me… like you, brother."

Gurdip smiled and nodded sagely. "Good. It is good. Now, I'll check my emails and see what's come back. Perhaps we can schedule a visit to Belmarsh ourselves?"

"Don't see why not. Can't do any harm. I'll organise it through official channels of course."

"And we may just get a bit of time in London," said Gurdip with a wink."

Kelland and Paulson finished their meals and gazed out at the beautiful vista and the sun glittering like sparkling jewels on the azure sea. "Look at that," murmured Kelland appreciatively. "Like someone has tipped a truck load of diamonds to frolic on the water."

Paulson raised his eyebrows in amazement, "Didn't know you were a poet!"

"I have my moments," said Kelland with a smile. "I'm not totally ignorant in the arts." He paused, "Another beer?"

"Why not?"

Kelland clicked his fingers at the waiter who scurried across, "Dýo býres, parakaló."

"Since when do you speak Greek?"

"Only essentials. I can just get by." He paused as the waiter returned with their drinks. "Efcharistó"

"So, what's the plan?"

"We finish our beers and head back to my hotel. Then we can decide what to do."

Paulson nodded. "We'll need to know the man's movements, his routine, where he lives, risk factors, family etc."

"Some of it, I already know. The rest we have to find out. We can't talk here. Let's wait until we get back."

Meredith Probert was at her window again. She had partially opened her net curtains and sat in her usual position with her cup of tea and tonight she had chocolate Hobnobs. The night was still, and she couldn't see any activity at all, anywhere. It was disappointing. She missed watching Stan Butterworth and wondered when he would be home. Tomorrow, she thought. I'll go and see him tomorrow. I'll take him some cupcakes.

There was a movement opposite and Meredith sat forward in her seat. She strained her eyes to see. There was someone with a small torch looking around the room. It looked like a man and another figure with him. She presumed it was men They didn't look female, and it wasn't the police. There was no one on duty outside now. She couldn't see the shadowy figures clearly but knew she had to phone the police. Meredith rose from her seat and peered through the window trying to see them more clearly. Suddenly the pencil flashlight held by one of the intruders turned in the direction of her window and shone onto her startled face.

Meredith scuttled downstairs; her heart was thumping wildly. She rushed to her front door and hastily put the chain on and secured the bolts inside before turning her attention to the back door and ensuring it was locked. She hurried around downstairs checking all the windows. She drew all her blinds and curtains and sat at the kitchen table, her heart thumping madly. She needed to calm herself. Her throat was so constricted she couldn't speak but she knew she must call the police.

Across the way in Stan Butterworth's house the two men were arguing. "I never signed up for this. I agreed to help you do a search. I am not into terrorising an innocent woman."

"You ain't got no choice mate. That there woman has seen us. It won't be long before she's on the blower to the cops."

"Then let's just go. Come back another time."

"She's seen us. Who knows what she knows, who knows what the old boy has told her. She needs shutting up."

"Now wait a minute. I am not going down for murder."

"I just want to frighten her a little. Make sure she doesn't call the cops. Put her out of action to let us complete the search and get away."

"No. I'm not getting involved."

"Suit yourself. Boss won't like it. I'm going across."

The man left standing swore softly. He knew he had to stop him. He couldn't live with himself otherwise. He groaned loudly before chasing after the other miscreant.

Meredith was still struggling to breathe normally. She rose from her seat and kept repeating to herself, "Call the police. I must call the police." Only then did she return to the hallway and pick up the phone. As she punched in the buttons, she was horrified to see her front door being rattled by an unseen hand and the letter box lifted. Someone was staring through the letterbox at her. She stifled a scream as the flap on the box rat-a-tat-tatted. Meredith dropped the phone and moved across the hall before slumping to the floor, shaking in fear.

Siri and Ronnie came out from the cinema holding hands looking happy and contented. Carried along by the exiting throng they found themselves propelled to a nearby coffee shop. Ronnie laughed, "Perhaps it's a sign that we should grab a coffee or whatever you would like?"

"What a lovely ending to a perfect evening before we get the bus home."

"So, what would you like?"

"I think coffee will keep me awake. I'd love a hot chocolate. It always seems a real treat." She added, "A bit of indulgence."

"And why not?"

They tumbled in through the door. It was fairly quiet inside and Siri easily found a table for two while Ronnie stood third in line to order their beverages. He kept glancing back at Siri scarcely trusting his eyes that she was out with him or believe his luck.

Siri smiled shyly back at him. It was their third date. He hadn't kissed her yet. She was hoping that would change tonight. The café door swung open and a drunken lout, staggered inside. He saw Siri and weaved his way to her table, "You will reserve that seat for me, please," he said slurring his words.

"I'm sorry, but that seat's taken."

"I can't see no one," said the drunk, plonking himself down.

Ronnie moved back to the table and tapped the drunk on the shoulder, "Sorry, mate. You need to find another seat."

"Who says?" he growled in a surly manner.

"I say. You're annoying my girlfriend."

"Your girlfriend, you say?"

"Yes."

"But I like sitting here. You move."

Siri rose. "It's all right Ronnie. I'll get us another table." She made to move past him, and he caught her by her wrist.

"I don't think so. You're the reason I want to sit here."

At this point, the manager came out from behind the counter. "Okay. Think you've had enough. Don't go annoying my customers, please. Just get up and be on your way."

"Or you'll what?"

"I'll call the police if I have to."

The drunk swore and shuffled to his feet. He let out a string of expletives and went back out into the street.

The manager turned to Ronnie, "Sorry about that, sir. Please accept my apologies. You, too, miss." He called back to the youth behind the counter. "No charge to these customers. It's on the house."

The youth nodded and Ronnie returned to the counter as Siri gazed out of the window. She could see the drunk stumbling across the street, where he appeared to lounge against the wall by the Burlington Arcade. He stared across the road at her with a leering grin.

Siri shivered.


Meredith was too frightened to speak. She was aware of someone walking around the outside of her house testing the windows and rattling the doors. She finally plucked up courage to crawl to the phone, dangling on its wire and retrieved it. She curtailed the bleeping line and dialled 999.

"Emergency, which service please?"

She swallowed hard and tried to generate some saliva into her dry mouth and finally managed to murmur. "Police."

The dispatcher could hardly hear her, "You'll have to speak up. What is your emergency?"

Meredith found her voice, "Someone is trying to get into my house."

"Right. Where are you?" Meredith gave her address. "Are you alone?"

"Yes." Her voice was little more than a squeak.

"Stay on the line with me. Someone will be with you shortly," said the dispatcher trying to calm her down. "Is the person known to you?"

"No."

The dispatcher continued to keep her talking before she announced. The police will arrive in a few minutes. You should be okay, now. Stay on the line until they arrive."

There was the sound of breaking glass and Meredith screamed. Sirens could be heard in the distance. She prayed they were approaching her house and that she would soon hear cars pulling up in her driveway.

Holly sat at a table with her friends Colin and Marcie, DCI Allison and, of course, Paul. She looked miserable, "What are you telling me?"

Colin looked at Paul, who nodded. "We think that somehow your biological grandmother's spirit has fastened onto you."

"*How* do you know?"

"Think about it, Holly. These absences you have, where you don't remember what has been happening or what has been said, the changes in your behaviour; happily taking on jobs that you normally loathe, the language you're using, the hymns you sing and recitation of Bible verses. That's not you. And we have seen more."

She looked across at Colin sharply, "What?"

Sometimes there is a subtle change in your features as if her face is being imprinted onto yours."

"That's impossible."

"I thought so, too," said Allison gently. "But I've seen things and I saw that tonight."

"So did I," said Marcie.

There was silence. Everyone's eyes were on Holly.

"So, what do I do?" she asked in a small tight voice.

"I'm going to speak to the Psychic school and see if they have any suggestions and do some more research, but…"

"But what?"

"I think we may need an exorcist."

# 4

Ronnie and Siri were in deep discussion about the drunk that was hanging around outside.

"So, what do we do?" asked Siri.

The manager walked across, "Is everything all right?"

"I'm not sure," said Ronnie cautiously.

"We close in half an hour. Do you want me to call the police?"

"That won't be necessary. I am with the police." He flashed his warrant card. "However, that drunk is intimidating. Is there another way out of here?

"What like a back door?"

Ronnie nodded, "Yes, something like that. We don't want the situation to become enflamed. If we can avoid the main entrance. I think it will help."

"There's a side door, which leads into the alley and yard between us and the next shop. It's where the bins are."

"That will do. He's watching the front door; we may escape his attention the other way."

"If you want to hang on a few more minutes, you can leave with the remaining staff. Walk out together. There is safety in numbers. Which way are you going?"

"Colmore Row to the night service."

"Jean and Fitzroy go that way. I have a motor scooter parked in the yard and usually take Tom home. If we all leave together it may confuse him."

"Good idea. We'll wait."

"I'll close the blinds and he won't see in," said the manager walking to the windows and drawing the slatted shutters across the window and sealing the café from prying eyes. They could hear the drunk screaming obscenities and Siri shivered again.

Meredith was terrified and shaking uncontrollably. With the sound of breaking glass, she knew, whoever it was, was gaining access to her house. She rapidly crawled across the floor towards the downstairs cloakroom, which had a lock inside. She carefully opened the door and shuffled inside and bolted it.

Hardly daring to breathe she shuddered as she heard footsteps coming along the short passageway opening doors and pausing. The intruder stopped outside the downstairs cloakroom and tried the door. It wouldn't open. Whoever it was began shouldering it and Meredith stifled a whimper before she fainted clean away in fright.

Ronnie and Siri moved out of the side entrance with the staff. They all waited until the manager had locked up. The manager and Tom mounted the motorcycle and set off; Siri and Ronnie walked out in the middle of the remaining staff and out into New Street, where they headed in different directions.

The drunk was on his feet watching the departure. He hurled obscenities at them and began staggering along the road after them. Siri turned to Ronnie, "I don't like this. Why is he doing this to us?"

Ronnie tried to calm her, "We'll be okay. He's a drunken troublemaker. We really need more Bobbies on the beat. That would help stop this kind of conduct, nip it in the bud before it starts."

"Why aren't there more?"

Ronnie shrugged, "Police cuts. Low recruitment. Just not got the manpower. It's alarming for anyone being on the end of this type of behaviour, even me."

They all walked on briskly. Siri heaved a sigh of relief when they reached the Night Service bus stop and joined the sparse queue.

The intruder at Meredith's had almost managed to splinter the lock of the under-stair cupboard when he heard the arrival of his conspirator who joined him in the house. They heard the police cars drawing nearer.

He turned to his reluctant, partner in crime, "It's every man for himself. We've got to get out of here." The perpetrator dashed to the back door and fiddled with the lock as the cop cars rolled up and soon someone was hammering on the door and ringing the bell. The other man looked about him and froze, while his partner made his escape.

The cops had brought the red enforcer. He knew he had to move. He hurried to the back where the other villain had got out, but he could see police with torches looking through windows and around the garden. He made a split second decision and darted for the stairs. He ran up them and disappeared from view just as the front door gave way.

The police called out, "Mrs Probert?" and began to search downstairs. They saw the phone hanging from its curling plastic cable in the kitchen. One picked it up to speak to dispatch and replaced the receiver. Two officers went upstairs to look around as one checked the doors in the passageway.

He tried the cloakroom door, "Mrs Probert? It's safe to come out now. It's the police."

Meredith groaned as she was just coming round. Her voice was weak and timid. "How do I know it's the police?"

"You called us, remember? You will see as soon as you come out."

"Are they still in the house?"

"It's being searched as we speak. I assure you, your safety is paramount."

Meredith slid back the loosened bolts and tentatively opened the door. An officer helped her out. She sighed in relief when she saw their uniforms, when there was a shout and a scuffle from upstairs.

Meredith started to breathe heavily as her heart kicked against her ribs. One of the policemen supported her as her legs began to buckle. She began to whimper, "What am I to do? I can't stay here. What if they come back? The front door's broken. I heard glass breaking earlier. He's broken a window, I'm sure of it."

"Mrs Probert, we will sort out your door and window. Have no fear."

"But I don't feel safe... in my own house... what do I do?"

The officer attempted to reassure her, "Is there anyone you can stay with until the repairs are done? Or someone who can come here?"

Meredith shook her head, "I don't think I can sleep in my house ever again." Meredith had been given a cup of hot sweet strong tea with a tot of brandy in it. A mixed-race WPC sat with her and promised she would remain with her throughout the night.

Meredith repeated, "But, I don't feel safe. Not anymore." She sighed, "How long will it take to fix the door and window?"

WPC Sidhu smiled. It was a kind and generous smile. She was strikingly attractive with huge dark almond eyes, the colour of nutmeg. "Don't worry yourself none. It will all be secured tonight, and the glazier, carpenter and locksmith will all be here in the morning."

There was another shout from upstairs and a man came hurtling down, ploughing past the cop standing at the door. Two officers gave chase, but the man was quick. He jumped over a garden wall and sped off. He was wiry with long greasy hair. He had a scarf pulled up over his face. One officer who had the nickname, 'The Bolt', had managed to catch up with the perpetrator, rugby tackled and floored him. He slapped on the cuffs and cautioned him. By the time he'd hauled the man to his feet, two more policemen joined them, and the intruder was led away towards a waiting police car.


Kelland and Paulson sat in Kelland's hotel room and discussed the way forward. "So how do we do this?" asked Paulson.

"Only one way. We have to do it ourselves with no one else to rely on."

"So, how?"

"We need to watch the Taverna for a week. Find out what we can. The man's name, his routine, where he lives. We can take it in turns."

"Won't that look suspicious? One of us there every day and night of the week?"

"We'll break it up. Alternate days and nights, and come together occasionally. We have to get a picture of this man's life. We need his name, where he lives, family and so on in order to assess the risks."

"I'll go back this evening and see when he knocks off."

"We can both go tonight, might as well have a meal together. You can follow him home. Get some basic information," said Kelland.

"And who is going to do the deed?" asked Paulson.

"We can't call on anyone else."

"I suppose that means me?"

"I can't do it," protested Kelland.

"No, you never get your hands dirty."

"Not if I can help it," agreed Kelland. "But Kira. She's a different matter. That will have to be me. And I'm not looking forward to it."

"What about the big boss? Surely he can get help? He must have someone in the islands."

"Probably. But let's see what we can do on our own first. If this is to work, we must be doubly careful. That's if we want our lives back."

"You mean yours. I'll be starting again as someone else."

"Put up with it. I pay you enough," growled Kelland getting surly.

Paulson squeezed his fists tightly as he stopped the remark that came readily to his lips. "Okay… Think I need a drink."

"Where?"

"Back to the Taverna."


Ronnie and Siri waited patiently at the bus stop. Ronnie had his arm around Siri, and he was feeling happier than he had ever been in his life. Siri nestled into his shoulder looking contented when there was a drunken roar. Siri's heart sank and Ronnie sighed heavily. He spoke softly to Siri, "Wait here, with Fitzroy and Trudy. I'll deal with this."

Ronnie turned and walked towards the inebriated man who was scowling viciously and waving a broken bottle about. "All right, mate. Do you really want to do this? Why don't you go home and sleep it off?"

"Or what?"

"I'll have to arrest you."

The drunk laughed derisively, "You? What is it? A citizen's arrest?"

"No, I am an off-duty officer." Ronnie flashed his warrant card.

"What? You? A puny strip of wind that's just hot air. All gas and gaiters. Ain't that what they say?"

"I wouldn't have a clue. I repeat, do you really want to do this?"

The drunk sneered and muttered, "You betcha!"

"Don't say I didn't warn you."

The drunk moved forward threateningly and barrelled towards Ronnie who neatly sidestepped and flipped the man over who fell on the ground. The thug scrambled up. He'd lost his bottle, which had smashed when he tumbled down. The glass had cut his hand quite badly. The yob yelled and powered towards Ronnie again with the same result. He landed flat on his back.

"Had enough?"

"I ain't started yet," the ruffian said scornfully, getting up. This time he was more wary dancing around on the pavement shouting threats. He put his head down and charged again, this time Ronnie countered and smashed his fist into the man's solar plexus winding him. The man slumped on the floor but didn't get up. He just groaned.

The others at the bus stop cheered loudly and clapped Ronnie on the back.

"I suggest someone call an ambulance for him to get his hand seen to," said Ronnie as the bus arrived.

No one took any notice and piled on the bus, so Ronnie took out his mobile and reported the incident. Siri snuggled into him again. She looked up at him with her smoky eyes and sighed. "I feel so safe with you." Ronnie smiled down at her and gazed back at her. Their faces were so close, he could feel her sweet breath on his skin and their lips met in their first tender kiss.


Allison set his mouth in a hard line and ruminated on the latest call from the top brass. How they had discovered that he was still curious over their shutting down his interest in the sad death of Gary Watson, he didn't know. He thought he'd covered his tracks over the last few years. *'Obviously not well enough,'* he thought.

Mary passed him a much-needed glass of red wine, "It's understandable, Greg. If it's a case of National Security. They don't want you dredging up new facts that could upset their own plans. They clearly have good reason."

Allison grunted and took a swig of his Merlot and said belligerently, "I know the case is closed. But everything has just been a bit too pat, too convenient, too neat. It riles me. Someone should be made to pay for Gary Watson's death. I'm damned sure the MRF is involved and that's the reason. One of their number did something and that's why they slammed the brakes on it."

"What good will it do you to ferret out the truth? You could lose your job, pension everything."

"It would give me satisfaction to know… just to know."

"But would you let it rest there? I don't think so."

Allison sighed, "No, I don't suppose I could."

"Then let it go. You can't drag anyone else into this. You will only jeopardise their careers, too. You have no right to do that," reasoned Mary.

Allison sighed, "I know… you're right. I must let it go. I will have to let the others know and put a stop to it. It just rankles, that's all."

"I know. But you can't lose anymore sleep over it. Put it to bed and forget it. Please, for me. Save some of your time for the girls coming home. Don't ruin it."

Allison swallowed down some more wine. "Okay. I'll try. But if something crops up…"

"I know, I know. Let's try and enjoy it while it lasts. It would be lovely if you could take some time out when they're all here. It won't happen again in a hurry."

"We had a holiday in Malta," Allison pointed out.

"Yes. That was a necessity to keep you safe. I know you have more leave owing. You should take it."

"I'll think about it." It was Allison's way to end the discussion, but Mary promised herself she would pursue the subject of time off again very soon.

Alex Wallace was immersed in his novel; the book was coming along well now he was over his writer's block. It was also proving useful to have a few other creative ideas for future works that he could dip into if he got stuck again. He turned to his cat who was resting peacefully on the sofa, "You know,

Snooks, coming here was one of the best things we could have done. Our lives have changed dramatically and all for the better. Whoever thought we would have a lady in our lives? And have one that we both like… The phone rang, interrupting his reverie.

"Alex?"

"Yes?"

"Call me on the other line. This one seems to have a fault on it." It was Roy Chapman, his contact and boss with the MRF and he was being cautious just in case other ears were listening. Roy was always wary and with good cause. Alex hung up and ran upstairs to where his other phone was on charge in the spare bedroom. He unplugged it and dialled back immediately.

"Roy? You have something for me?"

"I have. Remember before everything broke with the Kelland case?"

"Yes?"

"You told me you had suspicions about dealings in Ironbridge?"

"Yes."

"Can we meet?"

"Where?"

"Dale End Café? I'll be there in fifteen minutes."

Alex felt a pleasurable tingle of excitement run through his body now taut with tension. "I'll be there." He ended the call and pocketed his phone. Alex ran back downstairs, put a few cat treats out for Snooks whose eyes opened wide. She jumped off the sofa and padded to her dish and began to eat the Dreamies Alex had laid out for her. He picked up his keys and left.

Alex sat on one of the benches and tables outside Dale End café. He ordered a latte and a slice of their chocolate orange cake. He'd forgotten how hungry he was, he had been so immersed in his writing. He couldn't wait for Roy and took a large bite. It was heaven on a plate.

Seven minutes later Roy came and sat opposite him. He stared at the few crumbs left on Alex's plate. "Worth it?"

"Most definitely. In fact, if you are going in to order you can get me another slice. It's delicious."

Roy laughed and went inside to the counter. He returned with two slices and set them down.

Alex quipped, "Oh, I couldn't possibly manage two pieces."

Roy raised an eyebrow, let out a snort of derision before going back inside to bring out his coffee. Once he was settled, there was silence while they ate their cake.

Alex brushed the crumbs from his front and asked, "So, what's up?"

"We've got a fix on Paulson and Kelland."

"I thought Kelland had skipped to The Dominican Republic?"

"He did. He's popped up in Rhodes and so has Paulson."

Alex's eyes gleamed, "And?"

"Firstly, we want you to check out this connection with Ironbridge. Your girlfriend's an estate agent, isn't she?"

"She is. You can't think she's got anything to do with this?"

"Unlikely. But she may be useful. You could put out some feelers, see what you can learn. She may know something, something she's probably not even aware of."

"Yes?... Why do I think there's more to come?"

"You and I are off to Rhodes."

"When?"

"Flights booked from Birmingham two days from now. Give you time to prepare."

"What about weapons?"

"Leave that to me. We have a contact there to supply us."

"MRF?" Roy nodded. "What if I find out anything about the Ironbridge connection?"

"Pass that on to your cop friend."

"Stringer?"

"Yes, but we need the info, too. There are suspicions about a man inside the force who is warning those at the top of the OCG who don't want to get their hands dirty. If that's the case, we can get him and them. Your pal Stringer will be a good starting point."

"How do I do that?"

45

"You have your methods. I'm sure you'll manage." Roy drained his coffee cup. "That's it for now. Keep your phone with you. I'll let you know when and where. We are going on a little holiday. I'm sure you can work that into your need for research somehow."

Roy stood up. The meeting was over. He walked back through the park and left Alex looking thoughtful.

Paul was at his easel, working on a Worcester landscape. He could hear Holly launching into yet another hymn. This time it was 'Fight the good fight'. He frowned; things were becoming progressively more difficult. Holly was still Holly but these lapses into Grace Clifton's personality, or whatever it was, were becoming more frequent. He wished Friday would hurry up and come around. That is when they were expecting a visit from the catholic priest in the diocese responsible for exorcism. But first there was to be a medical examination to determine whether this possession by a person who was dead was not just some sort of mental illness. Colin's report as a psychologist was of paramount importance as to whether an exorcism could be performed. He had made an excellent clinical assessment and hoped it would do the trick. Everyone wanted Holly back full time not sporadically.

The preliminary report had been sent to the Church and Colin would be there to meet with the priest on Friday when they would come on to Cornflowers. Paul was wondering whether to ask Allison or not. He would check with Colin and Holly, when she was herself, later.

The man apprehended at Meredith Probert's house sat uncomfortably in his cell waiting for his solicitor to arrive when Angus Mackay strolled along the corridor where the holding cells were situated. He stopped, looked around and crossed to the cell. He lowered his voice, "Nesbitt?"

The man turned his head and saw Mackay; recognition flashed across his face. "What the ... What are you doing here?"

"I've transferred." Mackay looked shiftily around him as a uniformed copper walked past to release a drunk who had been sleeping it off in the next cell. The officer led the drunk away and barely took any notice of Mackay interacting with the prisoner. Mackay spoke quickly in low tones. "I know you from petty crime in my old manor, nothing more. Get it?" Nesbitt nodded. "Good we understand each other."

"Can you help me? They're transferring me to Winson Green remand centre this week."

"Maybe. But no more talk, not now. Let me think." Mackay marched off and returned to the squad room. He entered with a swagger, "Morning, lads." A few returned his greeting, looking up from their work stations. "What's on?"

Pooley looked up, "Dealt with your cases then?"

"Not seen them yet; remember I've only just transferred."

"I think you'll find you have a full in-tray, now. Plenty of work to go around. You been given a partner yet?"

"Not yet." Mackay rubbed his hands together in a brash pretence of glee, "Then, I'd better get onto it." He sat at his desk, booted up his computer and logged on before picking up the files, which he started to sort through. It seemed to be pretty routine stuff: burglaries, car thefts, a suspected chop shop, sexual assault and knife crime. He needed to pick one to begin with but what he really needed to know was why Nesbitt was in a holding cell.

# 5

ALEX HAD A COMPLETE FILE on the estate agent used by Kelland and his operatives in the sex trafficking cases and the solicitor who did the conveyancing of the properties they bought for such purposes. He was checking through Roy Chapman's notes and what the MRF had already learned about them. The solicitor, a Mr Matt Guard of Beech Tree Law had a number of high-profile clients, many of whom were on the wrong side of the law. He had a reputation as a highly intelligent man with sharp business practices that had earned him the nickname Slick. According to the file, Mr Guard was well connected and had managed, in each case, to retain a top-notch barrister who had a one hundred percent success rate with cases he'd fought. According to the police reports, a number of guilty suspects had got off Scott free with his help. He was a man that warranted further investigations. Alex thought it would be helpful to take a look at the man's financials and track the money that had come into his accounts. That could be the starting point.

Alex then turned his attention to the Estate Agents in Ironbridge, where Jane worked. It seemed the owners were two brothers, Jacob and Nathan Murch. Jacob was Jane's immediate boss and Nathan was more of a sleeping partner who was in the background. Nick Tart was just the person who had previously owned the company. It had been sold on and the brothers had kept the name, so no guilt for Mr Tart. The old man who founded the company had since died, so no leads there, either. Alex rubbed his chin. He didn't like the idea of Jane being involved and somehow he couldn't see it. He scanned the notes on the two men and discovered that one had a somewhat shady past.

Alex decided he would do a little ferreting himself and see what he could learn, satisfy himself that Jane was not involved and then pass his discoveries onto Mark. He would scan and copy the information onto a flash drive that he would send to Mark. He needed to do that before the end of the week.

Now, how could he engineer the conversation around to her role in the Estate Agents? Alex had an idea. His mouth began to tweak upwards. It would work. He was sure of it. He had to make it work before he left with Roy for Rhodes.

Ronnie and Gurdip were excited to be on the train to London on official business. They were expected at Belmarsh that afternoon at 3 o'clock to interview Fred Butterworth. Gurdip was grinning delightedly. "I've only ever been to London once," he said.

"That's once more than me," said Ronnie. "You'll have to guide us around the underground. I've bought a map, which should help as we have a few hours to kill. I'd love to see Covent Garden."

"And the West End," added Gurdip. "Woodward has recommended a few places for us to go. Here, I've got a list."

He pulled out a sheet of A4 paper and Ronnie took out his map. "Got the tickets?" asked eagle-eyed Ronnie as he spotted the ticket inspector moving through the carriage.

"Er… you've got them, haven't you?" said Gurdip looking at Ronnie who was suddenly in a panic and patting all his pockets. "Relax. I'm just winding you up. They're here somewhere." Gurdip took out his wallet and pulled out two second class tickets, seat tickets and return tickets and had to sort through them first to find the right ones and then shoved the rest back in his wallet. He held them up ready to pass the to the inspector. That all went without a hitch and the two young men began to plan their day. "Northern line from Euston to Leicester Square then hop on the Piccadilly line to Covent Garden. Sounds simple enough and the trains are regular."

"I'll be guided by you," asserted Ronnie. "I'm not going to get blamed if we go wrong."

"Oh, ye of little faith. We'll be fine. We won't be there at rush hour and from Covent Garden we can walk up Bow Street to La Ballerina Restaurant for an early lunch."

"What's that?"

"Woodward says, it's a nice Italian and we can afford the food on a cops' salary. None of your high-end stuff. They do all these early theatre dinner meals. It's just up from Covent Garden Market and The Royal Opera House and we'll have plenty of time to explore the area."

"I heard there's entertainment in the square; jugglers, fire eaters and magicians and such." Ronnie was bursting with excitement. Gurdip laughed. The two young men were intent on having a good time. "Mustn't forget what we're here to do, though," said Ronnie.

"No. We can work out exactly what we want to ask Fred Butterworth."

"I'm interested in looking at his list of visitors; maybe that will tell us something."

"Maybe."

"And maybe I can get a gift for Siri."

Gurdip smiled, "Then I will get something for Ayesha."


Meredith Probert sat nervously in her kitchen as her front door was repaired and the lock changed. A glazier was inserting a new piece of glass where the other had been broken.

"How are you feeling now?" asked WPC Sidhu, gently. Her tone was soothing and understanding. She had glossy ebony hair, with an olive dewy skin complexion. Her figure was neat and trim, and Meredith had noticed the way some of the coppers looked at her.

"I was going to make some cupcakes for Stan and take them into the hospital."

"I think that's a great idea. Why don't we make a start on it, now. I'll help you."

"Oh, I don't know. I can't think straight at the moment. I'm all of a jitter."

"Sure, you can. It will give you a focus. Take your mind off things. Come on, now. Where do we start?"

Reluctantly, Meredith rose from the table and began to fetch the ingredients from the cupboard. With WPC Sidhu's help and encouragement, Meredith began to mix up her cake sponge. "I thought I'd do a variety. He likes my cupcakes." The very normality of the routine seemed to calm her, and she started to enjoy the task and the company. "I can't keep calling you WPC Sidhu…"

"No, you can't. It's a bit of a mouthful isn't it? You can call me Dilly."

"Dilly… Dilly… Tell me, what is that short for?"

"I was Christened Pika, my mother is from Slovenia and my father is from India, but at school everyone called me Dilly… pika dilly – get it?"

Meredith laughed. "Oh, I see. I thought it was going to be Mathilda."

"No, I rather like Dilly, so I kept it."

"It's lovely but so is Pika," said Meredith with a warm smile."

Meredith continued to instruct Dilly in the art of making cupcakes and the workmen doing the repairs came into say they had all finished. "Would you like a cup of tea?" she asked them politely.

No one was going to turn down the offer, so while Meredith put the cakes in to cook, Dilly made the tea and Meredith went to her cake tin and set out slices of her Victoria cream sponge. Everyone sat around the kitchen table and Meredith felt calmer and had to admit to herself she was actually enjoying herself, listening to the lively banter between them.

Alex sat with Snooks and made a plan. He wrote down his ideas and story arcs for the characters. This is what he would present to Jane. He had the basic idea of a story subplot and knew she would believe it and anyway, he may even use it in his book. The discussion was bound to shed some light on any shady dealings at the Estate Agents. He just had to ask the right questions. He looked at his watch, she would be arriving soon for a coffee. His notes were spread across the table in readiness. He scratched Snooks behind her ears and she purred in appreciation. Alex put his hand in his pocket and pulled out a pack of Dreamies and tipped some onto his palm. Snooks rubbed her face into her master before dipping her mouth into the treats and eating them from his hand. Alex ruffled his cat's fur. Until Jane had come along Snooks was the only important thing in his life. Alex couldn't believe how his life had changed in only a year.

The doorbell chimed and Snooks jumped from Alex's lap and with her tail puffed up and straight in the air, she ran to the front door, followed by Alex. It was Jane who stooped down and petted Snooks who purred loudly and wrapped herself around Jane's legs.

"She knew it was you," said Alex. "She ran to the door to greet you, well I never!"

Jane cruised into the kitchen and began to fix coffee; she spotted all the papers and post it notes littering the table. "Oh dear, have I come at the wrong time? Am I interrupting your flow?"

"Actually, you have come exactly at the right time," said Alex.

"Oh?" Jane arched an eyebrow.

"Yes. I wanted to ask you something…"

"Why, sir this is so sudden," she said fooling around and fluttering her eyelashes.

Alex laughed, in spite of himself. "No… I mean…" he began to turn a deep shade of pink."

"I'm only kidding. What is it? Ask away."

"I'm working on a couple of subplots for my novel that's to link in with the assassin story."

"Yes…?" she said uncertainly.

"Not sure really, but the guy who wants a hit on his wife, needs to get rid of her because she's discovered his crooked dealings with his company."

"So?"

"His company is an estate agents."

"Oh, I see, I think…" Jane continued to busy herself with making coffee.

"Do you think it would be possible to launder money through an estate agents?"

"How do you mean?"

"By purchasing numerous properties without raising any suspicions?" Jane passed Alex a cup of coffee and sat with hers opposite him at the table. "I mean is that at all feasible?"

Jane stirred her coffee while she thought. "Hm... we have had the odd developer who has bought a string of properties to redevelop, usually a row of condemned houses to flatten and rebuild in places like Telford."

"I can see how that would work, but what about someone who buys houses in a variety of areas, some way out of the agent's catchment area?"

"I suppose that could work, if the agent had a vested interest. Controls are so tight now and with stamp duty and everything it's not that likely."

"Although, if this agent was hiding things and properties were bought for other means, the money could be cleaned by purporting to be part of a business venture, couldn't it?"

"I suppose."

"You've not come across anything like that?"

Jane wrinkled her nose as she thought... "Come to think of it. We do have a client that will only deal with Mr Murch." Alex shook his head as if he didn't know who she meant. "Jacob Murch, he and his brother Nathan started the agency. I have never seen Nathan; he doesn't have anything to do with the business."

"And Jacob?"

"He has a few select clients and one I am thinking of in Birmingham."

"Yes?"

"He's bought lots of properties all over the place. Don't know what he does with them. Probably rents them out."

"So, it is feasible that dirty money could be cleaned in purchasing property?"

"But there are so many checks to prevent that. They would have to provide bank details and where the money came from and so on. I know I sometimes have to ask clients awkward questions about earnings etc. Especially if there's a mortgage involved."

"What if the dealings were in cash and the agent was himself crooked. Could he circumvent the checks?"

"It's possible, I suppose. If they are in company names that are formed especially to purchase the property. I mean references can be faked, can't they? Then on Land Registry it wouldn't look like the same person. There would be no red flags. Yes, I think it's possible."

"Great! And you'd be happy to help me with all the jargon and ins and outs of what's involved in these types of sales?"

"Why, yes."

"Ideal. Then it could work. Thanks, Jane. You will get an acknowledgement in the book when I've finished."

"Ah! Now I see the reasoning behind this… it's just to secure a sale!" she said with a giggle.

"Tarnation, you saw through that, then?" Alex stood up and moved around to her and stroked her cheek. He kissed her neck and stopped himself. "That's no good I'll get too carried away to work."

"I haven't got long, so you've missed your chance," she said with a giggle before finishing her coffee. I'll have to scoot. I've got three viewings this afternoon. Oddly enough, one's way out of my zone, in Birmingham."

Alex perked up, "Oh?"

"Yes. A house in Church Road, used to be a drama school owned by some bigwig and he's selling up."

Alex kept his face impassive as his mind began to race. "What time?"

"Viewing's at 4:30. The other two before are local."

"Bummer that means you'll be late for dinner."

"I'll try not to be," she said. Jane stood up and wrapped her arms around Alex's neck. "In the meantime, this is to remember me by," and she kissed him tenderly before trying to step towards the door.

"You can't go now," he complained.

"Sorry," she said pouting as she slipped away from him and blew him a kiss.

Alex smiled ruefully and gave a little wave. As soon as Jane was out of the door he dived back to the kitchen table and took out his cell. He pulled up Mark's number and dialled.


Gurdip and Ronnie had arrived at Belmarsh Prison. They were in good spirits.

The weather was fine and sunny, which immediately put a smile on their faces. Their lunch at La Ballerina restaurant had gone down well as had their walk around Covent Garden and the market. Ronnie had bought Siri a beautiful silk screen printed scarf and Gurdip had bought Ayesha a child's leather shoulder bag in the shape of a cat. Their journey via the tube and rail had taken them just over twenty minutes and they had taken a taxi from Woolwich to the prison.

From the outside it was an impressive red brick building that looked modern in design. But there was an aura about the place that made Ronnie shiver. "I don't know, Gurdip, but this place gives me the creeps. I feel it's full of evil."

"It's just a building. The building isn't evil. It's the criminals inside."

"Yeah but the walls can act like a recorder. Or at least that's what I've read somewhere. Come on, best get signed in we have to see the governor first. Next stop, Fred Butterworth."


Mark whistled as he walked down the police corridor to the squad room. He was feeling particularly chipper today and attracted a few cheery hellos en route. His mobile vibrating in his shirt pocket stopped him dead as he tugged it out to answer. He looked at the screen and number. No name was attached to the caller ID, and he frowned.

"Stringer."

"Mark? Do you have a private email address that's safe to use?"

"Sorry? Who is..." Mark suddenly shook his head as if to clear it as realisation dawned. "It's Alex isn't it?"

Alex affirmed and went on, "Got something that may interest you and help you with one of your cases."

"What's that?"

"Email addy first, personal not professional."

Mark looked around him to see if anyone was listening or observing him before giving out his personal email.

Alex scribbled it down. "Okay, I'll be in touch. You'll find it interesting and useful. By the way, I won't be around for a week or two. I have a little job on."

"Right. Text me when you're back."

Alex ended the call and Mark thought carefully about what had been said. He wondered what it was all about.

He continued to the squad room where Angus Mackay was clowning around as usual. Mark bristled. He shared Allison's dislike of the man. He was just a bit too cocky for his liking. But, there, as long as he didn't get partnered with him he could put up with his childish banter.

At the cottage in Ironbridge Alex got to work and put everything onto a flash drive before scanning all the documents again. He collated them, attached them as a zip file and wrote a cryptic email to Mark:

*"You needn't say where any of this has come from. I'm sending the memory stick as evidence for you, marking it for your personal attention at the cop shop. It will look anonymous enough, but you can study the files beforehand at home and get a handle on them. This is big, make no mistake. For starters, you should have enough here to proceed with a money laundering case on the solicitor and the estate agent. I'll leave it with you. AW."*

Alex hoped he wasn't jumping the gun. He knew he needed to talk further with Jane but was convinced she was an innocent party in the criminal affairs.

Gurdip and Ronnie sat uncomfortably in front of the Governor of Belmarsh Prison. Neither of them were at ease. It reminded them both of their time in Featherstone Young Offenders Institution, when Ronnie went into work undercover. That job had turned out really well for both of them, but here, they still felt uneasy.

The Governor had a printout of all visitors who had been to see Fred Butterworth, since he'd been incarcerated, plus a complete copy of his prison file including trial transcripts, which he passed across to the two detectives.

"You can peruse these at your leisure. Understand that Butterworth is in here for a very serious crime and the gold from the heist has never been recovered, so we do keep a close eye on all his visitors. Even the doctor attending him is in there."

"Thank you. What can you tell us about the man that wouldn't be in these reports?" asked Gurdip.

The governor paused and sucked the air in through his teeth. "Fred Butterworth is more misguided than bad. He's kept his nose clean in here. Doesn't mix much with the other inmates. Keeps himself to himself. His prognosis isn't good. I've included his medical notes. It's all in there. Will there be anything else, detectives?" Ronnie and Gurdip, shook their heads. "Then I'll get an officer to take you down to him. I must warn you, he doesn't look good."

# 6

GURDIP AND RONNIE FOLLOWED OFFICER Thomas down a series of corridors and through locked doors and gates until they came to the hospital wing of Belmarsh Prison. Officer Thomas led the young detectives to the bedside of Fred Butterworth.

Ronnie and Gurdip exchanged a look as the officer stepped back and allowed them to approach the bed. "I'll wait over there." He indicated a desk in the corridor and crossed to talk to a nurse in attendance. Ronnie and Gurdip picked up a chair each from the stack and sat either side of Fred's bed. His skin was tinged yellow and his face gaunt almost skeletal. He was propped up on a mound of pillows looking very thin and frail. He opened one eye and stared at them. "Who are you?" he rasped. His voice was brittle like dried autumn leaves that crackled and scrunched underfoot.

"Detectives Soper and Singh, sir." His voice was polite and gentle.

"Coppers? What do you want with me?"

"We just wanted to ask a few questions."

"I got nothing to say."

"It's to do with your brother Stan."

"Stan? I ain't seen him in years. He don't never come to see me."

"No, sir. He is in the early to middle stages of Alzheimer's."

"So?"

"He was badly attacked and ended up in hospital fairly recently."

"I wouldn't know anything about that."

"No, sir. We just wondered if you knew of anyone that might want to harm him. We have reason to believe he was attacked by a young man and woman and his house was ransacked. They were clearly looking for something. Something important enough for them to send someone to terrorise an elderly lady living opposite."

Fred's eyes gleamed with cunning. He went to speak but he was hit with a sudden rack of coughing. Spittle drooled from his lips as he struggled to gasp for air. He cleared his throat and reached for a beaker of water with a straw, which Gurdip was quick to retrieve and pass into Fred's hands. Fred begrudgingly thanked him and began to sip his water as the two friends waited.

Fred eyed them both, "Look, I don't know what I can tell you, if anything. My brother has been lost to me for years since he stopped visiting. I don't see much of nobody no more. If someone's after Stan it could only be cos he has something they want."

"And what might that be?"

Fred shrugged, "Dunno." His eyes flicked between the two of them. "Maybe he has something he shouldn't have. Maybe he's got something they want. Why don't you ask him?"

"We have and he can't remember anything except for the glory days of the fair. Still living in the past, remembering his stunt shows and the wall of death."

Fred laughed a dry crackly laugh. "Them were the days. Stan was a real showman. In prime position, too, if you get my meaning."

Gurdip shook his head, "No. What do you mean?"

"Think about it. Travelling around the country, never stopping too long in one place. Ideal I'd say."

Gurdip looked at Ronnie as if to say, whatever's he talking about? Ronnie seemed to cotton on to what the old man was saying. "I see. Perfect for doing a few jobs and getting rid of the goods somewhere else."

"I never said that."

"But that's what you meant. About this gold…"

"Ah, the gold. Never got it back you know."

"No. and if Stan was involved…"

"They could never prove that."

"No, but supposing he was. And after all this time, it would be easier to dispose of it. If he'd been looking after it for you, then maybe that's what that couple were searching for."

Fred turned to Gurdip, and gestured to Ronnie with his head, "He's got a canny eye and nose, that one. Knows what's what, I'll be bound."

Gurdip spoke, "Is that what happened then? He stored the gold for you?"

"I'm saying nothing, just speaking hypothetically, that's all." Fred started again with his hacking cough. Once he'd recovered, he snapped, "Now go away and leave me be. I want to sleep."

Ronnie nodded, "Okay, Mr Butterworth, but we may be back." He picked up a photo on his bedside table and perused it. "These your children?"

"What if they are?"

"They bear a startling resemblance to the two intruders, that's all."

Ronnie took note of Fred's responses when he said this and noted the slight twitch of the old boy's lips and the fact he blinked rapidly before closing eyes.

"Go on, get out of here and leave me be. I can tell you, Sonny. You got that wrong."

It was clear the interview was over.


Martyn Kelland and Marcus Paulson sat in a hire car close to the taverna. It was yet another night of watching their victim. The night was bright with a silver waning gibbous moon. A myriad of stars crowded in the velvet midnight blue sky and the air was warm with a soft, balmy breeze.

They had carefully noted his routine, times of arrival to the taverna, his shifts and departure times. They had found out that his name was Giorgios Doukos. They knew his habits of meeting his cronies at another bar in Falaraki after work, where he would play Diloti, a game similar to Casino, alongside a variety of other fishing card games. They'd discovered he originated from Crete and was proud to be one of the Fsakia people from Western Crete, who claimed to be the direct descendants of the Dorians, who came down to Crete around 1100 BC where his few remaining family members lived. It was looking better and better, with no one close to him living in Rhodes, he would be much easier to deal with.

They noted his trips to a gym, GK Fitness Club and were wary of his strength and power. However, Paulson was delighted that he lived alone on the outskirts of Falaraki, in a small villa, close to the Sotirakis Hotel, where Paulson was now staying. That made things so much easier. They began to draw their plans together.

DCI Allison had left work early, clutching a file, after assigning Mark to take charge, while he went to meet Colin and Paul in Vinoteca's, a wine bar in the library complex that was something of a university student haunt, from UCB formerly known as The University of Central England. He picked a table just outside on the concourse and sat down to wait. It wasn't long before Colin arrived looking as dapper as ever.

"Morning, Chief. This is something new to my experience, and I don't mean this student bar but Holly."

"Mine, too. Having been a total sceptic all my life Holly has changed my views on that."

Colin rose, "I'll grab us a coffee. Paul shouldn't be long."

"Flat white please with one sugar."

Colin nodded and went up to the bar. Allison looked about him studying the people who filed past. He enjoyed people watching, the variety of clothes, shapes and sizes. As his eyes followed a large fit man, who walked with a swagger, meeting a statuesque brunette, Paul arrived with a notepad and sat with Allison. He looked glum and extremely worried.

"Colin's just getting a coffee, perhaps you can give him your order." Paul nodded and went to join Colin at the bar, before returning to the table. "So, what's been happening? How is Holly?"

"Weird. Sometimes she's the Holly I know and love but at other times, it's as if another personality is imprinting itself on her, her facial expressions, her voice, and all the out of character things she keeps doing." Paul put his head in his hands. "I don't know what to do. I've kept a diary of times that she has changed and for how long. Suffice it to say… it's getting more frequent."

Colin came back, "They're bringing the drinks across, and I've ordered some cake, too. That might lift our spirits."

"I need something, a bullet to the head, maybe," muttered Paul.

"Come on, Paul," said Colin. "This isn't like you."

"No? Perhaps this is a side of me, you've not seen."

Colin twisted his mouth and engaged Allison's eyes. Paul was always upbeat and even tempered. Whatever was going on with Holly it was dragging Paul down to the depths of despair.

The waitress arrived with their coffees and two slices of lemon drizzle cake and a portion of apple cake and laid them out as Colin muttered his thanks.

Paul groaned. "That's another thing, baking. Holly hardly ever bakes. Now we have lemon drizzle cake and apple muffins coming out of our ears." He glanced up at Allison, "Sorry, Chief. I just don't know how to handle this." He dropped his head again in anguish.

Colin, ever efficient, took charge and spoke in a firm, no nonsense tone. "This won't do. We need to talk about Holly and what we have planned to do. Okay?" The chief and Paul nodded. "I have made an appointment with Father Ignacia Lawrence. Fortunately, he will see all three of us together. I have compiled a psychiatric report to show that Holly is not suffering from any form of mental illness, and this can't be construed as demonic possession but that of spirit possession by her biological grandmother. He will meet with us later this week, as I informed you, and will require your statements and any evidence. If he agrees there is cause for concern…" Paul snorted derisively. "He will ask the bishop's permission to carry out an exorcism. This won't be an easy road to travel, and we have to get Holly's compliance and agreement in this." He turned to Paul, "Will that be a problem?"

"Not when she's Holly. But when she's in her altered state I wouldn't count on anything."

"You've got video evidence haven't you?"

"On my phone. I have taken a few, one of Holly being herself so he can see what she's really like and several at different times when she's … different."

He tapped his notepad, "I've got a list of dates, times and duration of her strange behaviour. It's all in here."

Colin nodded. "Good. Where's Holly now?"

"At home. Cooking." Paul sighed. "The sooner we get this done the better."

Colin turned to Allison, "Have you prepared the police report I asked for?"

Allison nodded, "All the evidence of her psychic work and, of course, about the incident, I witnessed. It's all in here." He tapped his folder.

"Good. So, we're clear on that."

"What's next?"

"I say we drink our coffee and eat our cake. Then we go to Cornflowers and see Holly. If she's herself we can get a statement of acceptance of treatment."

"And if she's not?" asked Paul.

"We'll cross that bridge when we come to it."


Ronnie and Gurdip had enjoyed their day in London and even managed to see a show in the evening, The Lion King. Ronnie made a promise that when they could, they would bring Siri and Ayesha to see it when they had a suitable amount of time off. They were now on the train from Euston travelling back to Brum.

They had spread the papers they'd received from Belmarsh on the table and were looking through them when a name caught Ronnie's eye. He tapped the list of visitors, "Look at this."

Gurdip peered at where Ronnie's finger was pointing. "Doctor Edgar Charles."

"Who's that?" Gurdip looked questioningly at Ronnie.

"I'm sure he's the guy who was arrested regarding that sex trafficking ring. And look," Ronnie ran his finger down the list. "He was replaced by another doctor after only four visits. We will have to ring the governor and find out why. And here, what was this bozo doing, visiting?"

Gurdip raised his eyebrows. "More questions to answer. Interestingly enough, Fred was visited by his son and daughter just two days before the attack on Stan."

"Think we'll have a lot to report when we get back," said Ronnie.

Kelland sat in the taverna, Paradosis with a group of visitors and locals and ... Giorgios. Kelland ensured Giorgios had his glass of Ouzo topped up amidst the laughter and revelry. He'd told Paulson he would drop Rohypnol and GHB into Giorgios' drink before Giorgios left. He promised he'd add ketamine too, if he had the chance.

It wasn't easy.

Paulson watched from the shadows.

Kelland checked the time. In fifteen to thirty minutes Giorgios would be on his way. Kelland ordered some plates of mezzes to share with his companions. As soon as they were delivered he went to the bar to get some more drinks. It was the perfect opportunity to doctor Giorgios' drink. With sleight of hand and no one observing he was able to deposit the drugs into the glass. It was made easier as Giorgios was the only one drinking Ouzo.

Kelland gave an agreed signal and rubbed his nose. Paulson left.

Kelland returned to the table and delivered the drinks. Giorgios protested, "No, όχι, no, no. No more."

Another Greek, Stavros called out drunkenly, "I'll drink it. If Giorgios can't take it." Stavros extended his hand for the glass after downing his Mythos beer.

Kelland felt a surge of panic and tried to cajole Giorgios, "Come on. You can't run out on us now. One more for the road. I want to hear more about Crete and the Fsakia people and legends. Just one last drink. I won't press you to take another."

"Don't say you can't hold your liquor," mocked a burly Greek called Andreas. The others joined in the banter and Giorgios finally succumbed, and amidst a cheer from everyone in the bar, he downed his shot in one swallow to the chant of "Down in one, down in one," with hands banging on the table in accompaniment.

Kelland sighed inwardly nervously and joined in the chatter amongst the other drinkers as Giorgios reeled out of the bar. Kelland's eyes followed him as he stumbled down the road. His part was now done. He could relax and have a few drinks himself and he joined in the teasing banter with gusto. He intended to stay there until the bar closed.

Paulson had to all intents and purposes hurried back and retired to his room in his studio apartment, where he quickly changed his clothes.. Once the lights in the main lobby had been extinguished he crept out and was dressed all in black. He carried a small rucksack containing various items including a bottle of sulphuric acid, a knife and an unusual Maxim 9 pistol with a built-in silencer manufactured in Utah. At his ankle was a tactical and functional Beretta M9A3.

As he escaped into the night, he didn't see the man, carrying a bag, who had entered the darkened hotel lobby. The man made his way to Paulson's room. He fiddled with a key card and slipped inside.

Once inside he got to work. He switched on a pencil light and exchanged the laptop on the table with one from his bag. They were identical. He swapped flash drives that rested by the computer and carelessly laid out some random CDs. He secreted files and papers including bank statements into the briefcase on the floor, before double checking the laptop before he left, ensuring the machine was left asleep rather than shut down.

Just as quietly the man slipped away into the dark.

Paulson was beginning to sweat as he pulled on his balaclava, the weather was warm and the moon was shrouded in cloud, perfect for doing dastardly deeds without detection. Crickets thrummed loudly in the balmy air. Paulson moved towards the road leading to the shack where Giorgios lived intending to surprise the man. He waited, hidden from view.

Giorgios sauntered along the road towards his abode, whistling cheerfully. He stopped suddenly and appeared to be disorientated. Paulson stiffened and watched as Giorgios seemed to stagger and stumble before collapsing on the ground. He struggled to get up, fell back and didn't move. It was Paulson's time to move.

Paulson looked about him swiftly. Apart from the sound of insects buzzing and crickets humming he could hear nothing, nor could he see anyone. He needed to get Giorgios out of sight in order to finish him off. He couldn't risk being seen so he moved across to the Greek and caught hold of him by his shoulders to drag him into the bushes. As soon as he bent over the man and touched him, Giorgios responded by flipping Paulson backwards onto the ground and jumping up. Paulson was dazed and winded. He groaned as Giorgios dusted himself down before disappearing down the road and into his shack. Paulson sat back and made to rise and follow Giorgios to his house just as another masked man hurtled towards him brandishing a hand gun with a silencer. He fired as Paulson was reaching for the Beretta strapped to his ankle. There was a soft 'pftt' sound. Paulson slumped back as the masked man fired again. Paulson's body jerked and then lay still. His eyes were open and staring with shocked surprise. No one stirred along the road. All was quiet.

The assassin crept off silently into the night.

The following morning, Kelland sat on the other side of security at Diagoras International Airport waiting for the departure board to reveal his flight's departure gate. A large man in a straw hat, carrying a newspaper, strolled closer and tipped his hat to Kelland who smiled in return. The man walked to the gents' toilets. Kelland rose and followed the man inside.

The man leaned back against the wash basins and locked eyes with Kelland, who turned away and checked the closets. They were alone.

"Any problems?"

"Nope. Everything went down sweet as a nut."

Kelland nodded, "Giorgios?"

"Played his part well. He had no idea, what was really happening."

Kelland nodded again. "Good. It is good.

"Second payment?"

"Will be done as promised."

"Good. I'd hate to come after you."

"No need for threats. It will be done in a few moments."

"Good." The man walked out of the restroom and Kelland settled himself in one of the closets, removed his phone and transferred the rest of the money for Paulson's hit. He couldn't avoid his mouth turning up at the corners. It was a job well done. Now he could soon return home. But, then there was Kira.

Alex and Roy exited their plane and crossed the concourse towards passport control where they were checked through before moving on to pick up their luggage. They entered the corridor following other passengers towards Arrivals. Alex glanced at those passengers waiting to depart on the other side of the glass. His eyes narrowed as he saw someone he recognised. He nudged Roy and whispered something. Roy turned his head to look at the person indicated and frowned. They walked on to where the carousel was already turning and their flight's luggage spilling out onto it.

They waited until they spotted their bags, tumbling down, hauled them off and turned to make their way through the hall. It was there Roy did a double take and nudged Alex. Their eyes followed a man in a light linen suit with a white Panama straw hat, which had a black band. He was dragging a smart cabin size bag on wheels on the other side of security heading towards an information board.

They stopped and stared before making their way to the taxis waiting outside. They hadn't yet spoken about the people they'd both recognised. That conversation would wait until they reached their hotel and were in their rooms.

Their journey passed in silence.

# 7

ALEX AND ROY CHAPMAN ARRIVED at their hotel in Falaraki, The Pegasus Beach Hotel. It was big enough to be anonymous. They carried their bags up to the family room after checking in and looked around. Alex stepped to the window and balcony. They were on the sixth floor and the views of the beach were magnificent as was the surrounding coastline. Alex sighed wishing he could be here on holiday rather than for work.

"Did you see, who I saw?" asked Alex eventually.

Roy nodded, "I thought he was dead."

"Me, too. What do you think he's doing over here?"

Roy chewed his cheek, "After he left our unit, he worked as a mercenary. Then I heard he was a gun for hire. A bit like you were."

"He disappeared off the radar in Panama and it was rumoured he'd been killed by drug runners. Haven't heard anything about him for about six years."

"Well, he's obviously not dead and is now back in the game."

"And dangerous. Always was something of a psycho."

"Do you think he's connected to Kelland?"

"Why else would they both be in Rhodes?"

"We better unpack and get out. See what we can learn."

They swung their bags on the bed, put away their clothes, arranged their toiletries and changed quickly into the more innocuous garb of holidaymakers and went out from the hotel and into the street.

This time of the year the resort wasn't too busy. It was before school holidays had kicked in and mainly older people and couples, who were taking advantage of lower prices. They donned their sun glasses and walked down the street towards a crowd of people gathered on the side of the road close to the Sotirakis Hotel. Red and white crime scene tape with Greek wording had been put up, police milled about, and a white tent had been erected with scene of crime officers coming in and out. An ambulance waited nearby and soon a gurney with a body emerged from the tent, which was loaded into the ambulance.

Roy approached a tourist to ask what was going on.

The silver haired gent standing with his wife shrugged, "Not entirely sure. Seems they found a body close to the hotel hidden behind all the refuse bins."

"Any idea, who?"

"Some bloke. I did hear someone say he was English. Don't know much more except police are pointing the finger at Golden Dawn or one of its offshoots."

"Yes," added the wife. "Cryptea or Combat 18 Hellas. It was something like that saying it's a hate crime."

"Chap must have been gay or trans. Don't hear anything about this sort of thing at home. I've never heard of Cryptea or any of the others."

"No, it's surprising. The wife's been googling it. Lots of killings and other atrocities. Wouldn't have come here if we'd known about these crank groups."

Alex murmured, "Greece and the islands are beautiful. I'm sure you'll be fine. They wouldn't want to upset the tourist trade. I shouldn't worry."

"No," replied Roy. "If it's a Neo Nazi group of some sort. They are just after the publicity not to attack holiday makers."

The couple looked doubtful. Roy and Alex moved on. "We may have to do a little grease palming."

Alex looked questioningly. "The Greek police are notorious for being corrupt. A little bribery will go a long way."

"Then we need to find a suitable Greek copper. And I'm sure the MRF can give us help with that."

Allison and Colin travelled together to Cornflowers, where Paul greeted them genially, but his face was haggard. "We're in the conservatory, come on through."

"Is the priest here yet?"

"Not yet."

They walked behind Paul into the spacious, airy and bright garden room, with its profusion of plants and rattan furniture. Paul and Colin each took a seat.

"No Holly?" questioned Colin.

"She'll be here in a minute."

"Is she Holly?" asked Allison uncertainly.

"At the moment," replied Paul.

"Good," said Colin. We need him to see her as Holly before anything else."

The bell rang.

Moments later Father Ignacia Lawrence came into the room. He was an enigmatic looking man of indeterminate age, whom Allison believed was younger than he looked. His line of work had clearly allowed lines and wrinkles of erudition, experience and weariness to form on his face. He had well-cut platinum grey hair, combed neatly and wore an expression of compassion. He was about five foot ten in height and of medium build. He was wearing a black cassock buttoned at the front and clerical collar, which raised Allison's eyebrows as it was unusual to see a priest in traditional dress outside the church. He wondered if it was anything to do with the occasion. He carried a black leather case and Paul invited him to sit.

Introductions were made and Father Lawrence settled in a wicker chair and perused those in the room seemingly to quietly assess them.

Paul asked, "Some refreshment, gentlemen?"

While Allison and Colin opted for tea, Father Lawrence requested a glass of iced water. Paul left them and Allison squirmed uncomfortably in his seat.

The priest's voice was deep and rich. Allison could imagine him giving a sermon and his voice filling the church. "To have a police report is unusual to say the least," said the Father turning his grey-blue eyes on the chief.

"Yes, well Holly is a respected consultant who has been instrumental in helping us solve many difficult cases. It's all in my report."

"Which I have read. However, I prefer to hear your assessment from your own lips."

Allison nodded. "We have noticed a subtle change in her behaviour and actions, which has grown stronger lately. She is saying and doing things out of character and by the nature of her sensitivities we are becoming increasingly concerned for her health and well-being."

"She has shown no sign of this before?"

"No. Never."

He turned to Colin, "You do not feel that she is suffering from any mental impairment? Psychological illness?"

"No. Holly has always been of sound mind. What is happening is something totally new."

The priest remained silent as he digested these facts.

Colin spoke up, "You need to meet Holly and see her as she is and see what happens to her."

"Oh, I intend to. But be assured, the Church takes cases like this very seriously indeed, which is why we have a designated priest in every diocese capable of dealing with such cases."

Paul returned with a tray of drinks and plate of biscuits, followed by Holly who eyed the priest curiously. She was looking particularly demure in a grey pinstripe dress with a white lace collar and button up boots reminiscent of nineteen-sixties' fashion.

The priest studied her. "So, you are Holly."

"I am."

"And do you feel as if you have a problem?"

Holly screwed up her face as she thought. "I don't know. I am me but I have periods where I am not me, if that makes sense? Lost times that I can't remember. Paul tells me things I have said and done, and I have no recollection or understanding of any of them."

"You know why I am here?"

"Yes. To assess me and to see if the Church can help me get rid of the spirit of my biological grandmother who is invading my body."

"That is extremely succinct, young lady."

"Call me, Holly, please."

"Very well. Holly." The conversation was stilted and difficult as Father Lawrence outlined the Church protocols. He invited witness statements from each and every one of them and shook his head. "What you are saying is very difficult to believe, when I see before me a delightful young woman, in complete control of her sensibilities and no sign of any aberrant behaviour. I'm sorry but without categorical proof that I have witnessed with my own eyes I cannot see how we are to progress."

Paul groaned, "Believe me. She really does need your help."

The priest drank his water and lay the glass down, his long, tapered fingers clutched the rosary that hung from his waist although he was not from a Dominican or Franciscan order.

"I have video footage of her when she is not herself," said Paul.

Father Lawrence rose and walked to the conservatory door. "Believe me, I am concerned for you and what you claim is happening to Holly but unless I see something myself, I am unable to help. I am not saying that nothing can be done. If, when she has another episode you call me, and I can bear witness to an attack then I will come. Of that I promise you. But for now, I will take the case under advisement from the bishop. I am afraid that is all I can do for the moment. I am sorry." He began to walk to the door. Paul followed him to show him out.

Paul tried to plead with the Father and persuade him to view his evidence as they approached the front door when suddenly there was an ear-splitting rendition of 'Fight the Good Fight' belting out in a thin strident voice heavily accented in Brummy tones. Paul stopped. "Wait! Listen! … That's not Holly. Quickly let's go back."

Father Lawrence stopped and turned, and they retraced their steps to the garden room. As they entered the room they could feel the change in room temperature, which had dropped considerably. Holly was singing, facing the window, as if her heart would burst while Allison and Colin looked on in disbelief.

As Father Lawrence re-entered the room Holly stopped singing. She spun around and faced him. Her face had undergone a subtle change as if another was imprinting itself over hers. She threw up her arms in welcome and cried out. "Trust in the Lord with all your heart and do not lean on your own understanding. In all your ways acknowledge him, and he will make straight your paths. Proverbs chapter 3 verses five to six."

Father Lawrence looked dumbstruck as Holly came closer to him. Her body moved seductively, and she swayed her hips as she walked and whispered lasciviously, "Delight yourself in the Lord and he will give you the desires of your heart. Commit your way to the Lord; trust in him, and he will act. Psalm thirty-seven verses four to five."

Holly pressed herself close to the priest, as her eyes beetled together and she murmured, "It is time. Time for my cleansing ritual. You must come with me."

"HOLLY!" shouted Paul and her eyes rolled back in her head, and she slumped to the floor. He turned to the priest, "Now do you believe us?"

"So, there's no doubt about it?"

Roy shook his head, "None. The stiff is definitely Marcus Paulson, verified by his prints and with warrants out on him. It was easy to identify him."

"I should let Mark know."

"They'll hear soon enough."

"I'll just give him a heads up," said Alex.

"Suit yourself." Roy shrugged as he spoke, "I don't suppose it can do any harm."

"It's a good job you speak Greek. What else did you learn?"

"They've taken his mobile phone, flash drives, briefcase and laptop. And they have officers checking his movements since he's been here." Roy paused and said, "Is your amiable cop going to keep us up to date?"

"I dare say. If he doesn't someone else will. So, what's your take on it?"

"It looks to me as though our friend, The Ghost, was here to do a job."

"And that job was Paulson."

"Under Kelland's instructions?"

"I reckon so. So, what now?"

"A little investigation ourselves. Find out from… what's this copper's name?"

"Kostas. Kostas Adamos."

"In the meantime, I'll contact Mark."


Allison had left Paul, Colin and Holly with the good Father and hurried to get home. His house in Gillhurst road was lit up like a Christmas tree. He saw a hire car in the drive, parked next to it, and wondered who it could belong to as he knew Mary was collecting Cally today from the station. And then he fully remembered. *Cally! Cally was home today.* This thought put a spring in his step. As he put his key in the front door lock, gales of girlish laughter reached his ears. He smiled, putting away all thoughts of Holly and what he had witnessed. Time enough for that later. He put on his brightest smile and went inside.

He entered the kitchen and to his surprise, not only was Cally there with Mary but Diana, too. They were enjoying a glass of wine together. Cally jumped up and ran to cuddle her father, "Popsie!" she exclaimed.

He returned her fierce hug a look of extreme pleasure manifesting on his face. Diana's cool voice interrupted him. "Have you got one of those for me, too, Dad?"

He opened his arms and his eldest daughter rose and snuggled into his shared embrace. His eyes filled up and his voice choked with emotion, "Diana! This is just…" stuck for words, he murmured, "Lovely."

His girls pulled him down into a seat. A glass was quickly found and filled, and the chief sat there with his wife and girls wearing a soppy look on his face and they shared a toast together. "To family."

"To family," they chorused and burst into excited chatter around the table.

Pooley went down to the cells to prepare prisoners on remand for transfer to Winson Green. He stopped short when he arrived at Nesbitt's cell. "You!" he exclaimed, recognising him. "What are you here for?"

Nesbitt groaned, "Wrong place, wrong time, Guv."

"I'll say," Pooley shook his head and drew in his cheeks. "You got a slew of charges waiting for you. What's this one, then?"

"What I got for trying to do the right thing," grunted Nesbitt. "I may have got mixed up in something I wasn't ready for. I ain't no killer."

"Then help yourself. Tell us what you know, and it will go better for you."

"Then I'm a dead man."

"Suit yourself. You'll go down for a long time."

Nesbitt shrugged, "Nothing no one can do now."

Pooley studied his list. He found Nesbitt's name and that he'd been apprehended during a break in to a witness' house. "I'll be back. Think on what I've said. There's still time to turn this around."

Nesbitt turned away and faced the wall. His inner turmoil was revealed in his face.


Ronnie and Gurdip were back at base and ploughing through their notes. They were hampered by Allison's absence and needed to report to him to check on how they were to proceed. Ronnie called across to Mark who signalled that he was on an important call and to give him a minute.

Ronnie chewed the end of his pen as he doodled the names of those they needed to follow up on including how they could speak to Dr Edgar Charles, already in custody for an unrelated crime, so what was the link?

They also had to interview, Fred's family. His sister, Sadie Baker, they would do first on a zoom call together with her twin daughters, Julie and Yvonne. Ronnie went about setting it up. Gurdip was trying to track down Fred's children, Jason Butterworth and Marilyn Spicer. This was trickier, Marilyn was divorced and had moved out of the family home, her husband had gained custody of their only child. Jason moved around a lot and his last known address was in Smethwick. Gurdip would need to go to the flat and see if there was any forwarding address. In the meantime, he'd join Ronnie on the Zoom call with Sadie Baker and her daughters.


Across the squad room, Mark was on the phone to Alex, "Nothing has come to us yet."

"It will."

"Are you sure it's Paulson?"

Fingerprints don't lie. Not when they are on the hand."

"Fair enough. What else?"

"We believe his death is the result of a hitman nicknamed 'The Ghost'. He's known to both of us, ex-military, we saw him walking through Departures as we were coming into Rhodes. We also saw Kelland leaving. It's too much of a coincidence and I don't believe in coincidences."

"Nor do we."

"I'll be in touch." Alex ended the call.

Mark replaced his phone thoughtfully. This was news. Allison wasn't around, so Mark sat at his desk and pulled up the Interpol file on Paulson and saw that his death had been reported in Rhodes and was under investigation. He needed to discover if any other evidence had been discovered at the crime scene or where Paulson had been staying. He immediately issued a request for the evidence to be shared with them.

Pooley walked into the squad room and crossed to Mark, "Can I have a word?" Mark looked up and nodded genially. "Got a prisoner downstairs waiting to go on remand to Winson Green."

"Yes?"

"Name of Nesbitt." At this name, Angus Mackay looked up and strained to listen.

"That's one of the men from Montague Road."

"The sex trafficking case?"

"Yes. I thought he'd escaped. But, it seems he's up on a different charge, breaking and entering a property and threatening a woman."

"Is he, by George?"

"Do you think we can delay his transfer? Get someone to accompany the CDO and meet the escort service to take the other two thugs to the prison and hold Nesbitt. He can be transferred later."

"Why?"

"I dunno. Just a hunch. Think we might get something out of him. He says, he won't talk but I reckon with a bit of friendly persuasion he might crack."

Mark thought for a moment, "Let me make a call. Get someone to accompany the handover to the CDO on duty and get Nesbitt in Interview Room 4." Mark looked around the squad room. "Mackay!" Mackay looked up. "Get yourself downstairs with…" he looked at Pooley. "Who was doing the handover with you?"

"Rennie, look up the CDO in the log. Go down with Mackay and introduce him to the officer taking the other prisoners to 'orse Road. Leave Nesbitt."

Mackay questioned, "Horse Road?"

"Just a nickname for the prison. Stop what you're doing. Do it now. Pooley, go and fetch Nesbitt. I'll see you downstairs."

"I've just got a quick call to make. I'll meet Bill downstairs, if that's okay?" said Mackay.

Mark nodded, gathered his notes and went after Pooley.

Alex and Roy sat at the Taverna where Kelland had entertained the locals. They soon discovered much more through gossip and bribery. Giorgios sat at the table with them. He spoke good English, as many Greeks do, and Roy was able to fill in any blanks in Greek. They were soon getting a picture of events that fateful night.

Giorgios continued, "Mr Forrest he wanted to play a prank on his friend and had a bet."

"Mr Forrest? Is this him?" He passed him a photo of Martyn Kelland.

"Yes, yes. Mr Forrest. That's him."

Roy and Alex exchanged a look and Roy continued. "He would pretend to ply me with drinks, but I only drank water. Ouzo looks like water. He even pretended to put drugs in my drink while his friend was supposed to be watching. I had to pretend to be drunk and fall about near home and then take him by surprise when he came to me. I know jujitsu and Taekwondo. This I did."

"What then?"

"I left him and went home. Mr Forrest was going to ambush him. I not know what really went down. I was shocked in morning when I find out what happened. I not say a word. I no want go prison. I keep quiet."

Roy nodded in understanding. "Who else knew about this?"

"No one. It just supposed to be a bit of fun. No fun for that guy."

Ronnie and Gurdip had finished their zoom call with Sadie Baker and her two daughters. They were pleasant ladies, and the detectives didn't believe they had anything to do with the attack on Stan. Sadie was at work that night at the local hospital, where she was a staff nurse and the twin sisters, Julie and Yvonne, had both been at home revising for their A level exams to which their father could testify as could a study buddy, Jeanette Carter. Who had been with them. Ronnie and Gurdip believed they were innocent of any offences.

They now had to look to Fred's children who they learned were Robert Butterworth and Marilyn Spicer. Thirty-two-year-old Rob had a history of minor offences, anti-social behaviour, petty theft, and being drunk and disorderly. Marilyn had a clean slate. They couldn't find anything about her anywhere. Sadie had given them their addresses and contact details, so the next step was to pay them both a visit. They agreed that they would check in on Meredith Probert at the same time.

Gurdip stood up, yawned and stretched and went to the windows and looked out over the city. Angus Mackay was still talking quietly on the phone to someone and had his head down. Gurdip was suspicious. The man was usually so full of himself and loud that Gurdip was curious and wondered who he was talking to.

Mackay turned as he felt Gurdip's presence and said into his phone, "Gotta run and get back to work. I'll call you later." He replaced the receiver and stared challengingly at Gurdip, "What?" There was a surliness to his tone.

Gurdip shrugged but caught the hostile look in Mackay's eyes and returned to his seat as Mackay glared after him. Mackay quickly changed his expression as Bill Rennie walked back into the squad room.

"Are you coming or what?" asked Bill.

Mackay grinned innocently up at Bill as if he was the Chief Chorister at St. Paul's Cathedral. He could see he had Bill hooked and was ready to reel him in, maybe even make him an ally.

Bill waited at the door as Mackay gathered his things. Bill was acting like an adoring puppy around Mackay, and they were soon engaged in lively banter and more of Mackay's tales. Ronnie glanced across at Mackay and Bill laughing together and frowned. As the officers left and made their way downstairs Ronnie studied his friend, Gurdip. "What? What is it?"

Gurdip shook his head, "Nothing. Don't worry about it."

But, Ronnie knew something had upset Gurdip. He had a feeling it was to do with systemic racism. He had seen it too many times before, and at some point he would tackle Gurdip to find out.

# 8

ALEX AND ROY SAT AT a table outside the Taverna Paradisi. They were in the company of Kostas Adamos from the local Hellenic police station where he was captain. They were talking softly in a mixture of Greek and English as they shared a few Mythos beers. Captain Adamos looked around furtively and passed Roy a local shopping bag and Roy passed Kostas a padded envelope, which he secreted in his jacket and shook Roy's hand.

"I need them back as soon as possible. The British police want them."

"I bet they do," said Roy. "Give us two days. Can you do that?"

Kostas nodded, "I can manage that. We meet here same time, two days from now?"

Roy nodded, "Agreed." They shook hands again and Kostas left. He turned to Alex, "Let's get these babies back to the hotel. See what we can learn."

Alex added, "And hope we can crack the passcodes easily." They paid their bill and made their way back to the hotel.

Once in their room they tipped out Paulson's laptop, flash drives and phone, put on surgical gloves and started work. Alex took the phone and Roy the laptop. Alex switched on the mobile and was surprised to see there was no security needed to open it up. He was straight in. He checked text messages and numbers, making a list of what he believed to be of relevance. Harder to access, he thought, would be deleted messages. He was wrong. There weren't any.

He crossed over to Roy who was working on the laptop and peered over his shoulder at the screen with the desktop files in view. Roy was systematically working through them. and copying the computer's contents onto a memory stick.

"Something's not right," said Alex.

Roy paused and looked up, "What?"

"It's too easy. It doesn't take a mastermind to get into his phone, no security, password, nothing. I think that's highly unusual."

"Maybe he's careless or not as bright as we thought."

"Maybe… or maybe we're being set up. What have you got?"

"I'm copying everything for us to study later but I must admit I'm surprised, too."

"Why?"

"Look at this." He highlighted a file and opened it up. "Unencrypted for a start. And it has details of sex trafficking, including the cases in Birmingham. This is on an international level, and I would have thought these business dealings would have been locked in secure files. It's as if someone wanted us to find them as it marks Paulson out as the brains behind the job and that I just can't believe."

"What about the flash drives?

"We'll copy them to our computers. We'll have to get the cyber unit onto them. These do look encrypted. Once we've copied everything over we can return them to Kostas. But I agree with you. Something is not right."

"Hmm. And it's convenient that there are text messages on the phone, talking about the black market organ donation and references to how his boss is unaware of what's going on under his own nose at West End Products."

"Like you say, it's just all too easy."


Ronnie and Gurdip had checked at the address in Smethwick and were given a forwarding address for Fred's son. They arrived at Jason Butterworth's house at 181, West Boulevard, Quinton. It was a respectable redbrick house in a row with others of the same design, a small front garden with a gate, and room to park on a gravel path. There was no vehicle parked there so Gurdip and

Ronnie parked on the hard standing, went to the front door and rang the bell.

A petite blonde holding a small baby answered the door. She looked harassed and careworn. "Mrs Butterworth?" enquired Ronnie.

"Who wants to know?" They showed their warrant cards, and she admitted them. "What's he done now?"

"Nothing as far as we know," said Ronnie politely.

"Then why are you here?"

"We just need to ask him a few questions."

"Good luck with that."

"Where is Mr Butterworth?"

"Gawd knows. I ain't seen him for the best part of two weeks."

"Then maybe you can help us. Where is he likely to be?"

The woman shrugged. "Don't know. You could try his sister. Thick as thieves those two are."

"Do you happen to know where he was," Ronnie checked his notebook, "last Tuesday?"

"No. He bunked off the Friday before. Sorry."

Gurdip asked, "Have you ever heard him mention his uncle? Stan Butterworth or his father Fred?"

The woman thought for a moment and said, "Look you might as well sit down. Looks like this could take a while and I need to feed this one. Do you mind?"

Both detectives sat muttering their thanks, exchanged a look and murmured that no they had no objections.

Mrs Butterworth turned away from them and adjusted her blouse, she wrapped a shawl around her and the baby and turned back to face them and sat on her nursing chair with a pillow underneath her arm and the little one. The baby sucked greedily, and little soft gulping sounds came from his throat. It was all done very discreetly.

"You wanted to know about his dad? Bad news that man. He's in Belmarsh. Been in and out of trouble all his life and that's what's rubbed off on my Jason. Always filling his head with stories of riches to come. Said he was doing time for theft and the loot will be his reward."

"Any idea what he meant by that?"

"He filled his head with some nonsense about the goose that laid the golden egg. Fairy tales, I told him. But he argued with me and said no, it was true, and his Uncle Stan had all the answers. Trouble was, his dad's terminally ill now. They're trying to get him out so he can die at home. When Fred gets out, if he gets out, all will be revealed. Jason and that sister of his, Marilyn went up to the smoke to visit him. When he came back he said he didn't like the look of his dad. Thought he was a gonner. Said he was going to have to take matters into his own hands. He had the names of some other blokes that had been involved in a job years ago. I thought they'd all be doddering fools now but seems some of the chaps have passed their knowledge onto their sons. So, he and Marilyn went off to visit his uncle and say hello. He came back like a raging bull, fair upset me and little 'un. Said his Uncle had gone barking. Didn't know what he was talking about. Old boy's got Alzheimer's and don't remember nothing. According to Jason he was supposed to be looking after Fred's share for him. A share that was to come to him and Marilyn. I told him, it was all pie in the sky, he told me to shut it and walked out. I ain't seen him since." She sighed heavily, "That's that then. No buried treasure nothing to make our lives any easier."

"Do you know where Marilyn lives?" asked Gurdip.

"Marilyn Spicer her name is. Somewhere in Selly Park, I believe. Not sure of the actual address. It'll be in the book by the phone." She jerked her head to a telephone table next to the settee. "In the drawer over there. Help yourself."

Gurdip reached in the drawer of the stand next to where he was sitting and opened it. Underneath a pile of bills and invoices was a little black book.

"That's it. In there. Take a look." Gurdip thumbed through the names and addresses and found an entry for Marilyn, several had been crossed out and the last one entered was in Selly Park Road, Selly Park. As he made a note of the full address and phone number he flicked through the book and a couple of other names caught his eye, one was Nesbitt. He quickly scanned the number repeating it in his head before closing the book and returning it.

"Is that it?" asked Mrs Butterworth. "There ain't no more I can tell you."

Ronnie rose, "No. Thank you, you've been very helpful. We'll see ourselves out. If you remember anything else, here's my card. He placed his card on the coffee table in front of him. If you do see or hear from Jason please let us know."

"I doubt it. I'm having the locks changed. He can go jump…I want nothing more to do with him."

Ronnie nodded politely and the two detectives left the house.


Martyn Kelland was back in the Dominican Republic and making plans to return to the UK. He was on the phone to Kira. "Darling, I don't know what happened. You should never have been put in that position."

"I've been threatened, the police are all over me."

"But, Kira. I am not involved. Paulson was the one who was using my business. I had no idea what was going on. Call me naïve."

"But, the girls. I saw them at the warehouse. Remember, you picked me out from one consignment? You saved me."

"Well, maybe I was aware of some things, but I didn't have anything to do with it. I thought he had some prostitution ring, was pimping or something. I didn't know all the details. Look I don't want to fight. I just want to put things straight. As it happens I can't get home yet, not until my name's cleared and I want you to come and live with me. I'll get a divorce and we'll be together." There was a pause on the other end of the line. "You haven't said anything to anyone, have you? Not talked to the cops?"

Kira hesitated, "I may have said something."

"Oh, Kira. What? What have you said?"

"Not much. Just that you protected me and gave me a job," she lied.

"I see. Pity you can't tell them that Paulson was behind it all."

"I can still do that."

"Can you?"

"Yes. Then we can be together. When can I see you?"

"Soon my darling, soon. Let me know when you've spoken to the police and set the record straight and I'll send for you. I promise."

"I will. I promise I'll call you."

Kelland put down the phone thoughtfully, and murmured, "I may have to call in The Ghost again."

It was then his phone rang. He looked at the screen and frowned. Number withheld. "Hello?"

Nesbitt sat in Interview Room 4 with Stringer and Pooley. He looked uncomfortable. His eyes were firmly fixed on the table between them, and he nibbled anxiously at his already badly bitten nails.

"In a spot of bother, Nesbitt." Nesbitt remained silent. "Remember me?" asked Pooley. Nesbitt's eyes flicked to Pooley's face and back to the table. "I noticed you wanted nothing to do with any of it, in the house where I was a prisoner, and so you scarpered. But we need your help to catch the real villains. Help us and it will go better for you." Nesbitt shrugged. "What were you hoping to achieve breaking into Mrs Probert's house? What has that got to do with trafficking young girls."

Nesbitt looked up and engaged eyes with Pooley, "You wouldn't believe me, if I told you."

"Try me."

"I'm no killer, a thief, maybe but not a killer."

"Then talk."

At that moment, Angus Mackay walked in. "Well, well, well. Nesbitt. Bit out of your league here, aren't you?"

Nesbitt shifted uncomfortably in his seat and Mark Stringer detected a flicker of alarm flash across his eyes.

"Mackay, what are you doing in here?" asked Mark.

"Thought I may be able to help. Nesbitt's a collar from my old manor. Do you want me to have a go at him?"

Mark bristled, "Thanks, but no thanks. We don't want past deeds muddying this investigation. We've got this."

"Suit yourself." He turned to Nesbitt. "Just remember they don't know you like I do. I know how slippery you can be." Mackay turned and left the room as Mark and Pooley exchanged a look.

"You were saying?" prompted Mark.

"I'm saying nothing. I want a lawyer." The change in Nesbitt's attitude was noticeable.

Pooley tried again, "There's something you're not telling us." Nesbitt remained stone-faced. "I understand you went to stop your partner from threatening Mrs Probert." Nesbitt rolled his eyes. "She was scared to death."

"He's no partner of mine. I'm not into threatening old ladies."

"No, I don't expect you are. What about trafficking young women?"

Nesbitt remained tight-lipped. "I've told you. I'm saying nothing."

Mark closed his file with a sweeping gesture, "This is getting us nowhere. Let him stew a while longer. We'll be back." They rose and walked to the door, when Nesbitt's voice stopped them.

"I thought I was going to Winson Green on remand."

Mark turned, "You are. But not yet. We've not quite finished."

"Then, you ought to get your own house in order. That's all I'm saying."

Mark and Pooley exchanged a look and Mark walked back to the table and rested his hands on it and stared at Nesbitt, "And just what do you mean by that?" Nesbitt was morosely silent. "Come on, Nesbitt. You can't throw something like that into the mix and not explain."

Nesbitt raised his eyes. "You need to look amongst your own."

"I don't follow," said Pooley.

Nesbitt drew in a breath, "Let's just say, not everyone can be trusted."

"Who? Who are you referring to?"

"Up to you to find out. I'm saying no more." Nesbitt fixed his eyes on the table again, ignoring further questions.

Stringer and Pooley left the room and spoke in low tones. "What do you think he meant?" asked Pooley.

"I'm not sure. Sounded like he was accusing one of our men of duplicity."

"It did. Did you notice his attitude when Mackay walked in?"

"I did. You don't think…?"

"I don't know but there was certainly a shift in his attitude."

"What do you know about Mackay?"

"Nothing much. Just that he'd transferred."

"Yes, but why? Why leave the Met for Brum?"

They fell silent as they approached the squad room. Pooley stopped. "Think I'll do a little digging, off the record, of course."

"Of course."

Mark sat looking thoughtfully ahead. He was wondering how he could persuade Nesbitt to talk when his desk phone rang jolting him back to the present. "Stringer... yes?" He sat upright looking concerned as he listened. "What?... Are you sure? But then why did you make a statement to the contrary?" He listened some more. "You will have to come in and redo it and you could be liable for perverting the course of justice." He listened some more and sighed heavily. "Very well. I'll expect you in later. Three o'clock? Fine." Mark ended the call and studied the receiver as he replaced it. He snapped his fingers at Pooley who looked up and Mark called him over.

"I've just had a very interesting conversation with a witness in the Kelland Paulson case."

Pooley looked interested. "Spill."

"Remember the woman who worked in the office?"

"Kira someone or other."

"Yes, her. She's just retracted her statement. She's coming in to make another."

"Why?"

"She said it was because she wanted to hurt him... revenge for him being married and not leaving his wife and for everything that happened to her."

"So, what's she saying now?"

"Said she'd lied and couldn't live with herself for doing that. She claimed Paulson was the brains and Kelland was just used. He was unaware of what was going on under his nose at West End Products."

"Do you believe her?"

"No... it's just a little too convenient, don't you think?"

"Think someone has got to her?"

"Quite possibly."

"I think you'll also be interested in what I'm learning, too."

"Yes?"

"Not here. Let me finish what I'm doing, and we'll take a break together."

Mark nodded and watched Pooley return to his desk and looked around. Everyone present seemed to be working. But not everyone was there. He knew that he needed to speak to Allison.

Jane sat in the estate agents, sorting out property details to be emailed to customers when the door opened. Jacob Murch, her immediate boss walked in.

"Morning, Jane. Have there been any calls for me?" He was a tall man, in his late forties, athletically built with a fine head of chestnut coloured hair. He was smartly dressed in a navy pinstripe suit and blue shirt with a royal blue tie.

Jane looked up and smiled, "Morning, Mr Murch. Your brother rang and wants you to call him back and a Mr Patterson left a message to say he couldn't make the three o'clock viewing could you make it later. I've jotted down the messages and numbers on your memo pad."

"Thank you. I wonder what Nathan wants. He rarely rings the office."

Jane looked up impishly, "Guess you'll have to call him to find out."

"Very funny. But, you're right. I'll phone him now."

Jacob disappeared into his office and Jane saw the switchboard light up telling her his line was in use and she carried on with placing property details in envelopes to be, franked and posted.

The light went out and almost immediately lit up again. Jane could hear Jacob had raised his voice in his office, but she couldn't make out what was being said even though she strained to listen. It was most unlike Jacob to shout, and she frowned.

He stormed out of his office, "Anyone rings. Take a message. I have to go out for a while."

"Is everything all right, sir?"

"Nothing I can't handle. Can you hold the fort, Jane?"

"Of course, sir."

With that he buttoned up his mackintosh and headed out. He turned at the door. "If I'm not back before closing, can you shut up shop for me, please?"

"Of course."

Jacob closed the door leaving the shop bell clanging in his wake.

# 9

MEREDITH PROBERT SAT AT STAN'S bedside. She placed a box of cupcakes on his nightstand and held his hand. "Come on, Stan. You need to get fit and well and then you can come home."

Stan squeezed Meredith's hand. "It won't be long. They've said that as soon as my bloods are normal, they'll let me go. Doctor is reviewing me today. Look at my arm. Like a pin cushion I am."

"The bruises will fade. At least you didn't break anything. Tell me, Stan. Who was it?"

Stan screwed up his face as he thought. "I've wracked me brains. I don't remember nothing. Honestly. But you, Meredith I remember you. And as soon as I get out of here I'm seeing a solicitor and putting you in my will. The rest of the family can go whistle. They've done nothing for me. Nowt. But you... You've always been there for me and helped me whenever you can."

"Oh, Stan. I don't want anything. It'll be enough to have you back home. You can help me with my coffee mornings."

"Ah, but you don't know what I got." Stan touched his nose with his first two fingers and winked. "What I got is worth having and it'll be yours when I've gone."

"Don't talk like that. Please. I don't care what you've got. I just want your friendship."

"You know my head's all over the place, these days and my mind gets foggier. I want to do this while I can still remember. Can you recommend a good solicitor… One that can be trusted?"

Jane was just putting away her files and about to close down her computer when Jacob Murch returned in a somewhat agitated state. She looked at him concerned, "Is everything all right, sir?"

"No, Jane it isn't and there isn't anything anyone can do about it. Except…"

"Yes?"

"Mr Patterson."

"What about him?"

"No, I couldn't ask you, it's time to go home."

"I don't mind, sir if I can help."

"Can you make the viewing with Mr Patterson at five-thirty? I have a shed load of work to do and…"

"Yes, sir. That's fine. Just tell me where and when?"

Jacob smiled in relief. "That will be such a help."

"No problem."

"It's an address in Quinton Birmingham. A bit out of your way, I know. 59, Glyn Farm Road. Nice property. He wants to add it to his portfolio of rental properties. I have the keys here." He fished in his pocket and pulled out a set of keys and passed them to her. "I'll just get the details." Jacob moved into his office and retrieved a set of sales details. "I know it's out of our area. I will phone him and explain that you will be meeting him instead of me. He's an important client. I don't want to upset him. I've written him a letter. Could you pass it on to him please." He handed her a sealed envelope, which she put in her bag.

"Of course," said Jane smiling. "I recognise the name. Doesn't he have properties all over the place?"

"Yes. He has quite a list from Shropshire to Bath. Luckily, this one is in Birmingham and it's not too far. Are you sure you don't mind?"

"Honestly, sir it's fine. I'll see you tomorrow."

Jacob sighed, "Ideal. I'll see you then. Have a good night."

Pooley finished his call with the Met and put down the phone, carefully. He rubbed his chin and went to find Mark. He found him in the chief's office, collecting some files. He slipped inside and closed the door, apologising to Maddie as he did so.

He spoke in low hushed tones, "Just had an interesting conversation with one of Mackay's old colleagues."

"Yes?"

"Now he's not accusing him of anything. Just saying that there were suspicions about his behaviour. He moved from Forest Gate to Clapham South. Some excuse or other about not getting on well with the crew there and some rumblings about his attitude towards ethnic minority members. Now it's not clear why, but he was something to do with a particular case involving the grooming of minors and lost an important piece of evidence. Caused something of a ruckus and as a result he put in a request to transfer to another force, preferably the Midlands. Hence, he is here."

Mark digested this information, "Any information on Nesbitt?"

Pooley nodded, "Petty crime and theft. Nothing violent. Interestingly, his father was well known to the force. Believed to have been involved in some major crimes. From what I've learned, he was something of a reluctant criminal."

Mark raised his eyebrows, "Seems in line with what he said to us. Let's go and have a word."

Jane sat in her car outside the property in Glyn Farm Road. She was early. She took out the details and studied them. It was a Georgian styled house with bay windows and a well-kept garden at the front and back. It had valuable parking spaces in the drive. It appeared to be a well-proportioned family house for a couple with children. It had schools nearby, not too far to the shops, and excellent public transport links. Perfect really.

She sent a quick text to Alex explaining where she was and that she may be able to question Mr Patterson about the problems involved with buying multiple properties and to ask him if he had ever come under any scrutiny from HMRC. It will help your research. She ended the text with miss you and a kiss, and tossed her phone on the passenger seat.

Jane took out Mr Murch's letter, picked up the paperwork, and house keys. She stepped out of the car, locked it and made her way up to the front door and opened it.

Back in the car, her phone vibrated and rang, The name Alex came up on screen, but Jane was too far away to hear anything.

Jane began to appraise the house. It was in good order and well laid out, some redecoration was needed but little else. She made mental notes as she walked around, possibilities for alterations, which she didn't believe were needed, but it was always good to have suitable responses on how to change things if someone didn't like the layout.

She glanced out of a bedroom window and saw a black Range Rover draw up outside and assumed that it must be Mr Patterson, so she made her way downstairs and opened the front door.

A chauffeur stepped out of the vehicle and opened the back passenger door and out stepped a sharply dressed tall man with a full head of salt and pepper grey hair. The chauffeur remained by the driver's door as Mr Patterson started up the drive.

"Mr Patterson?" Jane extended her hand, which he ignored.

He breezed past her into the house. Jane bit her tongue, she couldn't abide rudeness. "Mr Murch asked me to give you this. She passed him the letter, which he thrust into his inside pocket.

Jane noticed his hands were beautifully manicured. He had nails that shone as if coated with plain varnish. The skin looked soft, too. He wore a heavy gold signet ring on his right hand. His suit was expensive. She surmised it was a light wool mohair mix. Jane swallowed hard and tried to engage him in friendly conversation. "Mr Murch sends his apologies and said he would telephone you later to discuss the viewing."

Mr Patterson merely nodded, adding, "Damn nuisance Jacob not being here. I value his advice."

"Anything I can help with I will," said Jane pleasantly as she began extolling the virtues of the house.

"I can read the property details myself, thank you," he said brusquely. Jane bit her lip and looked positively crestfallen. Mr Patterson caught her expression and apologised. "I'm sorry. That sounded very rude. It's just I am in something of a hurry and somewhat annoyed that Jacob isn't here himself, although I had been forewarned. There is no need for me to take it out on you." He smiled radiantly at her, and Jane felt somewhat better.

"I know I'm not Mr Murch and you have a long association with him, but I will do my best to help you in any way I can. Any questions just ask away," and she beamed at him.

"Thank you. Lead the way."

Jane explored the house again with him, pointing out architectural features and feeling a little bolder decided to ask him a question. "Mr Patterson, I wonder if you can help me?"

"If I can. What is it?"

"My boyfriend is a writer, and he is working on a tricky part of his plot that involves estate agents and a criminal mastermind."

"My dear, I hope you are not suggesting I am some kind of crook?"

"No, no. Of course not. I just thought that as you have such a magnificent portfolio that you might be able to tell me the pitfalls of buying properties in large numbers… as far as HMRC and the law is concerned. Any problems you might have encountered…"

Mr Patterson paused and studied her. His smile was calculated. "Well, my dear, it's not a problem if you have a good estate agent and solicitor who work together. I suggest you talk to Mr Murch. He will be able to help you more than me. I always leave it capably in his hands."

Jane smiled and turned away. "Thank you, Mr Patterson. I will take your advice." She didn't notice the change in his eyes, which had become colder, nor his mouth, which twitched at one corner.


Alex was walking outside the studios frantically trying to contact Jane. He had responded to her text with an attempted warning. "No, don't ask him anything. Please. You never know who you are talking to. I'll call you later."

He tried to ring her, but the connection was bad and now his battery was low. He needed to charge up his phone. In something of a panic, he wondered what he could do. He dashed inside and put his phone on charge and managed to send another text. "Jane, please call me, ASAP."

He gave the numbers of the Hotel Pegasus and his room and sat and waited anxiously.

Kelland sat in a beachside bar in the Dominican Republic eating a local delicacy of empanadas and tostones, a side dish of twice fried plantain. He was talking quietly on the phone to someone. "Well, you better do something about it … I don't care … Very well… call him." Kelland ended the call, looking pensive. He appeared to come to a decision and scrolled through his phone until he found the number he was searching for and hit the call button.

"Hello, I may have another little job for you… Same arrangement as before … I'll send you the details in the usual way." Kelland curtailed the call.

Gurdip and Ronnie compared notes on what they had discovered and tried to piece things together and make sense of it. Ronnie stared out the window. It was raining with graphite grey skies. He watched as the raindrops chased each other down the glass. Where was the sun? Almost as if the heavens heard him the rain dribbled to a stop and a chink of blue appeared in the gloomy skies.

Ronnie scratched his head and groaned. "We need to run this by the chief."

"Agreed. But how?"

"What do you mean?"

"His daughters are across, and he has taken some time off."

"I thought he only had one daughter?" said Ronnie.

"No. One lives in the States, the other in Australia. He has grandchildren he hardly ever sees."

"How do you know all this?"

"From Mary."

Ronnie raised an eyebrow questioningly.

"I spent a lot of time in the kitchen with her when we stayed there. Heard all about her family. And, Sergeant Stringer let drop he was taking some personal time."

"How long?"

"Couple of weeks, I think."

"What do we do?"

"Take it to Mark. Get his advice."

"Is he in?"

"Haven't seen him."

"We need to speak to him away from here." Ronnie glanced around. "Not safe if our suspicions are correct."

"No," said Gurdip as he saw Mackay staring at him from across the squad room. "I think we'd better shut up. Perhaps take a break," he said meaningfully as Mackay began walking across the room towards them.

"Got a problem, lads? Anything I can help with?"

"Nope. We're fine. Thanks," said Ronnie with a grin.

Mackay tried to sneak a look at the paperwork on the desk, but Gurdip was too quick. He shuffled the papers together, sat forward on the desk and folded his arms over it.

"Thirsty work this," exclaimed Ronnie. "Come on, Gurdip. It's stopped raining. Let's take a break, grab a coffee." Ronnie closed down his computer and grinned at Mackay. "Catch you later, Angus." He stood up and tapped Gurdip on the shoulder, "Come on. Bring your notes. We can discuss them over coffee."

Gurdip rose and forced a smile and nodded at Mackay who stared distastefully at him. They left and took the stairs to the foyer and out into the road. "What now?"

"Let's get across to the chief."

"Without announcing ourselves?"

"He won't mind. Especially when he hears what we have to say."


Alex walked across his hotel room back and fore until Roy complained. "Quit with the pacing, will you? It's making me dizzy."

"Sorry." Alex sat down with a bump. "It's just…"

"I know. I'm sure she'll contact you as soon as she can. Remember there's a two-hour time difference. Not only that her phone may be switched off. It could be at the bottom of her handbag, and she can't hear it ring… could be anything."

"I just wish I'd never mentioned anything. I'll never forgive myself if anything happens to her."

"Let it rest. Worry about it when it happens. That's my philosophy. Anyway, we leave tomorrow."

Just then Alex's phone rang, and he snatched it up.

"Alex?"

"Jane? Are you okay?"

"I don't know…"

"Why? What's happened?"

"Nothing… but…"

"But what?"

"It's just a feeling."

"What? What are you feeling?"

"I came to feed Snooks, and I could swear someone was following me… watching me…"

"Who?"

"I don't know. No one I've ever seen before. It made me feel uneasy."

"Where are you now?"

"At work."

"Is anyone with you?"

"Just Mr Murch. He's in his office."

"Are you using the office phone?"

"No."

"Listen carefully… make an excuse. Say you have a migraine and get out of there. Is there anywhere you can go?"

"I could go to my mum and dad's. But I have to feed Snooks."

"Is there anyone else?"

"There's always my friend Clare. Why? What's happening?"

"I'll explain everything when I see you. Don't go out alone. When you go to feed Snooks take someone with you. When you're in the house or at Clare's lock all the doors and windows."

"Alex, you're frightening me…"

"I don't want to do that. I just need you to be careful. I will be home tomorrow. I want you to stay away from work and don't go out anywhere. Understand?"

"Yes, but…"

"No buts. Please do as I say. Promise?"

"I promise. Can't you tell me what it's all about?"

"Not on the phone. I'll see you tomorrow. If not before. I'll call you later. Be careful."

Alex ended the call and turned to Roy. "We have to try and get a flight back tonight. You can stay on until tomorrow. You have to return all the stuff to Kostas."

"I'm coming with you. I can give this lot back today. No arguments. Let's get packed up. I'll call Kostas and book a taxi to the airport. We'll have more chance of changing flights if we're at the airport."

Alex didn't argue. He just nodded.


Mary Allison opened the door to Ronnie and Gurdip. "How lovely to see you, both. Come on in."

The young detectives trooped in and could already hear laughter and excited chatter coming from the sitting room. They followed Mary inside. "Look who was at the door!"

Allison glanced up, "It must be important if you've come all the way here."

Ronnie blushed, "We don't wish to intrude, Chief."

Gurdip added, "No. We can come back another time, if we're interrupting."

"No, it's okay. I'll hear what you've got to say. Go on through to the kitchen."

Ronnie and Gurdip made their way through the house to the kitchen as Greg Allison heaved himself out of his chair and walked to the door. He turned to Mary and his daughters, "I won't be long. I want to hear more about your trip to Chile and Argentina on that wine tour, Diana, and more about your plans, Cally All the details. Leave nothing out." DCI Allison lumbered out through the door, closed it and from inside, the excited chatter resumed.

The chief entered the kitchen and faced Ronnie and Gurdip. He gestured them to sit, "Now, then... what's all this about?"

# 10

ALLISON LISTENED CAREFULLY TO WHAT his young detectives had to say and rubbed his chin, in the way that was peculiar to him and spoke quietly. "Have you talked to anyone else about this?" They exchanged a glance before they shook their heads. "Good. Keep it that way."

There was a silence.

"Sir, I think Pooley and Stringer have suspicions."

"Why is that?"

"From conversations."

Allison eyed up the two young men. "This is not going to be easy. We have to get absolute proof. Internal Affairs will have to be involved at the right time. We'll get Mark and Pooley in on this, but no one else. The less people know the better. What about Nesbitt?"

"Soon to be transferred to Horse Road."

"Do we know the Custody Detention Officer who is taking him from the custody suite to the security service?"

"CDO Birling took the other two prisoners with another CDO. They change all the time. We can never be sure who will be on the escort team. Mackay went along to meet the security group to see what's what. And who's who. He was interested in how we do transfers here he said."

"Wish we weren't so short staffed. Thank you for coming to see me with this. You know I have taken leave as my family is home?"

"Yes, sir," they chorused.

"It's not ideal. But Mary would skin me alive if I came back to work now. Please keep me informed. And… watch your backs."


Alex was in something of a state. He was fidgety on the plane, anxious going through passport control and couldn't wait to get back to Ironbridge. Roy tried to calm him en route.

"I won't drop you off. I'll get out with you and see you in. Stop panicking. It's not like you. You need a cool head."

"It's all right for you, you have a family. I've never had anyone. All I have is Snooks and now, Jane. How did you manage it? Keeping your family safe in this line of work?"

"I just did, and I kept them separate. Sally knew what I was involved in after I left the military but no specifics, so she understood and never asked questions. It was safer that way. If it's serious with Jane you should tell her."

Alex blew out of his mouth as he considered what was said. "I've never been serious about anyone."

"Are you serious about her?"

"I am."

"Then bite the bullet and tell her."

"Then what?"

"Explain about your other life. She'll understand. She already knows you do something for the Government."

Alex nodded, "She's guessed a bit. Knows I'm not just trying to be an author. Teases me sometimes, about my James Bond activities, calls me a spy!"

"You'll work out what to say. Now relax. It won't be long, and you'll be able to see her. Does she know you're coming home early?"

"I sent her a text at the airport. She hasn't replied."

"That doesn't necessarily mean something has happened."

"But what if it has?"

"We'll cross that bridge when we come to it."

Meredith Probert was in tears. She had arrived at the hospital that evening with some more treats for Stan to discover he had suffered a massive heart attack in the night and had passed away. The nurse tried to comfort her in the family room. "He thought a lot of you. He left you this."

Staff Nurse Payne passed Meredith a buff envelope, which Meredith eyed curiously. It had a logo on the front and a name, Samuel's Solicitors. "Aren't you going to open it?"

Meredith nodded, "In a moment. I will. What about his body and the funeral? His next of kin will need to be contacted. None of his family live close by."

"I hope I can leave that to you?" she asked.

Meredith nodded miserably. "Yes, I'll see to it." She dabbed at her nose with her hankie and began to open the letter. The nurse watched her. As Meredith began to read, she gasped. "I don't believe it." Nurse Payne looked at her. "He has made me executor of his will and has left me all his tools and motorcycles, the contents of his bank accounts and safety deposit box. Not only that, he has bequeathed his house and contents to me and I am instructed that when that is sold that I am to donate fifty thousand pounds from the proceeds of the sale to Macmillan, fifty thousand to his sister, Sadie Baker and twenty-five thousand each to her twin daughters, Julie and Yvonne."

"That's wonderful!"

"But I told him I didn't want anything."

"If it's any comfort, he said he wanted to repay all your kindness and he didn't want anything to go to the rest of his family. You'll be carrying out his wishes. He was a nice old boy."

"Yes, he was. He should never have passed like this. If it hadn't been for those two thugs..." she stifled another sob. "Macmillan will be very grateful, I know. We used to do coffee mornings. Stan used to help me."

"Yes, he told me."

"I'm going to miss him."

Staff Nurse Payne patted her hand, "I know you will. But, he's left you a lovely legacy that you can do something with."

Meredith sniffed, "I suppose."

"I'll just go and get his few possessions, watch, wallet and so on." Nurse Payne rose and left.

Meredith murmured, "Oh, Stan. Why did this have to happen?"


Roy approached Alex's cottage in Ironbridge and parked at the front on the road. Alex stiffened. "Jane's car is there parked next to mine. There are lights on in the house."

"That's great. She's here waiting for you. You can have that talk. Then, I'll get out of your hair."

"No, something's not right."

"What makes you say that?"

"That car parked just ahead."

"What about it?"

"I've never seen it before."

"So, someone's visiting a friend."

"No. An old biddy lives up there. She never has visitors."

"What are you thinking?"

"I don't know, it's just a feeling. Come with me, Roy. Bring your service weapon." Roy removed a box from under his seat. He took a handgun and passed another to Alex. They checked they were both loaded and stepped out of the car and quietly closed the doors before slipping silently towards the gate, which was open. He whispered to Roy, "We never leave the gate open. We don't want Snooks going out on the road. Something is definitely off."

They trod gingerly along the path and ducked down low by the window. The blind had been pulled down but there was enough space left at the bottom to see into the room, where there were two men, dressed all in black wearing balaclavas, They were both holding weapons and moving slowly around the kitchen. There was no sign of Jane or Snooks.

"Looks like your hunch was right," whispered Roy. "Come on."


Jane was shaking in fright sitting inside a wardrobe in an upstairs bedroom with Snooks. Snooks was none too happy and let out a plaintive mew. Jane tried to calm the cat by smoothing her down, but Snooks wriggled out of her arms and scratched at the wardrobe door.

Jane could hear the men moving around downstairs, now. *What the heck was going on?* She risked opening the door of the wardrobe a fraction to allow Snooks out and prayed she was doing the right thing. She watched as Snooks shook herself and jumped back up on the bed and curled up seemingly oblivious to what was happening.

Jane had been in the bedroom changing and had seen two figures with flashlights creeping along the path at the side of the house. She had hurriedly switched the light off and watched as the two men, they looked like men, examined the windows and doors on that side. Jane knew she needed to get to a phone, but her mobile was downstairs charging. The house phone was in the kitchen. She needed to stay put and keep quiet that's if she could control her breathing, which was coming out in juddering gasps. Once she had heard glass breaking she had looked for somewhere to hide and had dived in the wardrobe taking the surprised cat from off the bed with her.

Her mind was working overtime as she struggled to reason through what was happening. *'How can I get out? Was it safe to get out? When I get out what can I do?'* She finally decided that she was just waiting for trouble if she stayed in hiding. Whoever it was seemed to be searching for something or someone. Suddenly, there was a huge crash and some shouts. Jane crept out of the wardrobe and Snooks shot off the bed at the noise and took herself back inside the wardrobe that she had just escaped. Jane moved tentatively out of the room and towards the landing. She peered through the wooden rails on the landing that looked down into the hallway and saw four men engaged in a fight. She recognised Alex immediately and heaved a sigh of relief but was horrified when one man appeared to be knocked out and went down. The intruder that he had been fighting with, removed a knife and was about to strike Alex in the back and she screamed out, "Alex, look out!"

Alex turned and leapt out of the way just in time, and Roy, who was on the floor raised his service weapon and fired at the perpetrator hitting him in the shoulder. The man staggered forward and fell onto the other intruder. Roy scrambled up and secured the man as Alex dealt with other. Jane was now practically hysterical and sobbing. She came running down the stairs. Alex called out, "Jane, in the kitchen table drawer, there are some cable ties. Get them quickly." She ran past the struggling men and flew into the kitchen. She rummaged in the drawer and pulled out some white cable ties and gave some to Alex, which he used to tie the man's hands behind his back, and his feet. The others she gave to Roy, who did the same. Both men were now secured face down on the floor.

Alex pulled off the men's balaclavas. They were no one he recognised. "Jane, call 999, get an ambulance and the police here. You can tell them what happened."

He turned to the man, "Who are you? Who sent you?" There was no response.

Jane dashed back to the kitchen and made the call. She returned to the hallway, "Who the hell are these people? Why is this happening? What's going on?" She ran into Alex's arms, nestled her head in his shoulder and her tears began to flow.

Alex looked across at Roy who nodded. "I'll explain later. But, firstly are you all right? Did they hurt you? What about Snooks?"

"Snooks is safe. She's upstairs. I'm okay, just upset. I hid to begin with until I heard you both coming in. I didn't know what was going on and then I had to come and see."

"Thank God you did," said Roy. "If you hadn't Alex would be dead."

"Alex, who is this?" said Jane uncertainly indicating Roy.

"This is Roy, he's my boss. Roy will keep an eye on these two, let's get into the kitchen and make a brew. I promise you I'll explain as much as I can once the police have gone. Please be patient."

The sound of sirens approaching the house assailed their ears.

The blue flashing lights had been and gone. The intruders had been taken away and initial statements taken. The police and ambulance had finally left. Jane sat with Snooks on her lap in the sitting room and eyed Alex and Roy. "Now, tell me what just happened here?"

Alex looked at Roy for help who sighed and rolled his eyes as if to say, 'you better speak up'. Alex looked abashed, "I don't know what to tell you, Jane."

"Try me." Jane's gaze was steely. "No one can have moves, fighting skills such as I witnessed here… what are you? You're not who you say you are, are you?"

"Yes and no."

"What do you mean, yes and no?"

"I am who I am. You know me. I'm Alex and an aspiring writer…"

"With a military side-line or something…" She sighed, "I know we joked about James Bond and spying, but what I saw terrified me." She fixed him with despairing stare.

Alex shifted uncomfortably in his seat and Roy felt the need to speak up. "Jane, Alex is not lying to you."

"No, he just didn't say anything. He avoided telling me the truth. That's just as bad."

"Because he couldn't. It is a case of national security. He legally can't tell you everything."

"It all seemed a bit of a game. I didn't believe he was a spy. Not really."

"That's because I'm not."

Jane studied Alex hard, "I want to believe you. Tell me something… anything…"

"Jane, Alex is a member of an elite military force run by the government that goes in to troubleshoot in all kinds of areas. He also works with the police in some instances. He is involved in an investigation now that has inadvertently involved you."

"What do you mean?"

Alex jumped in, "I didn't know that you were going to ask questions."

"Questions?"

"I told you I was working on a subplot…"

"And that was a lie."

"No, I am, but…"

"But?"

Roy stepped in again, "Those men were not after Alex. They were after you."

"What?"

"You are not safe, the questions you asked that client must have really rattled them."

Jane went white, "Oh my God. I don't understand... What...? How...? What do I do?"

Alex crossed to Jane and sat next to her. "I tried to stop you. You didn't get my texts."

"I left my phone in the car, when I showed him around."

"I'm so sorry, Jane. We have suspicions about your estate agency being involved in money laundering and more. I just asked you a few questions to see if you were aware..."

"What? You thought I might be involved?"

"No, of course not. I was just seeing if you knew of anything happening at the agency that might ring alarm bells. I never meant for you to be drawn in."

"I was trying to help you..."

"I know, I know..."

"Is that why you became involved with me? Was this your plan all along?"

"No, no. I knew nothing about this when I met you. Our relationship is real."

"How do I know that? How do I trust you?"

"I promise you, my feelings are genuine."

Tears streamed down Jane's face. "So, what do I do?"

Roy moved to a chair and sat facing Jane. "How well do you know your boss?"

"Jacob?" Roy nodded. "Not very well. Only in a professional capacity. It's a small agency. Why?"

"We believe he is involved in major criminal activity. How brave are you?"

'Sorry?"

Alex interrupted, "No. You are not involving Jane in this. No way."

"Hear me out. Jane is not safe. They believe she has insider knowledge of what has been going on. They don't know yet that the attack on her has failed."

"They soon will. Fancy lawyers will get them out on bail, and they will just disappear."

"You need to contact your mate in the force. Tell him to speak to the chief in Telford. Get them to hold those two as long as possible. Jane should go into work as if nothing has happened."

"You are not going to use her as bait," insisted Alex.

"Not exactly. We need to rattle Jacob Murch. See what he does. We will be there to protect her. I will pose as a prospective client. I will be there. What time do you go to work?"

"Now hang on a minute," blustered Alex.

Jane wiped away her tears. "No, let's hear what he has to say. I get there around 8:45 and open up, make a cup of tea or coffee and open the office at 9:00 a.m."

"What time does Mr Murch get in?"

"It varies. Usually about ten."

"But he will be expecting you not to make an appearance…"

"On my days off. Mr Murch opens up."

"Then you will have to get in extra early. I'll be waiting outside. I will come in with you. I shall put listening devices in his office. When he arrives, I will already be sitting with you with a previously arranged out of hours' appointment. Nothing will happen to you. Alex will phone the office with some kind of emergency, better still, will say he has got back to find his home ransacked and in disarray, you will get permission to leave."

"Then what?" asked Alex.

"I'll do it," said Jane. "Bugger it, I'll do it."

# 11

DCI ALLISON LEFT THE HOUSE with his girls and Mary chattering excitedly waiting for the arrival of Rosemary, Andrew and the children. He heard Mary's voice ringing in his ears. "Try not to be too long. You really should be here to meet them, Greg. Please."

"Sorry, Mary. You know this is important."

"It always is," she had murmured in reply.

Greg Allison felt some guilt. He knew she was right. He hadn't seen her so happy in a long time. But he also knew the importance of being present at the first intervention of the Church in Holly's case, Paul had pleaded for his moral support, and he felt he owed it to her. On another note, he knew he needed to catch up with Mark and his other detectives regarding Angus Mackay. It was a bad time for him to be on annual leave. There was just too much going on.

Allison got into his car. He would have time to think on the journey to Cornflowers. He didn't know what to expect and so would use that time to catch up with his DS and Ronnie and Gurdip. He started the car, made sure his hands free was connected and set off down the drive.

At Cornflowers Paul was waiting anxiously. Colin had already arrived. They were both in the sitting room and Holly was in the kitchen singing lustily, 'Hills of the North rejoice' but he felt he had nothing to rejoice about. Allison was on his way and the priest; Father Ignacia Lawrence was expected within the next half an hour.

A room had been prepared in advance: large cathedral candles had been lit, incense burned, and a Bible and prayer book sat on a makeshift altar with a large wooden cross. Images of Christ and the Virgin Mary hung on the wall behind, and angel and cherub ornaments were strategically placed. There were three chairs in front of the altar and a further two chairs placed by the door. The room was locked and awaiting the arrival of everyone.

The bell rang, Paul leapt up and hurried to welcome Greg Allison who had arrived along with the priest. They convened in the sitting room and sat. Father Lawrence was dressed in his robes and carried a large leather bag containing things he needed.

"Before we start, I need to bring you up to speed with what I have discovered so far."

Just then, Holly breezed in still humming happily. "Ah, I see we have guests. I will pop the kettle on. Tea or coffee, anyone?"

Father Lawrence declined. He had brought his own flask of water. The others accepted Holly's offer and she went out giving them time to talk.

"This is not a simple case of demonic possession, although demonic possession is never simple. What we have is highly unusual… that of a dead person's soul invading a living body but a dead person who has committed such evil that although she appears to be God fearing she is as close to Hell and the devil himself that I believe it is likely that it is not only her grandmother residing in her body but a demon or demons, too." Father Lawrence turned to Paul and asked, "Perhaps, you had better explain what has been happening here."

Paul shifted uncomfortably in his seat. "Father Lawrence is right. He has visited on a number of occasions since we all met. He had to ensure that Holly was not mentally ill. On some of the visits, Holly changed."

"How do you mean, changed?" asked Colin.

"Religious artefacts became anathema, abhorrent. She would make unholy sounds and growl. But all of these changes were fleeting and when Holly was Holly she had no recollection of them. Unfortunately, these occurrences are getting more frequent and stronger. I am very afraid and sick to my stomach at what I have witnessed."

"Why haven't you told us?" asked Allison.

"He told me," said Colin. "I think we both hoped it was just a temporary thing and he didn't want to worry you, Greg."

Allison nodded, "So what now?"

"I will begin the exorcism prayer and whatever you see or hear, you are to remain silent and not interfere. Is that understood?"

Allison spoke, "I know we are to remain quiet during the ceremony and not interrupt but what if things become physical, what then?"

"I pray that they won't."

Holly returned with a tray of tea things and a lemon drizzle cake. Holly was now Holly and being her usual self. "Here, I won't stand on ceremony," she giggled. "Sorry didn't mean to make such an awful pun. Help yourselves. There's plenty more in the kitchen."

Father Lawrence turned to her, "Holly you do understand what is going to happen?"

"Yes, you have explained it fully. The sooner this awful business is over with the better. I am not used to all this domesticity."

She shot a look at Paul, who rose and took her hands. "We are all here for you. All of us."

Father Lawrence added, "But, it may not be easy, and it may take longer than we've hoped."


The CDO, Andrew Birling was a tall well-built young man who clearly worked out. He was a popular character and got on well with the police officers he knew at the station. He had been assigned to collect Nesbitt from his holding cell to hand him to the security service that would take him to Winson Green. The officer on duty opened up the cell door and Birling barked, "Okay, Nesbitt. On your feet." Nesbitt was stretched out on his cot. "No time for napping, now. Up you get." Nesbitt didn't move. Birling went across and shook the man. Nothing. He checked his pulse and airways before shouting at the officer, P.C. Brian Balment, "Get a medic here, now. Call an ambulance. Move. This prisoner is still breathing, but, there's something wrong."

The young copper dashed away, and Birling could hear him ringing for help. Birling, tried to sit the prisoner up, but his head flopped forward. Birling looked around the cell. There was vomit in the lavatory pan and tufts of hair on the pillow. Birling went to see if anything had been drunk or ingested. There was the remains of breakfast and mug of tea on a tray and half a bar of milk chocolate. He could see nothing that could have caused the man's collapse. Nevertheless, he bagged the chocolate, and tea mug and dinner plate to submit for forensic inspection.

PC Balment came running back. "Ambulance is on its way."

"When was Nesbitt last checked?"

Balment looked at the list, "An hour ago. He was fine then."

"Has anyone been down to see him, given him anything?"

Balment shook his head. Not that I'd know of. I've only just come on duty."

"Who was on before you?"

"I'm not sure. There was no one here when I arrived."

"Someone must have seen something."


Holly sat on a chair in front of the altar facing the wooden cross. Father Lawrence stood between her and the altar. He laid his right hand on her head in blessing and a voice rasped in a deep unearthly voice, "Get out! Leave! She is mine." Holly began twisting her body, contorting it into grotesque shapes.

The priest began to recite a prayer holding a Bible in his left hand, "Soul of Christ, sanctify me; body of Christ, save me; blood of Christ, inebriate me; water from the side of Christ, wash me; passion of Christ, strengthen me;" The sunlight seemed to flee the room and the blinds that were up rolled down of their own accord. "O good Jesus, hear me; within Thy wounds, hide me; let me never be separated from Thee; from the evil one, deliver me; at the hour of my death, call me and bid me come to Thee, that with Thy saints, I may praise Thee forever and ever. Amen." Dark shadows appeared to fill the room and a cool wind rushed through.

Throughout the prayer the others watched in horror as Holly growled and made sub-human noises. He lifted his right hand and raised his crucifix. "As I breathe holy air into this woman before me, let her body be cleansed of evil." He gently blew into Holly's face, and she roared in rasping anger. Holly and the seat she was sitting in went flying back across the wooden floor as if propelled by some great force and her eyes rolled back in her head. She appeared to be muttering in another language.

Paul leapt up in terror. Father Lawrence put his hand up to stop Paul from intervening. Allison and Colin just sat there in shock.


The results had come through to the squad room that traces of thallium had been found in Nesbitt's tea. The forensic scientist's report explained that this compound was odourless, colourless and tasteless, so easy to administer. A strand of hair with its root from the clump had been microscopically tested and indicated that the substance had been administered in low doses possibly through his time there at the station. It appeared that a much heavier last dose had been administered in an attempt to kill him. This had been deduced from looking at the evidence of his stomach contents, which had been pumped. Ronnie and Gurdip were sent to the hospital, where they were waiting to speak to Nesbitt.

The doctor overseeing Nesbitt's treatment confirmed they had tested his urine, which also revealed thallium poisoning. He was being treated with Prussian Blue, a solid ion exchange material, which absorbed thallium. Twenty grams a day was being fed by mouth, which would pass through the digestive tract and come out in his stools when he defecated.

The young officers listened carefully as the doctor explained that any peripheral nerve damage would be slow to recover and was often permanent together with sensory loss. Nesbitt had complained that his feet felt like they were walking on hot coals.

The two officers listened carefully to everything they were being told and then asked if they could see Nesbitt.

"He's very weak and tired but as long as you don't stress him out, yes, you can both go in."

Ronnie and Gurdip made their way to the private room, where Nesbitt had just returned from a session of hemoperfusion, where doctors used a machine that filtered his blood and cleaned out the toxins.

They tapped lightly on the door and entered.

Nesbitt was wired up to various pieces of equipment, which displayed his vitals. He looked deathly pale with no colour at all. He groaned when he saw them. "What do you want now?"

Ronnie drew up a chair as Gurdip stood by the door. His tone was gentle and confidential, "Listen, mate, someone wants you dead. You must know something that frightens a lot of people. We can help you."

"How?"

"Tell us what you know, and we can protect you."

Nesbitt snorted, "I'm no grass. Besides, they would find me and kill me and there wouldn't be anything you could do. They would be aware of every move I made."

"If that's the case, you've got nothing to lose. Tell us what we need to know."

"If I'm risking my life, I want something in return."

"What?"

"These charges to go away for a start."

"I can't do that."

"There must be someone who can…"

"Our DCI is currently on leave."

"Then you'll have to wait until he's back. I'm okay here for the moment."

Gurdip intervened, "There'll be a copper on the door making sure only regular medical personnel will be allowed in or out."

"That's what I'm afraid of. Someone could quite easily get to me before your boss is back."

"If it will make you feel any better I can ring the chief. See if there's any strings he can pull. Gurdip will sit with you. Just hold on." Ronnie went out into the corridor and let Gurdip take his seat.

Gurdip eyed the man who looked exhausted and fragile before speaking. "You know, I believe there's someone you are worried about at the station."

"I never said that."

"No, but we heard that you intimated it in interview."

"What if I did? It was a foolish mistake."

"Listen, if there's a rotten apple in the barrel, you root it out. If it's a bad copper we need to know."

Nesbitt rolled his eyes, "And just how do you do that.? You lot look after your own."

"Not in the case of a dirty cop," Gurdip persisted. Nesbitt flinched and Gurdip continued, "So, you can verify that there is someone on the force you're afraid of?"

"I'm saying nothing."

"Foolish, I'd say." Gurdip paused and said slowly, "I shouldn't be saying this, but I've got my own suspicions. It would be good to have them confirmed."

Nesbitt remained quiet and closed his eyes.

Gurdip spoke quietly and commented, "I wonder what you'd say, if we said that we would put Angus Mackay here, on your bed-watch?"

Nesbitt opened his eyes and Gurdip detected a flicker of fear in them. Nesbitt looked away, hurriedly, closed his eyes again and murmured, "They wouldn't give a sergeant bed watch duty."

Gurdip studied Nesbitt's face and noticed a vein pulsing in the man's cheek that was not apparent before.

Ronnie breezed in and announced, "Chief is still out. Can't be contacted till later. I've spoken to Mark. He's going to see what he can do."

"Not good enough," said Nesbitt. "Now, clear off and let me sleep."

"We just want to know who brought you your meals and tea."

"I don't know all of their names. Shouldn't you have a duty list somewhere?"

Ronnie and Gurdip exchanged a glance and Ronnie continued, "Yes, more than likely but we need to know if anyone not on the list visited you." Nesbitt remained silent. "You do realise that someone is out to kill you, to stop you talking. What makes you think they won't try again?"

Nesbitt thought carefully but was still unresponsive. Ronnie stood up.

"Come on, Gurdip. Let's go. We're wasting our time here." Both officers walked to the door.

"Wait!" Ronnie stopped and turned. "Are you sure you can keep me safe? Not some namby-pamby promise but something solid. These people can get to you anywhere, even in prison or in the cop shop in a cell."

"I've told you Mark is going to see what he can do. Then we'll run it by the chief."

"If he comes back with something concrete and guaranteed, I'll talk but not until then."

Ronnie nodded, "Understood. We'll get back to you. Come on, Gurdip."


In Cornflowers, everyone was in a state of shock. Holly was now a spitting ball of fury. She screeched in a subhuman voice, "Get out! Now! I am stronger than you. Leave!"

Father Ignacia Lawrence raised his Bible. Holly hissed. She stood up glowering and growling, stepped backwards to the wall. With strength from another world and defying gravity she proceeded to walk backwards up the wall before flopping down and levitating three foot above the floor. Her eyes had rolled back in her head, spittle hung from her lips as her mouth frothed.

The Father took his Holy water and made the sign of the cross on her forehead. Her skin sizzled, her eyes refocused. She began to writhe and scream. She fell on the floor and wailed at the priest's words that thundered above the surging wind that had sprung up from nowhere and was rushing through the room.

"My Lord, you are all powerful, you are God, you are Father. We beg you through the intercession and help of the archangels Michael, Raphael and Gabriel, for the deliverance of our brothers and sisters who are enslaved by the evil one. All saints of Heaven, come to our aid."

Holly snarled and growled, in an unholy demonic voice, roared, "You will not win. We are too powerful." The priest continued and pushed the Bible towards her. Red welts began to appear on her face and body.

"From anxiety, sadness and obsessions, we beg You. Free us, O Lord. From hatred, fornication, envy, we beg You, Free us, O Lord. From thoughts of jealousy, rage, and death, we beg You, Free us, O Lord." Holly growled and roared. "From every thought of suicide and abortion, we beg You, Free us, O Lord. From every form of sinful sexuality, we beg You, Free us, O Lord." Holly hissed and spat kicking her legs out as if playing some imagined ball game. "From every division in our family, and every harmful friendship, we beg You, Free us, O Lord. From every sort of spell, malefic, witchcraft, and every form of the occult, we beg You, Free us, O Lord."

Holly thrashed around on the floor, her body contorting into monstrous shapes before she fell quiet, and her movements subsided although her head still moved swiftly from side to side. Strange groans and moans escaped from her body as dark shadows and faces of spirits in torment surged from her diaphragm and dissolved into the air.

"Oh, Lord bless this your servant Holly, deliver her from the grip of the demons and the spirit of Grace Clifton. Bring her to a place of grace and deliverance." Holly gradually became still but her breathing was shallow. "Lord, You Who said, 'I leave you peace, My peace I give you,' grant that, through the intercession of the Virgin Mary, we may be liberated from every evil spell and enjoy your peace always. In the name of Christ, our Lord. Amen."

Father Lawrence blessed her and drew the sign of the cross on her forehead with Holy water. This time her skin did not sizzle and the livid red mark from before healed before their eyes. He raised his arms in supplication, "All you demons and evil spirits return to the depths of Hell. Leave this woman in peace." There was a collective sigh, like a breath of wind, that dissipated into the air.

The priest turned to them. "She will need to sleep. Don't be surprised if she sleeps until tomorrow. Watch over her. Keep her safe.. Lay this cross on her body." He passed Paul a wooden crucifix. "I will retrieve it at my next visit. Keep the Holy water and sprinkle it onto her throughout the night. I will return in the morning. And if you need to… pray. I don't believe this is over." And as if to prove his words a cool breeze spun through the room like a whirling dervish and lifted the curtains at the window, so they blew out at an angle before finally fluttering back down once more. "We will try again, soon."

Allison and Colin watched as Paul ushered, the Father to the door with his black bag. They stared in amazement and incredulity at what they had just witnessed.

The following day was sublimely warm with clear blue skies and magnificent sunshine that bathed everything in its golden glow. Meredith Probert opened her curtains and looked out. She smiled to herself and hummed a little ditty as she finished drying herself after her shower and dressed.

She trilled a song from her teenage years, back in the fifties when she had been to dances at the local youth club, the Locarno and the West End Ballroom on a Saturday night. She sighed; they were happy times. Meredith walked into the spare bedroom and out of habit looked across at Stan's house. It was hard to think he wouldn't be there anymore. She was very fond of him and already missed him dreadfully.

She was just about to turn away when she saw a movement opposite and she peered carefully through the curtains. It was that same woman and man she had seen, who had attacked Stan. She was sure of it and continued to watch.

They continued to rummage through Stan's belongings. Meredith knew she had to call it in but this time she would not be spotted. She knew she had to move quickly and bristled at the nerve of the people coming back.

Meredith ignored the telephone in her bedroom just in case they looked across and she would be seen. She ran down the stairs to the hallway and dialled. She spoke to the dispatcher, gave her name and explained that two people were disturbing the scene of crime, which was still cordoned off with yellow police tape. She advised them not to have their sirens blaring or it would scare them off. Meredith was not given to swearing but she allowed herself an expletive, "Bastards!" Meredith hung onto the phone as instructed and waited for the police to arrive. She half hoped she would see WPC Sidhu again whom she personally thought was a lovely girl.

Three police cars drew up outside Stan's house with lights flashing. The dispatcher told Meredith that she would be all right now and hung up the call. Meredith dashed back upstairs to see what was going on.

She peered out of the window and saw four uniformed coppers alighting and two in plain clothes, one was wearing a turban. To her huge gratification one of team was WPC Sidhu. Meredith knocked on her window and Dilly looked up and acknowledged her with a wave.

Meredith was delighted. She watched as the police constables entered Stan's property.

The two plain clothes detectives crossed the road and walked over to her drive and began to stride up it. Meredith dashed down to answer the door as the bell rang.

As she opened it there were several shouts coming from Stan's house and to her extreme relief and pleasure she saw a man and woman being led away and put into a police car.

Ronnie murmured, "Well, well… Marilyn Spicer and Jason Butterworth. That's no surprise." Ronnie turned to Meredith and smiled. "Is it all right if we come inside for a moment?"

"Of course." Meredith opened the door wider to admit them. "Would you like a cup of tea?"

"That would be lovely, thank you." They followed Meredith into the kitchen, where she set about filling the kettle and setting out the tea things.

"I don't know what it's coming to. People not feeling safe in their own homes. It's all wrong."

"You say they were the same people you saw initially, after Mr Butterworth's attack?"

"Certainly looked like it," said Meredith.

"Could you swear to that?" asked Ronnie.

"I think so, yes."

"You'll need to be one hundred percent," said Gurdip.

"I am."

The doorbell rang, "Now who can that be?" said Meredith.

"It's all right, I'll go," said Gurdip leaving Meredith to pour out the tea.

He returned moments later with Dilly. She breezed into the kitchen and smiled at them all, "I had to come and see how you were doing, Meredith."

Meredith beamed at her. "I was so hoping you would be coming."

"Yes, well… when I heard the call I knew it was you so had to come, didn't I?" She looked at the two officers, "Sorry, Detectives. I should say, I'm Dilly."

"Ronnie Soper and Gurdip Singh," said Ronnie.

"If we're being formal I'm WPC Sidhu."

Gurdip looked up. "That's a Punjabi name."

Dilly smiled and said, "Yes, my father's family is from that region. My mother is from Slovenia. I'm a bit of a mish-mash really." She beamed again and Gurdip felt himself smiling back.

"Come and sit down, Dilly. You might as well join us for a cuppa and a piece of cake."

"Yes. I can recommend it," said Gurdip munching on a cupcake, and he grinned at Dilly again. Ronnie flicked his eyes across to him and back at Dilly who was also smiling, and Ronnie smiled a secret smile to himself.

"So, Meredith… what has been happening?"

"You know that Stan has passed away?"

Dilly nodded, "I had heard. You'll miss him."

"Yes, I will. Do you think it was the attack that did it?"

"It certainly didn't help. I expect those two will have manslaughter attached to their charges."

"Good. They deserve it. Did you know, Stan made me his executor of his will and left everything to me with instructions to give money from the house sale to Macmillian and his sister and her twin daughters. Everything else is to come to me. All his tools and motorbikes. I won't know what to do with them."

Ronnie perked up, "Those Indian Scout motorbikes will be worth a fortune."

"That's what Stan told me."

"They are extremely rare. You should get a really good price for them. Wow. What a stroke of good luck."

"Maybe. But, I'd rather have my neighbour back. He was such a good friend."

"Of course," said Ronnie suitably chastened. "If you like, I could do some research for you?"

"Aw, would you? That would be grand. Thank you, I don't know where to begin with them or with the tools."

"Don't worry Ms Probert. I'll see what I can do."

"Meredith, please."

"Meredith."

"That would be lovely."

"There you are, Meredith. DC Soper will help you, I'm sure," said Dilly.

"I will. I'll have to drop by again and take an inventory of all his tools and stuff."

"You'll be most welcome whenever you want. There'll be a cup of tea and cake when you come."

"Sold!" said Ronnie with a cheeky wink. "Maybe, Dilly can drop by again, too."

This time it was Gurdip who looked at Ronnie.

# 1 2

JANE, AS INSTRUCTED, ARRIVED FOR work early. It was 7:30 a.m. Her tummy was bubbling like a hot pan on a stove. She convinced herself that it was now she should bring her GCSE drama skills into operation. She wiped her sweaty hands down her skirt and went to make a cup of tea and hoped Roy would be on time as he had promised.

Almost as if he had heard her, the office bell clanged, and Roy slipped inside. He worked quickly, putting listening devices into the phones and under desks. Tiny cameras were secreted in other areas, in Jacob Murch's office and the main area. Just as quickly as he had arrived, he left and waited close by for the appearance of Jacob Murch, while Jane continued doing what she always did every morning.

They didn't have long to wait.

Jacob Murch came striding down the street, jangling his keys as he walked. His steps were long and loping. His unbuttoned navy raincoat flapped around him like bats' wings as the wind caught it. Head down he marched on until he reached the estate agent's door. He stopped to select a key before noticing the lights were on and someone was moving around inside. He tried the door tentatively. It opened and he stepped into the main office.

"Morning, Mr Murch," said Jane cheerfully as he entered.

The expression on Jacob's face confirmed to Jane that he was not expecting to see her. He started guiltily, "Jane? But how... what..." He hurriedly composed himself and forced a smile. "Er... what are you doing in so early?"

"Oh, I have an early out of hours' appointment with a client. Should be here any minute. Would you like a coffee? The kettle's just boiled."

"Er, yes. Thank you. I'll be in my office."

Jane busied herself making her boss's coffee as the door opened, and Roy came in. Jane turned and beamed at him, "Ah, Mr Elliot. Please sit down." She gestured to the seat in front of her desk. "I won't be a moment. Would you like a drink?"

"Thank you. That's most kind. A coffee would be lovely." Jane nodded and afforded him a quick wink before asking, "How do you take it?"

"Milk, no sugar. Thank you."

Jane made the coffees and took one into the inner office and returned closing the door behind her. She picked up the second, passed it to Roy and went behind her desk and sat.

Her switchboard lit up and she could see her boss was on the phone. Jane shuffled some estate agent's notes and whispered, "What now?"

"You're doing great. We just have to wait for Alex's call. Now, pretend to tell me more about properties in Telford and Ironbridge."

Jane launched into an enthusiastic recital of the merits of various houses that the agents represented. Roy pretended to listen avidly.


In Gillhurst Road, Allison and Mary were having an early elevenses. The sky was a depressingly dull, grey leaden mass and threatened rain. The conversation was intense.

"And is Holly all right now? Is she Holly?" asked Mary who was horrified at what her husband had recounted to her.

"I've never seen anything like it. Mary. She really was possessed, like all those horror films we've seen over the years."

"As long as her head didn't revolve three hundred and sixty degrees," said Mary.

"No, but it was just as frightening. When she walked backwards up the wall I was reminded of that magician Dynamo."

"And you always said he did the impossible."

"Was blessed by God or was in league with the devil."

"So, what now?"

"I don't know. I'll ring Paul soon and see if she's all right. It would be a terrible loss to the department if she had to give up her consultancy. Even more so as she is our friend."

Mary eyed her husband quizzically, "There's something else you're not telling me...?"

"I'm sorry, Mary. I really am. But there is so much going on at the moment. I really have to get back to work."

Mary groaned. "I knew you'd say that."

Greg looked at her beseechingly. "I'm so sorry..."

"Can't Mark handle it?"

"Not all of it."

Mary sighed stoically. "Well, if you must, you must. Just promise me one thing."

"What's that?"

"You'll make the family meal with everyone, and the day out planned with the grandchildren. Come on, Greg. We never see them, and goodness knows how long it will be before we see them all again."

"Cally's wedding, I presume."

"Don't be flippant. You know what I mean."

"Yes. Okay. Please try to understand..."

"I am always understanding... all the time. But, Greg this is special. Very special. You know, I always bow to your needs; I have done all our married life, but this is very important to me." Greg lumbered from his seat and put his arms around his wife who was close to tears. "And don't try and soft soap me with some flannel."

Greg took her face between his hands, and studied it closely. "Don't think I don't know what you gave up for me. I know it's been hard for you. I couldn't have a better wife and I don't know what I'd do without you."

Mary struggled to stifle her tears. "Please, Greg. A little compromise here."

Greg sighed again, "I know you're right. I tell you what. Just give me the mornings to work and the rest of the day I'll be yours. Yours and the kids."

Mary sniffed. "We will have that day out with the grandchildren. Alton Towers, wasn't it? And the family bash. And I promise you, I will try my hardest to spend some more time with everyone while they are here."

"Heavens, Greg. I don't expect you to be with us all the time. I know girl chatter will drive you mad. Just a little more consideration, please. A better life work balance while the girls are home."

Greg nodded, "I'll do my best." His face furrowed in a frown knowing how much was at stake and how much there was to be done with the varied cases, which he believed to be linked in some strange way. Why he thought that he couldn't say. It was just a hunch.

There was a sharp crack of thunder and then it began to rain.


Nesbitt looked suspiciously at the white-coated doctor who had stepped into his room to check his vitals. He couldn't explain it, but he felt uneasy. He hadn't seen this doctor before. His hand felt for his buzzer. He felt more secure with it in his hand and waited.

The doctor was a tall man, powerfully built. There was just something about him. The way he moved and his hands. There was something off about him. Nesbitt was just about to push the button when a nurse walked in. "Oh, sorry, doctor. I've just come to give the patient some fresh water." She deposited the fresh jug and picked up the other one on his table. Nesbitt stopped her, "Sorry, Nurse. Can you do my pillows for me? I keep sliding down and it's not very comfortable."

The nurse replaced the jug and attended to Nesbitt's needs. Helping him to sit up against a bank of pillows. The doctor finished scrutinising the chart and announced, "All seems good. I'll stop by again later." And he left the room passing the officer on duty.

"Which doctor was that?" asked Nesbitt.

The nurse shook her head, "I don't know. I haven't seen him before. Must be a locum. I know there are a few doctors off sick with some bug going around."

Nesbitt was becoming more alarmed, "Can you tell the officer outside I want to speak to him?"

"Of course."

The nurse hurried away with the empty jug as a bell was ringing elsewhere and the constable on duty outside came in. "You wanted to see me."

"Yes, can you get a message to those two detectives who were here yesterday? Tell them I've reconsidered."

Jason Butterworth and Marilyn Spicer were being held at the police station, protesting their innocence, saying that they were relatives who just wanted to check out the whereabouts of Stan's will and had no malicious intent. They continued to deny any wrongdoing... and their stories kept changing. Pooley was fed up with going round in circles and getting nowhere. He terminated the interview with Jason Butterworth and slipped next door to see how Woodward was getting on with Marilyn Spicer. It seemed he was having no luck either.

Pooley stopped as he received a call notifying him of Stan Butterworth's death. "Oh, no! Poor old boy. This changes things..." exclaimed Pooley. Now they would have something to hold them on, so before solicitors came knocking and getting the siblings out he could have another go at the two of them with this new ammunition. He went back into Woodward and whispered in his ear. Woodward could hardly stop himself from grinning. "Well, Mrs Spicer... you better decide to talk now your charges have been upped to Manslaughter."

"What? But, I haven't killed anyone," she protested.

"Stan Butterworth is dead."

"What?"

"Get used to it. You're not going anywhere, yet."

"I want my solicitor."

Woodward snorted, picked up his papers and left the room.

Pooley was outside. "We'll let them stew awhile. Let them get used to the new charges." Woodward acknowledged and bounded up the stairs.

Pooley returned to the Squad room bumping into Gurdip and Ronnie on their way out to the hospital. They informed him that Nesbitt was keen to see them again, so they were off to talk to him. As they chatted, Angus Mackay strolled past towards the coffee machine and caught the word Nesbitt.

"What's up, lads? Has my crim from the smoke been causing trouble?"

Ronnie was quick to deflect the comment. "Nah. Nothing like that. Bloke's got a defective memory. Won't say a word. We're just going to have one last crack at him before he's moved to the prison infirmary."

"Don't hold your breath. He's a tricky one, that one. You mark my words, slippery as a barrel of eels. I wouldn't trust a word he says. I'll tag along if you like. I'll know whether he's lying or not."

Pooley jumped in, "I don't think that's wise. Three of you is overkill. No. You two be on your way. I have something else for you, Mackay. Follow me."

Ronnie and Gurdip hurriedly made their escape and left Pooley to deal with Angus Mackay.


Jacob Murch was sweating. He didn't know what had happened or how Jane was still alive. He wasn't sorry, he liked Jane. He was pleased she wasn't dead, but he knew it wouldn't be long before she was, and he wasn't liking the odds stacked against him. He could hear her lively chatter through the door. She was an excellent employee. Could he persuade Patterson to change his mind? He had tried but had to admit he hadn't been whole hearted about it. He needed to try again. He picked up the phone and played with it in his hand before he gathered enough courage to dial. It was answered quickly.

"Yes?"

"Patterson?"

"It is."

"Jane came to work this morning."

"What? ... Those idiots. I wondered why I hadn't heard from them. What the hell's happened?"

"How should I know? Look, I wanted a word. Can't you take the hit off her?"

"Why?"

"She's an innocent in this. She doesn't know anything. Her reason for asking those questions is true. Her boyfriend is a writer."

"It wouldn't be long before she put things together. She's not stupid."

"No, but to do away with her would only bring the police and more questions, can we risk that? I'm asking you to reconsider. I feel it was a bit of a knee jerk reaction."

"And if you'd done your job and been there, we wouldn't be having this conversation."

Laughter filtered through from the outer office. Jacob's mouth set in a hard line. "Well, I don't like it." He dropped his voice to barely a whisper. "I am not into murder."

"Bit late for that now. You're in this up to your neck. You get paid well."

"I'm not denying that, but I don't know what's going on."

"Nor should you."

Jacob heard Jane's ring tone with the Mission Impossible theme filtering through to his office. He heard a stifled scream. "Something's happened… that man… you haven't sent anyone here, have you?"

Patterson's exasperated tones came through, "No. Why?"

"I don't know. Something's happened in the other office. Look, Jane doesn't know anything, call off your men, please."

In the outer office, Jane's face flooded with a manifestation of shock and horror, "I am so sorry, Mr Elliot. I have to leave. Would you excuse me, and I will ask my boss to take over. Sorry."

Jane hurried to Jacob's office and knocked. She put her head around the door looking the epitome of distress and simulating a sob she said, "Sir, I am so sorry. Is it all right if I leave? My boyfriend has just rung, and his house has been broken into and ransacked. He heard from a neighbour that the police were called last night and there was some kind of fight. He's in a terrible state… writers, you know, are very sensitive."

Jacob murmured sympathetically, "Of course, of course." He spoke into the phone, "I'll call you back," and ended the call.

"Can you finish up with Mr Elliot, please? I have been going through the available houses for sale and gathered together an information pack regarding his requests. I'll be back as soon as I can."

"Certainly, no rush. I'll come through. I hope your boyfriend is all right."

"So, do I, sir. I will be as quick as possible."

"No problem. Take the rest of the day. I'll be fine. I'll see you tomorrow."

"Very good, sir. Thank you, sir."

Jacob rose to help the new client. He would ring Patterson back later.

Jane grabbed her coat and fled the office as quickly as she could, with another quick wink at Roy.

Jacob Murch emerged from his office his face wreathed in smiles. "Now, Mr Elliot, how can I help?"

Roy smiled, "I think young Jane has done a grand job. She's been an absolute gem helping me. You're lucky to have her."


Ronnie and Gurdip had arrived at the hospital and to their surprise they found DCI Allison there. He was talking to Nesbitt as Gurdip and Ronnie walked in.

"Chief! We weren't expecting to see you here," said Ronnie.

"No, and I don't want it broadcast that you have," said Allison gruffly.

"I have come to an arrangement with my superiors and, of course, with Nesbitt. He's being taken to a safehouse until this is all over. He'll be testifying and Internal Affairs will be investigating along with the Independent Office for Police Conduct into Mackay. If, as I suspect, this is something far reaching, Nesbitt is getting a new identity and will be relocated. Work can begin on that at Stone Haven. He's happy with that. Aren't you, Nesbitt?"

Nesbitt nodded, "I want to be well out of it. This is bigger than you think."

"Then you better start talking. Ronnie, Gurdip?"

"Sir?"

"You are to take him to Stone Heaven in an unmarked car. Pick him up, once he's cleared to leave. The doc's coming round in…" he checked his watch, "about twenty minutes. I suggest, you, Ronnie stay here and Gurdip take your car back and change it."

"We must be psychic," said Ronnie with his lopsided grin. "We've got an unmarked car outside."

"Good. In that case, you better take some notes. You can finish up with your questions when you reach Stone Haven. You know the drill. Get your notebooks out and listen. Fire away, Nesbitt."

Alex took Jane in his arms, "I'm so sorry you got dragged into this."

"It's not your fault, me and my big mouth. I was only trying to help."

"And you did, you are. We may have uncovered something really big but…"

"But?" Jane released herself and stared into Alex's eyes.

"It's not safe for you now. These are brutal men. They don't care who they hurt to keep themselves and their criminal dealings safe." Alex took a deep breath, "I want you to move in with me. You will be safe. I can look after you. It's not wise for you to go home or go to work."

"What? How will I live? I can't afford not to work. It wasn't my flat they trashed, it was here."

"Let me worry about that. I can afford it. You must know, they will be watching. They will take the first chance they can. You'll be safer with me."

"Until you're off on a mission or something."

"In that eventuality we will work something out. I am not going to let anything happen to you."

"What about Mr Murch? How will he manage?"

"I believe Mr Murch is up to his neck in it."

"Into what, exactly?"

"Money laundering and much more."

"I can't believe it."

"Maybe not. But he's involved. Roy will be here soon, and I believe he will have proof. We'll see how innocent or guilty Jacob Murch really is."

As if on cue, there was a tap on the window as a prearranged signal and a ring on the doorbell. Alex opened the door to admit Roy. He breezed in with his equipment and set it up in the kitchen, little was said. When he'd finished, he finally spoke, "You need to hear this." He set his recorder going and Jane listened in disbelief as she heard her boss talking to Patterson on the phone about her.

"At least he seemed reluctant to do away with me," she murmured after a moment. "What now?"

"We'll do as I said."

Jane was quiet and on the verge of tears. "… I really liked my job…"

"When this is over you can go back to it, there are other estate agents," said Alex softly.

"I can copy this onto a flash drive. You can get it to your cop friend. We're bound to get more intel as time goes on as long as they don't spot the bugs," said Roy.

"Let's see what's happening now," added Alex.

Roy twiddled with his screen, and they could see Jacob Murch in his office pacing around in an agitated fashion. "He doesn't look too happy," Roy observed. "He's just answered his phone."

"What's he saying?"

"Hang on…" Roy fiddled with his audio recorder and Jacob's voice came through loud and clear.

"You've done what? … That's crazy. I've told you; Jane is no danger to anyone. Call it off… What do you mean, you can't?... You have to try." Jacob stared at his phone in disbelief. "I guarantee she won't be a problem." There was a pause. At, first it seemed that the other person has hung up. "Damn and blast!" Murch put his phone onto loudspeaker. "Hello, are you there?"

"I am. I'm thinking… All right, I take your point about the cops. I'm not promising but I'll see if I can call it off." The call ended.

Jacob ran his fingers through his hair and appeared to come to some sort of decision. He picked up his keys and left the office. The camera in the outer office picked him up turning the open sign to closed and out he went, locking the door behind him.


Nesbitt was cleared by the doctor so Ronnie and Gurdip hustled him away to their unmarked car outside the hospital. They proceeded to the Hagley Road and fell into the line of busy traffic taking them up towards Halesowen and the Clent Hills.

Nesbitt was twitchy throughout the whole journey and refused to be drawn into any conversation. His only contribution to the questions asked was, "Wait till we get there." And he stubbornly fixed his eyes out of the window and played deaf to everything else around him.

Ronnie and Gurdip stared ahead of them and eventually their chatter lapsed into silence. Ronnie turned off towards the Clent Hills and kept a watch out of the window for any suspicious vehicles following them. The roads around Clent were quiet and there were none. Ronnie turned safely into Stone Haven Farm.

They drove up the long farm track to a five-bar gate. Gurdip jumped out and opened it for Ronnie to drive through and then diligently closed it behind him and they made their way towards the farmhouse and outbuildings and parked outside the front. Clive Cooper, who ran the show at Stone Haven came out to greet them. He was a short stocky man with intensely dark features and weather-browned skin. "Clive Cooper." He extended his hand for all three to shake. "I've been expecting you. Come on in." The young detectives ushered Nesbitt in front of them and they followed Clive through to the large farmhouse kitchen, where his team was assembled. "Let me introduce you to the team and then I have set aside a room for you two to continue with your questions. The chief said that was the arrangement."

Ronnie, nodded, "Appreciate that, sir. Thank you."

Clive gestured to each of the ones seated at the table, "This is Jilly."

Jilly was a slim attractive blonde in her late forties. She nodded, "I'm your acting coach. I'll be working with you on your voice, mannerisms, the way you walk and identity background. You'll have a complete makeover and the first thing we'll do is cut your hair. That's a dead giveaway."

"Hello, I'm Meg, Meg Hines." Meg was short and plump with a homely manner. "Your own mother won't recognise you once Jilly has finished with you. I will be working with you on finding a job, creating your qualifications and trying to find something you'll enjoy doing. You'll be going straight from now on and no mixing with members of the criminal underworld past or present. It'll be an honest job for you. You must leave your old life behind, starting now."

Nesbitt nodded and sniffed as the two women studied him and made mental notes. He turned his head to look at the tall dark man leaning against the range. The man stood up, "I'm Phil Brewer. I do the research, find you somewhere to live, once we know where you are working and find a name that will work for you. We usually keep your Christian name and change the surname. What is your first name?"

Nesbitt sniffed again and said, "Tim, Timothy."

"Okay, Tim. Catch you later."

"You will see other people around the farm that are genuine farm workers. You will meet them later at supper. Anyone else that you don't recognise report them immediately to me," said Clive. "For now, I'll show you to your room and you can talk with our two friends." He indicated Ronnie and Gurdip.

He led the trio to a row of stone cottages and opened up the first one and gave Nesbitt the key. "Breakfast is at nine, lunch at one and supper at seven. You can go in the kitchen, when you like for tea or coffee and snacks. Jilly usually puts the kettle on around four. She makes great cakes. Right, I'll leave you to it. Come and let me know when you're leaving, lads. You, Tim need to settle in. You'll find suitable clothes in the wardrobe and toiletries in the bathroom en suite. I think there's everything you need. I'll leave you to it. Your first session with Jill is at two-thirty."

"Where do I go for that?"

"Meet her in the kitchen and she'll take you to her studio."

"Bloody hell! Makes it sound like a full production for the telly or something," said Nesbitt.

"Something like that," said Clive with a laugh. "Cheerio."

Clive strode off and the trio went inside the stone cottage.

Nesbitt looked around. It was a clean, comfortably furnished sitting room and diner with a small kitchen at the back. There was a downstairs cloakroom with a toilet, and upstairs had a good-sized bedroom and ensuite.

"This'll do," said Nesbitt with a grin. Better than my place. How long will I be here for?"

"That depends on you," said Gurdip.

"And what you've got to tell us," added Ronnie. "How quickly do you learn?"

Nesbitt sniffed again, "Well then we'd better sit down. This could take a while."

# 1 3

"LEAVE NOW! I AM STRONGER than you," rasped an inhuman voice that emanated from the bowels of the earth, but seemingly spewed out of Holly's mouth. "You will not defeat me." The temperature in the room dropped close to freezing, so cold the priest and those witnessing this event could see their breath in the air as if it was a winter's day.

In contrast, Father Ignacia Lawrence was hit in the face by a fiery blast of air exploding from Holly's mouth in a scream and he continued to pray. Paul watched anxiously as Holly's face contorted and changed, there were three distinct faces, one a masculine skeletal deathly white face with sharp pointed features baring needle sharp teeth behind rimless red lips that blurred into the beetling brows of Grace Clifton and her cobra hooded eyes, and the other of a woman with a full head of wavy chestnut hair, demonic blood red eyes that darkened to black attached to a snake-like body.

Colin sat mesmerised by the spectacle in front of him and appeared to be holding his breath. His arms were crossed protectively in front of him again as if to prevent anything entering him. DCI Allison sat in another chair, in stunned disbelief, at what he was witnessing. They had both thought it was over, but Paul had rung them both again as signs of Grace Clifton had started to come through Holly once more. They had dropped everything to support Paul and Holly and to witness the next session with the priest.

Father Lawrence continued, "Saint Michael the Archangel, defend us in battle; be our protection against the wickedness and snares of the devil." Holly hissed and spat. "May God rebuke him, we humbly pray, and do thou, O Prince of the heavenly host, by the power of God, thrust into hell Satan and all the evil spirits who prowl about the world seeking the ruin of souls. Amen."

The priest laid his hand on Holly's head and she twisted as if burnt. With his other hand he made the sign of the cross. There was a guttural bellow of rage as Father Lawrence began to incant, "In the Name of the Father, and of the Son, and of the Holy Ghost. We drive you from us, whoever you may be, unclean spirits, all satanic powers, all infernal invaders, and all wicked legions. Stoop beneath the all-powerful Hand of God; tremble and flee when we invoke the Holy and powerful Name of Jesus, this Name which causes hell to tremble." Holly began to pant and growl. "Begone Satan, inventor and master of all deceit, enemy of man's salvation. Begone evil spirits that torment this soul, this child of God." Holly's eyes rolled back in her head. "In the Name and by the power of Our Lord Jesus Christ, begone Grace Clifton; may you be snatched away and driven from the Church of God and from the souls made to the image and likeness of God and redeemed by the Precious Blood of the Divine Lamb."

Father Lawrence removed his hand as Holly twisted and writhed and blood began to drip from her eyes. She started to rise from her seat unaided and levitated into the air, her head thrashed from side to side. The Father splashed holy water over her, which sizzled and smoked as it singed her clothing and skin. Unrelenting he continued saying his prayers.

A twisted black grotesque shadowy shape bellowed in an agonised groan as it emerged from Holly's body and disappeared into the air once it was struck with Holy water. Everyone watched transfixed as a serpentine coiling curl of smoke, writhed and hissed as it looped and bowed when it was expelled from Holly's stomach, and she floated back down to her chair. Her face dripped in sweat and her hair hung in damp rats tails on her head.

The priest lifted his Bible and rosary cross, "God arises; His enemies are scattered and those who hate Him flee before Him. As smoke is driven away, so are they driven; as wax melts before the fire, so the wicked perish at the presence of God."

The malevolent face of evil that was Grace Clifton was the last to emerge and came from inside Holly's head, chased away by the prayers of the Father, when a cry so terrible it must have come from hell itself, erupted as Grace Clifton fought against her expulsion and strived to resist the Priest's demands.

"Leave me be!" she hurled the words at the priest in a screech, "You cannot make me leave. She is mine."

Father Lawrence took a deep breath and raised his arms in supplication and pleaded, "O Lord, You Who love man, we beg You to reach out Your powerful hands and Your most high and mighty arms and send the angel of peace over us, to protect us, body and soul. May he keep at bay and vanquish every evil power, every poison or malice invoked against us. Under the protection of Your authority may we pray in gratitude, the Lord is my salvation; I will not fear evil because You are with me, my God, my strength, my powerful Lord, Lord of peace, Father of all ages."

The Father drew down his hands and made the sign of the cross in front of Holly and placed his rosary around her neck. "Lord our God, be merciful to us, and save your servant, Holly, from every threat or harm from the evil one, and protect her by raising her above all evil. We ask You this through the intercession of our Most Blessed, glorious Lady, Mary ever Virgin, Mother of God, of the most splendid archangels and all Your saints. Amen!"

There was a rush of wind and the drapes in the room fluttered and the icy cold temperature in the room rose back to normal. Holly's head fell forward onto her chest and Paul rushed to her side.

Father Lawrence staggered back and made his way to a seat; he was mentally and physically exhausted. For a moment, the others were totally speechless.

Allison finally spoke, "Are you all right, Father?"

The priest nodded, "I could do with something to drink."

"Of course," said Colin rising. "What would you like?"

"Some cool water please."

"Certainly, and I'll put the kettle on while I'm in the kitchen."

Paul turned to the priest, "Is that it? Will Holly be all right now?"

"She will need to rest. Sleep is a great healer. Keep an eye on her, let me know how she is in the morning. I will come back tomorrow afternoon just to check on her. They were powerful forces. I didn't know if there was more than one entity, although I suspected it."

"Is that usual?" asked Paul.

"I've seen it before, but the strength of the three was phenomenal."

"I cannot thank you enough," said Paul. "I dread to think what would have happened if we hadn't called you."

"To think I almost believed it unnecessary."

Colin returned with a glass of water. "I'm making tea, would everyone like a cup? We can try and digest what just happened."

"There are more things in heaven and earth…" murmured Allison.

"Shakespeare's Hamlet isn't it?" said Colin as he left the room.

"It is. And to think I never believed any of this," said Allison.

"Hocus-pocus, you called it," reminded Paul.

"I did. I have never seen anything like it. It's opened my eyes and mind."

"Not so quick to pooh-pooh things now?"

"No. But, I won't be talking about it with anyone else, that's for sure. No one would believe me anyway. They'd think I'd gone off my head."

"Early senility," quipped Paul.

Father Lawrence spoke, "I will leave some Holy water with you. You have the Bible?" Paul nodded, "And the book of common prayer?"

"I have."

"Keep them close, and if you are able, pray." He looked at them all, "All of you… Pray."


As Nesbitt began to talk Ronnie and Gurdip's eyes grew wider and wider. "I grew up in a family where my father freely mixed with the criminal fraternity. He was by profession a locksmith who graduated into petty crime that escalated when he became an adept safe cracker and was then useful to the criminal gangs. I was just a nipper, but I remember meetings at the house, men coming and going and my mom bringing in refreshments, tea, coffee, sometimes beer. As I grew up, I became more aware of what my dad was involved in. He'd always been what was called a 'Commy Burg', a commercial burglar who broke into warehouses, factories or shops. Non-violent crimes as there was rarely anyone present when they committed the robbery and so considered an impersonal offence; acquisitive rather than violent. But, the Wembley mob wanted his particular talent for a big job. He was persuaded to take part because the rewards were massive. He thought he's do it once and get out, make the big score and retire. It didn't happen. After he'd taken part in a really big heist that netted precious stones, gold bars and cash. The spoils were distributed between the gang members but dad gave his share of the gold and jewels to another associate to smelt and break down so it could be used to make new jewellery and the money safely recouped. In fact, a few of the gang did that. He worked with the Wembley mob that were a crash bang-gang. They called their crimes going 'Across the pavement.' They would drive their getaway vehicle up onto the pavement outside a bank and block the entrance. They'd rely on the element of surprise by crashing the bank doors, firing a shotgun into the ceiling in order to elicit fear and compliance. I tried hard to stay away from that life. I didn't want to end up in prison. It was only when Dad was dying he called me to him and gave me all this information. Told me to retrieve what was my and mom's inheritance, his dues, and I made a promise to do that. One of the other crew's sons was Angus Mackay."

Ronnie's mouth dropped open, "Angus Mackay? The detective assigned to us?" Nesbitt nodded. "So that's how he knows you?"

"He's a bent copper, through and through, working on both sides of the law."

"Have you got proof of this?"

"It'd be my word against his, but many times he had a hand in helping get crims off, losing vital evidence in cases. You'd have to look at his records, cases he was involved in or ones at his base in the Met where no convictions were made. Mackay was at the root of them. That's for sure. That's why I couldn't say anything. Something would have happened to me. I'd be done for. I know too much." He paused, "The only thing I have got..."

"Yes?"

"A recording of him threatening me and making me go to the house of the old boy who had the stash and get it back. He partnered me with some nut job who was going to off the old lady who witnessed a previous attack on the chap. I refused, but when I saw the nutter was still going ahead with it. I knew I had to stop him. He escaped and I got caught. Mackay warned me to keep my mouth shut or else … he knows some nasty characters."

"Have you still got this recording?" asked Gurdip.

"On my phone. In the evidence locker unless Mackay has got there first."

"Does he know about it?" asked Ronnie.

"Not sure."

"Then we need to get it and quickly," said Gurdip. "Never trusted that bloke. Seems I was right."

"I wonder why he was moved from the Met?" mused Ronnie.

Nesbitt looked up, "I can tell you that. Things were getting too hot for him, so he asked to transfer but he had another reason and that is to recoup his share of the spoils. His father, like mine, was involved in the same heist. And wanted his loot."

"What about your involvement with Kelland?"

"I fell into that by accident. I did a driving job across the border to collect a cargo. I didn't know it was human. I couldn't get out of it and then I was condemned to work for the team; it was either that or be killed. I was lucky when your guy came snooping in Montague Road. I finally managed to get away and intended to stay away. But then I was picked up and stuck in your nick. That's where I saw Mackay and he threatened me."

Ronnie sat up. "We need to get your phone."

"Yes," agreed Gurdip. "Before Mackay."

"Then you'll need my password. Got a pen?"


Kelland relaxed in the sunshine in the Dominican Republic. He sipped a cocktail in a beach front bar and his phone rang. He answered and listened. Whatever he was told made him sit up straight and become tense. "Well, where is he?... You need to find him and get rid of him... I don't care if it's difficult, it's not impossible, see what you can find out..." Kelland disconnected the call. He rang another number. "It's me. I'm bringing our job forward. Is that a problem?" He listened some more. "I'll transfer half now..."

Kelland's mouth twisted as he listened and then curtailed the call. He dialled another number and purred into the phone. "Hello, darling... Thanks for talking to the cops and recanting... Yes, I'm fine. Missing you. I've organised your plane ticket... Yes, emailing you all the details.... Great! I'll see you at the weekend... can't wait. Love you." Kelland sighed a self-satisfied sigh and perked up, calling over the waiter and ordering another cocktail.

As Gurdip drove, Ronnie dialled a number and waited, "Chief, you won't believe what we've learned from Nesbitt." He went on to detail the conversation he and Gurdip had had with Nesbitt at Stone Haven.

There was a pause as Allison weighed up what he had been told. "We must get hold of that phone."

"We're on our way to retrieve it now, sir."

"Good. I'll meet you there." He ended the call.

"We need to step on it. We've no time to waste."

"Then, I'll put on the siren. It is an emergency," said Gurdip. The lights flashed and the siren wailed as they weaved through the traffic to get to the station.

Angus Mackay was feeling twitchy. He didn't know if he'd managed to make Nesbitt ill and needed to see. He marched down to the holding cells. Good, Nesbitt was gone. He nodded at WPC Sidhu on duty and picked up the roster. He frowned and turned to Dilly, "Can't see what time Nesbitt was picked up..."

"Not sure. I've only just come on duty." She wasn't giving anything away.

Mackay frowned again. "Did he go to Horse Road or not?" His tone was unpleasant.

Dilly kept her face impassive. "You know as much as I do."

Mackay swore and his heart had begun to race. He moved away and went to the stairs to return to the squad room as if hoping to find answers there. Dilly didn't like his tone or attitude and wondered why he was so interested in a prisoner.

Mackay took the stairs two at a time and swaggered into the squad room and looked around, gauging who was there and who would be most forthcoming. He spotted Bill Rennie poring through paperwork and crossed to him. "Hi, Billy-boy. What you doing?"

"Worst part of the job." He sat back in his chair and eyed Angus and noted his expression. "What's up?"

"Not much. Just wondering…"

"Wondering what?" asked Bill curiously.

"I just came up from the cells and see Nesbitt has gone."

"Haven't you heard?"

"Heard what?"

"He went to hospital." Bill said.

"Why?"

"Someone tried to poison him."

"Is that right?" Mackay said, "Know him from my old manor. I was just going to tell him to keep his nose clean. Thought maybe I'd persuade him to talk. Is he all right?"

Bill shrugged, "I haven't heard. Rumour has it someone tried to off him again in the hospital."

Mackay sucked in a gasp of air through his teeth. "Wow. Someone wants to shut him up, he must know something."

"More than likely. If that's the case, think I'd talk, wouldn't you?"

Sweat broke out on Mackay's brow, "Yeah, yeah. Course. If your bosses want you dead then there's nothing to lose."

"Exactly."

"What do you think the chief has done?"

"Maybe a safe house or witness protection."

"Oh, really?" Mackay's mind was working overtime. He didn't like what he was hearing. "Where's that then?"

"Not sure, why?"

"Just curious."

"If I hear anything I'll give you a shout." He turned back to his paperwork.

"Ta, mate." Mackay was now visibly sweating. "Cor, it's hot in here, innit?"

"Is it? I haven't noticed."

"Think, I'll just pop out, get a breath of fresh air. Hope I'm not coming down with something."

Mackay had started to panic. Could anything be traced back to him? He didn't think so, but maybe just in case, he ought to check Nesbitt's belongings, find out what was in the evidence locker and remove anything that might attract attention to him. Why wasn't the bloke dead? He was like a cat with nine lives. Still if someone else was working to eliminate him, like the person in the hospital, perhaps they would succeed and soon. Mackay tried to appear nonchalant and regulate his breathing. He mopped his brow now laden with perspiration and tried to calm his fluttering insides.

Feeling marginally better, Mackay steadied himself and strolled back and went downstairs to the evidence locker. He spoke to the constable behind the desk. "Just need to check something on the Nesbitt case."

"And why would you want to do that?" came the tones of DCI Allison behind him.

"Er..." He was floundering and blustered, "I heard he was in hospital and thought I might be able to help since I know him so well."

"Haven't you got enough work of your own? This isn't your case."

"No, sir. I just wanted to help." His manner was crushed and his face flushed red. He skulked away silently fuming.

Allison growled at the PC, "Nesbitt case, everything you've got. Has anyone else asked for this evidence?"

The PC checked the log and shook his head. "No, sir. Just you and that other detective."

"Good. If anyone requests it, refer them straight to me. I want to know about it. Flag it in the book."

"Yes, sir."

Allison picked up the bag with Nesbitt's phone and statements regarding the break-in at the Butterworth house and started back up the stairs. He reached the squad room and moved to his office. He was aware that Mackay was watching him covertly. He closed his door firmly and drew down the window blind that overlooked his detectives.

Still standing, he picked up a report on his desk from the duty officer. Jason Butterworth had been put on remand at Winson Green. He was saying nothing, closed up tighter than a lady's Victorian corset. But Marilyn Spicer was a different matter. With the new charges hanging over her, she was prepared to talk now and had stopped bleating about her rights. Woodward had taken her to a safe house in Erdington.

Allison sighed and sat down. He studied what had come from the evidence locker and picked up the phone and switched it on. It was password protected. He groaned and opened his desk drawer to reach for a Mars Bar. The sound of the paper ripping was extremely satisfying but not as fulfilling as the taste of the chocolate itself. He sighed out loud and leaned back in his chair intending to savour the moment, which didn't last long as Ronnie and Gurdip were at his door. He hurriedly finished his mouthful and put the remains in the drawer.

The two detectives were bursting to tell the chief all they had learned. Ronnie glanced at the phone in his hand, "Sir, is that the phone?"

"It is but it's no use without a password."

"Which I have got," said Gurdip wiggling his eyebrows. He read out the code, Allison typed it in and began to scroll through until he found the recording. They sat back to listen.

# 14

KELLAND WAITED AT PUNTA CANA airport for Kira's arrival. Although it was at a less busy time, which was good, the plane had been delayed and Kelland was getting impatient. He tapped his foot as he sat watching the arrival board. He took note of the electronic updates and sighed in relief when the letters and numbers for Kira's flight changed and it read, landed.

Kelland moved into the arrivals hall and waited. He knew she had Customs to get through and that could take a while.

Eventually, passengers streamed through, all wearing masks as was the rule at this time. Amongst them was a tall man wearing a Panama hat, who Kelland instantly recognised. He gave Kelland a barely imperceptible nod and passed through the gate, travelled across the concourse to the main entrance, and the taxis waiting outside.

Kira was in the middle of a throng of Major League Baseball players returning from an international game. Even masked she was unmistakeable by her luxuriant hair. She was practically carried through the gate by the sportsmen, and she looked around eagerly for Kelland and waved madly when she spotted him waiting.

He waved back and she dashed quickly towards him pulling along her case on wheels. He gave her an enormous hug when she met him, a hug that on his part was tinged with regret. He took her case. "I've a car waiting outside. Let's get back to the villa and you can settle in. We can decide what we want to do tomorrow. Maybe, we will visit San Domingo and see the sights."

"I don't care, as long as I am with you," Kira purred.

They reached the car and Kelland packed her case into the boot and they set off for the villa. It was only a short drive and Kira chattered excitedly as they drove to the villa close to Playa Blanca – white sand beach. They entered a gated community, and drove to a magnificent villa with five bedrooms and seven bathrooms. It was luxurious and had a live-in maid. Kira explored the villa. She was as excited and as full of enthusiasm as a kiddie. She oohed and aahed as she went from room to room. She was majorly impressed with the swimming pool and danced around Kelland. Her child-like delight was infectious, and Kelland realised why he cared about her as much as he did.

He made up his mind to give her the time of her life, while he could.


Allison smiled grimly, "I think we have more than enough, don't you, lads?" Gurdip and Ronnie nodded. "I'll get a warrant and I'm sure that Gurdip would like to make the arrest, wouldn't you, Detective Singh?"

Gurdip grinned, "You betcha. Thank you, Chief."

"I think there will be a few relieved to get rid of him. His sort isn't good for the force or our reputation. Now, before you do that there's a message here from a Constable Sidhu," Ronnie and Gurdip exchanged a glance, "who says that Mrs Probert has everything in hand and just needs the inventory of all the items in the garage that you said you'd do."

"Yes, sir. I did. I promised to help," said Ronnie.

Allison sat back in his chair and thought hard, "Sidhu.... Sidhu... that name rings a bell. It's an unusual name."

"It's Punjabi," offered Gurdip.

"I wonder..."

"Wonder what, sir?"

"There was a Dr Sidhu involved in one of my early cases after my promotion to DCI. He was a doctor, a psychiatrist and clinical lead at The Old Birmingham City Asylum."

"Asylum?" said Ronnie. "Do they still have those?"

"They don't call them that anymore… Maybe, you could ask the constable when you see her, again? Ask if they're related?"

"Yes, sir," they choroused.

"And, gentlemen… don't mention a word about our evidence on Mackay. Not to anyone. Understood?"

"Yes, sir," said Ronnie.

"Let it come as a surprise… and I want to be there."

"Of course, sir."

"Better get off to Mrs Probert."

"Sir."

They left Allison's office and moved out into the squad room. Mackay looked at them both suspiciously and Gurdip gave him a cheeky grin and breezed out.


Martyn Kelland and Kira had disappeared into the bedroom. He was determined to make the most of her visit and intended to enjoy himself, while he could, before he deemed it safe to return to the UK. He was also waiting on a call from Patterson who was his contact at the OCG, with which he was involved.

He fell onto the bed with Kira and caressed and kissed her face tenderly whispering sweet nothings in her ear until the urge became too great and he began to undress her and she him.

He nuzzled her neck and ears, showering her with words of love and smothering her with kisses. Their passions heightened and they were soon moving rhythmically together until he had satisfied her first and then allowed himself to climax. They rolled apart on the bed and he exclaimed, "My legs have gone. And now, I need a shower. There's another bathroom just across the landing." He dashed off to the en suite leaving Kira lying there with a dreamy expression on her face.

She rose and wrapped a towel around her and made her way to a large family bathroom and locked the door. She basked in the refreshing water and hummed happily as she washed her lithe body and glorious hair feeling contented. She sighed, a faraway expression on her face and hugged herself as if she was in Martyn's arms. She felt deliriously happy, switched off the power shower, grabbed a fluffy towel, and wrapped it around her. She took another from the rail and wrapped it turban style around her hair and padded back towards the bedroom, where she could hear Martyn on the phone. She paused outside as she heard her name mentioned. She couldn't quite hear what was being said but there was an urgency in Martyn's tone that made her feel alarmed.

Intending to confront him she swanned into the bedroom, and he flushed guiltily, hastily ending the call. "Kira!"

"I heard my name mentioned. Is anything wrong?"

He blustered, "No, no. Nothing that can't be fixed."

"Who was it?"

His reply was swift and glib, "My solicitor. He is trying to dissuade me from ending my marriage."

"Oh? Why?"

"Repercussions for me financially, you know the score. It won't be easy."

"But, Martyn... you promised..."

"I know..." he went to her and gently caressed her face. "You know I'm a man of my word, don't you? I won't let you down. You will just need to be patient with me. My affairs will need a lot of sorting out."

Seeming happy with the explanation, Kira arched her back seductively and pressed her body against him. "So, what now?"

"You get dressed and dry your hair. I am taking you out tonight, on the town." He laughed as she wriggled against him and said, "Don't make this difficult for me or we will never leave the bedroom."

Kira smiled and sashayed away to the dressing table, where the hairdryer sat, and she began to do her hair. She tossed back the comment, "Just making sure you won't forget me."

"In five minutes?"

"Know that I am the best. Isn't that what you've told me?"

He nodded and grinned. "The very best. No one has anything on you." Kelland left the bedroom and ran lightly down the stairs. He was sweating and it wasn't with the heat as the air conditioning was on. He was feeling light headed. He thought, '*The sooner this is over with, the better.*'

Gurdip and Ronnie arrived at Meredith Probert's house and knocked. To their surprise, Dilly answered the door. Gurdip swallowed hard and was momentarily stuck for words.

"Thanks so much for coming. Perhaps you can do the inventory and let Meredith know exactly what she is dealing with."

"I've checked on line and an Indian Scout motorbike in tip-top condition is worth $48,000. That's around £39,000 and you have two bikes in immaculate condition... almost eighty grand," said Ronnie. "The ones belonging to Mr Butterworth are immaculate."

"That much?" said Mrs Probert shocked.

"I don't know about the tools yet, but I'll make a list and then check them against online valuations. That's a small fortune, that is."

Meredith sighed. "It's such a responsibility."

"Don't worry. I'll help you. The house sale will be the biggest responsibility. You will need it valued by a reputable estate agent."

"Oh dear, I've never done anything like it before. My husband, when he was alive, did all that."

"It will be fine," assured Gurdip. "And with Dilly to help you. It won't be a problem. Now, do you have the house keys?"

"I'll just get them." Meredith scuttled away leaving Gurdip and Dilly looking awkward until Ronnie stepped in.

"Dilly, we were just wondering... if you would like to come to our house for dinner sometime? Gurdip is a cracking cook you could meet Siri, my girlfriend who is Gurdip's sister. His little sister will also be around, we are just like a family. It would be good to get to know you." Gurdip looked embarrassed and turned to Ronnie raising his eyebrows meaningfully.

"That would be lovely. I'd like that."

"Great!" said Ronnie. "Then I'll leave Gurdip to sort out the date. By the way, our DCI wondered if you were any relation to Dr Sidhu, psychiatrist and clinical lead at, where was it again, Gurdip?"

Gurdip floundered, "It was the Old City Asylum, I believe. It's called something else now."

"All Saints," said Dilly. "Yes, we're related. He's my grandfather."

"Small world," said Ronnie and beamed as Meredith returned with the keys. He turned to Gurdip, "I'll get across now. Leave you to sort out the details with Dilly. You can come across when you're ready." And he left quickly leaving an embarrassed Gurdip struggling for something to say.

Ronnie let himself out and dashed across the road, which was relatively quiet. He let himself in and made his way into the garage and switched on the light. He pulled the dust sheets off the bikes and whistled between his teeth. They were absolute beauties. What he wouldn't give for one himself. He sat astride one and pretended to ride it making motorcycle sounds. He got off and tried to move the bike out of the way to get at the large metal toolbox behind and was surprised at the weight of the bike. "Thought these were lightweight?" he said aloud before leaning down to examine it more carefully. "Shouldn't be this heavy."

He stood the bike up and covered it over before opening the metal tool box. Again, the lid was very heavy. The box had been painted with a heat-treated powder-coat cover. There was a faint scratch mark that had been painted over. Ronnie picked up a screwdriver and scraped away a little of the paint revealing a gold-coloured metal. He examined the tools on the wall and lifted off a lump hammer that was also incredibly heavy, even for a lump hammer. He took the screw driver again and scratched the end of the hammer head. And a gold colour shone through.

Ronnie replaced the tool and leaned back against the tool chest in disbelief. Everything he had learned about the case could only lead him to one conclusion. "Christ! We've hit the bloody jackpot."

"What are you talking about?" asked Gurdip entering.

"These bikes, the tool station and the tools."

"What about them?"

"They're all gold."

"What?"

"Must be from that heist all those years ago. No wonder it was never found. It was turned into tools and bike parts… ingenious. Here help me cover these up. We must get back to the nick. I'll just take one tool to show the chief."

"Well lock up securely, I've just heard from the chief. The warrant's been rushed through."

Ronnie nodded, "Let's get going then. Your collar, isn't it?"

Gurdip grinned and wiggled his eyebrows, "And am I going to enjoy it? You bet I am."


Roy Chapman, Alex and Jane sat at the kitchen table in Alex's house. "Life is going to be difficult for you. We have to get you somewhere safe. There is a bounty on your head."

"How long does that last?"

"The bounty or the safe house?"

"Both."

"Depends."

"You're saying I can't go back to work?"

"I'm saying we have to keep you safe. I'm not letting anything happen to you," said Alex.

"Until this OCG is dealt with…"

"OCG?" questioned Jane.

"Organised Crime Gang. It's far reaching. They are involved in all kinds of things. They care little for life that's why I feel you need to think seriously about walking away and starting again, new identity and fresh start."

"But, what about my family? My brother, my mum and dad?"

"That will be tough but if you want to keep them safe, you need to leave. People like that use family against you. If you start again, they won't know anything. They will be safer," assured Roy.

"So, I won't be able to stay in Ironbridge?"

"Not unless the crims are caught."

Jane sighed; her eyes filled with tears. "I don't know if I can do that… Leave everyone and everything behind. What about Alex?"

Alex looked at Roy, "I don't want to lose Jane."

"You might not have to. Let's see if we can keep Jane out of circulation and sight until this case is solved."

"And just how do we do that?"

Roy and Alex looked at each other and Jane began to cry.

Roy said softly, "Jane, I promise you we will do all we can. I'll keep monitoring the office. In fact, we'll check the latest recordings, now. Alex won't leave your side until we know how best to proceed."

Roy fiddled with the equipment and pulled up the latest recordings and they began to run through them. He turned up the volume on one call, where Jacob appeared to look relieved and was smiling.

"You won't regret it. I promise you. Jane is an innocent. She knows nothing.... Of course, yes... I will keep an eye on her. She's due back to work tomorrow... yes, I assure you, you're doing the right thing." The call now over, Jacob rubbed his hands together and sighed in satisfaction.

"Can you trace who he's talking to?" asked Jane.

"The cyber unit will be able to help triangulate the call. I'll need his phone to make it easier."

Jane went to speak but Alex pre-empted her, "No, you don't. You're not doing anything else that can put you in danger. No arguments."

"Alex is right. Wait..." Roy studied the image of the office. A man in a balaclava entered the estate agents. He gently closed the door and turned the sign to read closed and bolted the door from the inside. He moved stealthily to Jacob's office door. From his trouser waistband he withdrew a pistol. Jane gasped. The camera showed him attaching a silencer to the gun barrel. The man opened the door, aimed the gun and fired. The camera in the next room picked up the image of Jacob at his desk, his look of surprise and him falling forward with a hole in the centre of his forehead.

"Oh my God!" swore Jane.

"We need to call this in, now."

"And this settles it, Jane. This man is getting rid of loose ends. You cannot go back to work."


Gurdip and Ronnie arrived back at the station and made their way to the squad room. Ronnie looked around the room, Everyone was working. Mackay was poring over a computer studying the screen. He didn't even look up. Ronnie went into the outer office and knocked at Allison's door.

Ronnie heard the instruction to enter and popped his head around it. "Sir, we're back."

Allison heaved himself out of his chair and manoeuvred his way to his office door and waited. He nodded at Gurdip who acknowledged with an inclination of his head.

Gurdip marched to Mackay's desk and said, "Angus Mackay, I am arresting you on suspicion of attempted murder, witness tampering, attempted removal of evidence and perverting the course of justice. You do not have to say anything unless you wish to do so, but anything you do say will be taken down and maybe given in evidence."

"You're having a laugh, aren't you?" growled Mackay.

Gurdip put his hand on his shoulder, "Stand, please."

"Get your filthy hands off me."

"You better comply unless you want resisting arrest added to the list," said Allison intervening.

Mackay's head snapped around, "What is this? I've done nothing wrong."

"That's for a judge and jury to sort out, don't you think?" said Allison.

The squad room was deathly quiet as the detectives present watched Gurdip haul Mackay to his feet and march him away to a holding cell.

As soon as they had exited there was a burst of fevered whispering. "All right, all right," said Allison. "Settle down. Get back to work. Soper! In here with me, now."

Ronnie retreated to Allison's office, and he indicated that Ronnie should sit. He pressed his intercom, "Maddie can you get two teas in here and look out for Singh. As soon as he returns, send him in to me."

"Yes, sir."

"Now then, what have you got to tell me? What on earth are you doing with a lump hammer?" said Allison inching forward in his seat.

Ronnie's mischievous grin appeared. He licked his lips and began to recount the events that had occurred at Meredith Probert's house and enjoyed stringing it out for the best possible effect.

Allison rolled his eyes, "Okay, Ronnie. I'll run with it. Finish your story."

Kira was now dressed and looking lovely in a primrose cotton jumpsuit. She wore comfortable flatties, and her glorious hair was loosely tied back. Martyn stepped back to admire her. "You look stunning. Now wait there, I have something to complete the picture." Martyn disappeared into the bedroom and returned with a black velvet case and gave it to Kira. "Open it." She gasped as the light hit the emerald stones set in a platinum necklace.

Martyn removed it from the box and fastened it around her neck. "There. That completes the picture. In the words of Eric Clapton, you look wonderful tonight."

"Oh, Martyn. It's beautiful."

"Only the best for you my sweet. After all, you are going to be my wife aren't you?" Kira nodded her head vigorously. "Did you pack an overnight bag?"

"Yes. It's just there," she indicated a small bag by the bedroom door. "Where are we going?"

"I thought we could go to Santo Domingo. I've booked an apartment. We can do a little sightseeing, The 3 Eyes, National Park, the Basilica Cathedral of Santa Maria la Menor and many more and…." He playfully tapped the end of her nose, "We can do a little shopping for an engagement ring."

"Oh, Martyn. You really mean it?" She threw her arms around his neck.

"Of course. My wife has received the divorce papers. It will take a little time but at least you know my true intentions. Right let's get on the road, we have quite a way to go. Best get started. I want to make this trip special to thank you for changing your statement to the police." He removed her arms from around her neck, picked up his bag and retrieved Kira's bag.

Kira chattered lightly as they walked downstairs, "It wasn't easy, but they accepted the fact that I lied because you were married."

"Perfect."

"In fact, I shouldn't have left the country. I was terrified that someone would stop me, but I got on the plane without any fuss."

"That's good. I'm sure you're going to like it here and when the time is right we can return home together."

Kira sighed happily and they left the villa together.

The sunshine turned Kira's tresses almost blue black. Martyn opened the door of the Mercedes sports car to admit Kira and ran around to the driver's side. They processed along the drive to the electric gates, which opened, and the vehicle roared out onto the road. They had travelled a short distance when a black Range Rover pulled out behind them and motored a discreet distance behind them. Martyn glanced in his rear-view mirror and slowly a smile began to manifest on his face.

Angus Mackay was sounding off to anyone who'd listen about how his rights had been violated. He insisted that they had made a mistake and demanded his phone call and a solicitor.

On the phone he spoke quietly to someone, "I'm in trouble. You have to get me out of here... yeah... who? Matt Guard? Great... I don't know what they've got unless Nesbitt has spilled his guts... Will you? Thanks... no witness, no case." Mackay grinned. '*Matt Guard, eh? The best for the best,*" and he instantly felt calmer.

He sat on the bunk in the cell and wracked his brains for what could have given him away and made the others suspicious of him. He couldn't think... He'd been more than careful when dosing Nesbitt with Thallium. He was sure no one had seen him doctor the tea. There was just one occasion when he had almost been caught but he convinced himself that no one witnessed this. He was more concerned about a search of his flat and if anyone was to look through his desk drawer at the station. The thallium was in an unlabelled bottle. It could be anything and it was in a small brown glass bottle tucked right at the back of his drawer. He had every faith that Matt Guard would get him out, then he would have an opportunity to get his things, surely? If the bottle was found he could pass it off as colloidal silver that came in brown bottles, but then he knew it would be tested. Of course, he could deny it and accuse Singh or one of the others of planting it. His mind was running through all the possibilities. He had to admit it didn't look good. He just hoped the bottle wouldn't be found until it was too late. He was also pleased that the OCG would be after Nesbitt. Getting rid of him would solve the problem or at least make things easier for him.

Holly had slept right through the night and half of the next day. Paul brought her a cup of tea and sat on the side of the bed. he stroked her hair, and she slowly came to and smiled up at him.

"How are you feeling?"

"A bit rough and bruised but much calmer."

"Good. Father Lawrence will be arriving in a couple of hours."

"Not another session?"

"I'm not sure. I think he just wants to check on you. I believe he drove out the demons last time."

"And Grace Clifton?"

"I certainly hope so."

"So, do I." Holly sat up and took her tea, which she sipped slowly before she turned her huge dark eyes on Paul. "Paul, I am so scared. What if it happens again?"

"We'll cross that bridge when we come to it, and we will face it together."

"I don't know why you haven't given up on me already, but I'm glad you haven't."

"I'll never do that," assured Paul. Holly didn't say anything, but her eyes filled with love and brightened with unshed tears. "I'll let you drink your tea and get showered and dressed. I'm sure then, you'll feel a whole lot better."

"I'm sure I will, too," murmured Holly biting her bottom lip as she did in times of uncertainty. "We will get through this," she said more vehemently.

"Yes, we will. I was going to say, 'that's the spirit' but it didn't seem appropriate."

Holly smiled. "You and your puns... no... spirits are something I don't want to think about unless they're with tonic from a vodka or gin bottle," and she laughed.

"That's my girl." Paul leaned over and kissed her gently on her forehead and stood up. "Back to work, now. See you in a bit."

# 15

THE LOCAL POLICE HAD FINISHED interviewing Jane. The news of this seemingly random killing was the talk of Ironbridge and all over the local news. As Jacob Murch was a person of interest who had been flagged up by the West Midlands' police force they had been informed and Mark Stringer was on his way to speak to Jane.

Jane sat back in the kitchen and addressed Alex, "What do I say?"

"Tell the truth. At least Mark is someone you know and can trust."

"I suppose so. What about you? How much does he know about you?"

"Enough for you not to worry." He clasped a flash drive in his hand. The footage, the conversations are all on here. We'll let him run with them."

Jane's mobile rang insistently. She picked it up and answered switching it onto loudspeaker. "Hello?"

"Jane?"

"Yes?"

"Nathan Murch."

"Yes, Mr Murch. I am so sorry for your loss."

"Thank you. It is a sad and damnable state of affairs, but I didn't ring about that. Circumstances, of which you are aware, mean the agency has no one on duty or at the helm. Look, I know you've had a dreadful shock but is it possible for you to come back to work? I will have to come in and replace Jacob and I know nothing about the business, how it works or anything and I would really appreciate your help. The police have been in and removed all sorts of things. Could you possibly help me out here, please?"

Jane looked at Alex who shook his head vehemently. Jane hesitated and said reluctantly, "Um, yes... I suppose so."

The relief in Nathan's voice was apparent. "Thank goodness for that. I don't know what else to do. My own business can be left safely in my partner's hands. Thank you. When can I expect you?"

"I can get there after my interview with the detective from the West Midlands. I'll come after that."

"Wonderful. I'll see you then." The call ended.

Alex was almost tearing his hair out. "Why on earth did you agree to that?"

"I'm sorry. I couldn't help myself. He sounded so sad. You haven't found anything on him, have you?"

"Not yet. But it's too dangerous, Jane. You saw what happened to Jacob."

"I know, but I can't turn my back on the business I love."

"Very well. If you're going to be stubborn about it. I will come with you."

"You can't."

"Why not? A concerned boyfriend just looking out for his partner... You can give me some filing to do or something. You just never know. Better to be safe than sorry. No arguments. I insist."

Just then the doorbell rang.

Kira had been wined and dined and was feeling contented. They were staying in a luxury apartment in the Arroyo area of Santo Domingo, and she had no idea how dangerous this area of the city could be. But, Martyn was showing her the time of her life. They had spent three days there sightseeing and were to move onto Jimaní, that day. It was a city in South Western Dominican Republic, a hilly region between the western shore of Lake Enriquillo and the border of Haiti. It was a place specially chosen by Kelland.

Kelland had dressed casually and waited downstairs; he was feeling nervous. As Kira descended, she quite took his breath away. She really was exceptionally beautiful but now, now there was no going back. The last four days had not only delighted Kira but had treated Martyn to a good time, too.

They were going to Cabarete to Nectar Restaurant with views of the beach and just had to wait for the taxi to take them there. "Darling, why aren't you wearing your necklace?"

"When we were out, I overheard someone say that maybe it was dangerous to wear expensive jewellery in this part of the world. So, I thought it might be safer not to."

"Oh, don't be silly, darling. We'll be perfectly safe. We're going there and back by cab. I want to show you off. I will be with you, remember? Every man will envy me, and it will set your dress off beautifully."

Kira laughed girlishly and said, "I'll go and get it. You'll have to put it on for me."

Kelland checked his watch. His stomach was bubbling like a shaken soda bottle. He could feel it rising and swallowed hard to suppress the urge to belch. The corner of his mouth began to twitch as Kira returned with the emerald necklace and he fastened it around her neck.

His hands slid around her throat as he kissed and caressed her from her dainty earlobes, down her neck to her décolleté. Kira melted under his touch and sighed his name, "Oh, Martyn." There was a toot, toot outside as the taxi arrived, and the couple left the apartment for their night out.


Jane had insisted on returning to work so Alex and Roy had been monitoring events at the Estate Agents. So far, there seemed to be nothing out of the ordinary. Jane had continued safely in her job and was teaching Nathan Murch as best she could about the running of the business.

Alex and Roy had to agree that Nathan Murch seemed not to be a part of Jacob's enterprises. However, they didn't completely trust the man. They had intercepted his calls, and everything appeared to be above board. The clients that came in were just ordinary people looking to buy a new home or sell one. Then, there was a surprise visitor.

Jane glanced up from her work and saw Mr Patterson entering the agency. "Ah, Jane. Is Mr Murch in?" he forced a smile.

"Mr Murch?"

"Yes, Mr Nathan Murch."

"Er… yes. I'll just let him know you're here." She picked up the phone and dialled his extension. "Mr Murch. Mr Patterson is here to see you… Yes, sir… Of course, sir." She turned to Mr Patterson as she replaced the receiver, "Please go in, sir."

Patterson managed another smile, knocked and entered, closing the door firmly behind him. Jane took her mobile and quickly dialled Alex's number. She lowered her voice, "Alex? Patterson's here to see Mr Murch… yes…" She hurriedly ended the call.

After that, Jane couldn't concentrate she fidgeted and fiddled and was relieved when a client walked in looking for literature on three bed houses available to rent in Shropshire. It gave her something to do and on which to focus. Jane sat the client down and made notes of his full requirements and his personal details.

Nathan's office door opened, and he spoke quietly to Jane, "Sorry to interrupt, I can continue here. Mr Patterson needs your help. Can you pop into my office?"

Jane's complexion paled and she trembled as she apologised to the gentleman opposite, "So sorry, sir. Mr Murch will be able to help you." Jane rose and went into Nathan's office.

Jeremy Patterson was standing by the window staring out onto the road that led to the square. He turned as Jane entered and she felt a creeping vine like fear wrapping around her squeezing her chest. She attempted a bright smile but stuttered as she spoke, "M... M... Mr. Patterson," she said bravely with strained brightness as she attempted to control her speech and facial expression. "How can I help?"

"Ah, Jane… Yes. As you are aware I have dealt with this estate agency for many years and Jacob was a personal friend. I am more than sorry for what happened to him."

Jane wanted to retort that she didn't believe anything of the sort, but instead, she smiled sweetly and said, "Yes. It was a great shock."

"I am transferring my business to another estate agent more local to me and wanted to collect the files dealing with my transactions." He spoke with authority that warranted no dissent.

"I see. If you would like to give me the new agent's address I can have them couriered to them." Jane still had that fixed smile on her face.

"No, I would prefer to take them now, if possible?"

"Ah, it will take some time to find them all, with Mr Murch's very tricky filing system. Unfortunately, he doesn't file in his client's name but by the areas of property."

"I'll wait."

"But, it could take hours, sir. May I respectfully suggest that you go for a coffee somewhere. There are plenty of places available. I will try and find them as quickly as I can. We only keep current files here. Past transactions are kept by law for accounting and tax, and they're all boxed up in the store room through here." A vein began to pulse in Patterson's cheek. Jane felt that same serpentine coiling of fear that she had felt earlier.

Patterson considered these new facts and sighed in exasperation. "Very well, I will return in an hour."

"But, sir; it could take much longer."

"Very well, I will ring in an hour and see how far you have got."

"Yes, sir, Mr Patterson."

Jeremy Patterson turned abruptly and stalked out of the offices and into the street.

Jane hurriedly dashed into the main office where Nathan was still sitting with the new client, and she retrieved her handbag with her phone. "Sorry, sir. It looks like I'll be commandeering your office for a while."

"That's fine. Do whatever you need to do."

Jane went back into the inner sanctum and closed the door. She took out her phone and rung Alex. "Did you get all that?"

"Every word. There must be something he wants hidden. Get his files. Can you check them at all?"

"I'll do my best."

"Good girl. Be careful. Roy will drop by as Mr Elliot and make sure you're okay."

"Fine." Jane quickly hung up. '*What on earth did he want with them all? Why now? Alex must be right. The man had something to hide.*' She did however feel safe in Nathan's company. If he was involved in Jacob's shady business, Alex would have warned her and certainly Nathan wouldn't have asked her to deal with it.

Kira stepped out of Nectar restaurant. They walked a little way down the street. Kelland paused. "Taxi's late. We better wait here, don't want to walk too far around the streets at night."

Kelland took her in his arms and kissed her tenderly then held her close. "You really are very beautiful," he whispered as he looked over her shoulder to two men walking towards them. Behind them was the man Kelland recognised and had engaged for the job. A frown creased his forehead, '*Who were the other two?*'

He didn't have long to wait and find out. One native Haitian grabbed Kira snatching the necklace from around her neck, the other attacked Kelland knocking him to the floor. The attacker leaned over him and smashed his fist into his windpipe. This man freed Kelland's wallet from his inside pocket, his Rolex from his wrist and ran, dragging the now screaming Kira with the help of his conspirator away down the deserted night street that hid the evils of men, enfolding them in its dark shadowy mantle.

The Ghost sprinted to Kelland now choking on his own blood. "Kira..." he rasped out.

"I shouldn't worry. We need to get you to a hospital."

"But Kira..."

"I don't believe she will be a problem for you," reassured the Ghost helping Kelland back to his feet. "Let's get you to safety. We can argue later."

The taxi Kelland had ordered cruised up to them and they climbed in leaving Kira to her fate.

Jane had found a box in storage that contained many of Patterson's files and his acquisitions. She rummaged through them looking for anything that might look suspicious or untoward. Many had different names of buyers with Patterson and differing bank details. She managed to take screen shots of some and momentarily set the box aside and hunted through the filing cabinet looking for areas not local to Ironbridge, fortunately nearly all of these were indeed, Patterson's transactions. Jane took as many pictures as she could before moving onto current files on property. It was here she found some notes in Jacob's handwriting clipped to various property details. These looked more promising, and she took photos of them as well. They appeared to be coded and some names cropped up time and time again. Jane heard the clamour of the shop bell and warily continued looking through files.

The office door opened, and Patterson appeared with another two men who just stood there.

"I didn't ring. I couldn't wait. Are those mine?" asked Patterson.

Jane jumped nervously as she heard his voice. She tried to appear calm, "I believe so, I have found this one box in storage and these files, so far." She pointed to a pile on the desk.

"Is that it?"

"I'm not sure. There may be more…"

"Very well. I'll take these and if you discover anymore, keep them safe and one of my men will collect them. I will ring tomorrow. That should give you enough time, shouldn't it?"

"Er… yes, sir. I expect so." Jane's heart was now thundering so loudly it resonated in her ears and she was feeling sick to her stomach.

Patterson snapped his fingers and gestured to the men to collect them. One picked up the box while the other grappled with the loose files and they followed Patterson to the door to the street and left.

Nathan Murch watched curiously. He rose from Jane's desk and crossed to her, "Who *is* that man?"

"Mr Jeremy Patterson," answered Jane promptly.

"I know that's what he says, but who is he really? What was my brother mixed up in, here?"

"Nothing that I know of, sir," replied Jane.

"Hmm… I'm not so sure. Something is not right. That man is not right, and Jacob must have been involved in, whatever it is, up to his neck. I reckon that's why he was killed."

# 16

THE GHOST HAD DROPPED KELLAND off at the nearest hospital, which was an hour away. He was in a side room of Clinica Brugal in Puerto Plata, considered to be one of the best hospitals in the Dominican Republic. He was being interviewed by the local police. The language barrier made it difficult. He described as best he could his attackers who had taken Kira and didn't have to lie about any of it as they had both been surprised. His voice was raspy, and he found it very painful to talk. He was short of breath and wheezed a lot as the air rattled in his throat. He tried to describe Kira's necklace that had been snatched and his Rolex and wallet.

Martyn was waiting to go into surgery when more news came to the police in attendance. One young policeman whispered to his superior who sighed stoically and dismissed the man. He turned to Martyn and spoke gravely in Spanish. Martyn shook his head and a nurse at his side translated. "I am so sorry, signor. The lady you were with, she has been found."

"Is she all right?"

"The nurse shook her head and said slowly, "Her body was found on the border with Haiti." Martyn shuddered and looked distraught. "I'm afraid she has been raped and murdered by the men that took her."

"No, no, no!" said Martyn in horror.

"Is there anyone we can contact for you?"

Martyn shook his head. "Her parents are dead. There's only me."

The nurse intervened and told the police that he had to go down to surgery and any other questions would have to wait. She wheeled the bed from the room and Martyn stifled a sob. '*It wasn't supposed to happen like this.*' Her death was one thing, but rape and murder was almost too much for him to bear and genuine tears began to roll down his cheek.

The police were busy removing tools, the bikes and other items from Stan Butterworth's house. "It's a real pity," said Ronnie. Those bikes are worth a mint without the gold. We should find somewhere that can safely remove the gold and replace the parts with aluminium. Then Meredith would still have her bikes to sell."

"I'm sure you can help her with that," said Gurdip.

"Possibly. I might know someone."

"From your mad bad days?" said Gurdip with a grin.

"Maybe. My uncle, Mum's brother he works in a garage that specialises in classics. I could give him a ring. When is Dilly coming over?"

If Gurdip was fazed by the change of topic he didn't show it, "The weekend. We've both got Saturday off. Seemed the best chance for us to get together."

"Then you didn't mind me suggesting it then? In spite of your protestations?" said Ronnie with a grin.

"I suppose not. And she is very pleasant."

"Very pleasant? That's putting it mildly. She's lovely."

"Don't raise your hopes, she might not like me that way."

"I think there's a good chance she does; otherwise why come at all?"

"Oh yes? I almost forgot. You know we never checked Stan's shed in the garden?"

"Yes?" said Ronnie curiously.

"Well, you'll never guess what they found in there?"

"What?"

"A smelting pot and moulds for gold. Reckon if we'd finished our search we'd have discovered the truth about those bikes much earlier."

"At least we did discover the truth."

"Chief said there's a reward for the recovery of the gold."

"That's great news for Meredith. She can use that to help her charity. Good luck to her. Still it's a pity…"

"What?"

"That we couldn't get a slice of it."

"Not really. Thinking like that will get you into trouble, Ronnie boy."

"Guess you're right. We'll just have to keep playing the lottery."

"We don't play the lottery."

"Then we've no chance, have we?" said Ronnie with a laugh. "Still it's nice to dream."

Angus Mackay was sweating he had just been to court for his PTPH, plea and trial preparation hearing, otherwise known as arraignment. At this preliminary hearing, he had pleaded, not guilty on all counts, and was being placed on remand at Winson Green. Matt Guard of Beech Tree Law had argued that putting a serving officer inside with other prisoners was very risky, but Judge Babette Cooper believed the criminal justice system had a point to prove in the light of many headlines of police corruption and felons serving within the police force. She waived the protests away and Mackay was taken down to the cells to await transportation to the prison.

He didn't know why but he was feeling unnaturally nervous. Yes, he was worried and yes, he knew things were going to be tough for him, but this was something else. Call it a sixth sense or something similar but he had a sense of impending doom.

The leaden skies had all but vanished and now the sun was clearly visible in the sapphire sky. A few wisps of angel hair cirrus clouds drifted high in the heavens promising a fine day.

Allison and Mary were waiting for the arrival of their grandchildren who were being dropped off while their daughters were going on a shopping trip to be joined by Mary in the afternoon. Andrew, Rosemary's husband, would be on hand to help Allison with the children in the afternoon. He had armed himself with story books, colouring paper and crayons all sourced by Mary who had even borrowed a gaming console and games, if they ran out of things to do, after she had gone. Mary had baking organised in the kitchen for the morning and Allison could see how delighted she was to spend time with them. He gazed at her with pride and hoped that after Cally was married she might start a family and let Mary be a proper grandmother. Diana was never likely to have children now being an absolute career woman and with Rosemary living in Australia Mary hadn't had a chance to form a suitable bond with Rosemary's children. He knew it was something she dearly wished for.

Their hire car rolled up on the drive and Mary was as excited as the children who burst into the house laughing with glee. Allison could feel himself flummoxed. He wasn't used to children but knew he had to try his best for Mary's sake. Luke and Amy ran to Mary and threw themselves into her arms. She could barely hold back the tears of joy that filled her eyes.

Allison promised himself he would try his best to be as accommodating as he could and managed to plaster a smile on his face to welcome them all.

Cally had breezed downstairs with Diana and said hi to the kids before joining Rosemary in the car and off they went. Allison couldn't believe how alive the house was with the laughter of children. He lumbered to the kitchen and watched from the doorway as Mary put aprons on the two of them and rolled up their sleeves before measuring out the flour, which clouded up, much to their amusement, as it was sifted into bowls. Then, came the eggs, which was when the telephone rang.

Allison rolled to the phone and answered, "Greg Allison."

"Sir."

"Mark. What's happening?"

"Report's come in. It's about Mackay."

"What about him?"

"He's been granted bail."

"I expected that."

"There's more. You're not going to like this. He was involved in a hit and run on his release."

"What? How?"

"When he was released he was crossing the road and a large four by four came from nowhere, knocked him down and sped off."

"What sort of four by four?"

"Don't know. The two witnesses were elderly ladies who just said it was a big box shaped car with tinted windows and no, they didn't get a plate number."

"Bugger. Is he all right?"

"He's in Queen Elizabeth hospital in a coma. It's touch and go."

"You better get someone across to search his home address pronto and his desk at work."

"On it. Are you coming in today?"

"Tied up at the moment. I'll see what I can do… Damn and blast!"

"Greg!" came Mary's voice. "Mind your language."

He put his hand over the phone, "I was minding my language… it could have been much worse I assure you." He continued speaking to Mark. "Sorry, Mark. I have to go. Can you keep me posted?"

"Of course."

Allison replaced the receiver looking grim. He manoeuvred his way to the kitchen. "Mary?"

"I don't want to hear it…"

"Mary, please… Angus Mackay has been run over. He's in a coma."

"Then there's nothing you can do."

"I need to visit his house. I promise you I will be back in time to look after the children." Mary said nothing but her face spoke a thousand words and more.

Amy ran to him flour all over, "Please Grandpa. Don't go. Please." Mary continued to look accusingly at him.

"I'm sorry, Mary."

"You always are."

"I'll only be gone an hour or two at the most."

"Promise you'll be back, Grandpa," said Amy, pouting. "You said you'd read to us."

"And do painting," added Luke.

"And we will. I promise." He checked his watch. I will be back inside two hours. I promise," and without waiting for any more to be said he grabbed his coat and headed for the front door.


Allison got in his car and drove. He accessed his hands free and called Mark. "Have you got Mackay's address?"

"It's a house in Carisbrooke Road."

"Carisbrooke Road?"

"Near the parade of shops in Hagley Road. Close to Stanmore Road where that undertaker lived. Remember him?"

"Clement Pugh, if I remember correctly. I think I know where it is. What number?"

"Twenty-eight."

"I'll meet you there."

"On my way."

The traffic was fairly light, and he didn't have too much trouble getting out from Gillhurst Road and into Lordswood Road. He drove up to The Kings Head and waited for the lights before taking a right down the busy Hagley Road, a left into Barnsley Road and then right into Sandon Road and soon came across Carisbrooke Road, which was second on the left. He cruised around to a magnificent six-bedroom property on the first bend in the road. He drove into the paved drive and waited for Mark. '*There was no way a cop could afford a house like this on his salary unless he'd won the lottery.*'

A few moments later Mark drove in from the opposite direction. He shook a set of keys at the chief. "Pooley got them from the hospital. Let's get in." They walked up to the arched opening and attractive white wood studded door. Mark opened up and they went inside.

They stood looking in shock as the place had been ransacked. Drawers from tables and sideboard had been turned out, chairs were upside down cushions ripped apart. The glass of the French Windows at the back had been cut with a glass cutter and the doors were still open.

"So that's how they got in. Get a team of SOCOs here. They obviously think he had something dangerous to them. We will look upstairs next and see if we can find anything, laptop, tablet or PC. Any memory sticks, paperwork or anything. What about his personal effects at the nick? Anyone cleared his desk, yet?"

"I'll get Pooley onto it."

"Fine. Look I've got to get back. Mary will roast me if I don't keep my word. Why does everything happen at once? … Has anyone checked CCTV? We'll need doorbell footage and street cameras. See if we can find something, anything to find who has done this and find footage from Horse Road at the time of the accident." Allison felt in his pocket and groaned he hadn't picked up a Mars Bar and a Mars Bar was just what he needed right now.


Allison hurried back to Gillhurst Road as quickly as he dared and parked. He opened the door and announced cheerfully, "I'm back." The smell of baking wafted through the hall and squeals of delight emanated from the kitchen. He hurried through to the kitchen where there was a tray of his favourite butter shortbread biscuits cooling down. He reached out his hand, but Mary slapped it away, "No! If the children can't have one yet then neither can you."

"Point taken," said Allison studying Mary's face as she spoke. "Am I forgiven? I did keep my word…"

"Yes," Mary's tone was measured. "But the test will be when that phone rings again."

"I'm not going anywhere. I'll pop the kettle on and then maybe we can all have one of those delicious looking biscuits. What would you like, kids? Orange juice? Or?..."

"Yes, please, Grandpa."

"Orange it is." Allison walked to the fridge and took out the carton of juice. He glanced back at Mary and her face was softening. He managed a warm smile for his wife, and she looked down quickly. Retrieving the glasses from the cupboard, he poured them each a drink before filling the kettle and switching it onto boil.

"All right. You don't have to go overboard," murmured Mary with a wry smile as she fetched the teapot. She went into the cupboard and removed some side plates before going to a cake tin full of sweets and Mars Bars. She passed one to Allison, "Here."

Allison grinned. "I take it I'm forgiven, then?"

"Just about." It was then the phone rang.

Mark was going through Angus Mackay's desk while Josh Linton was staring at Mackay's computer. Pooley had gone to do a search of Mackay's locker. Mark attempted to empty the contents of one drawer onto the top of the desk. He pulled it out as far as he could. Amongst some stationery items there was a scrap of paper with a couple of phone numbers. He set them to one side but stuffed right at the back of the drawer, something was wedged preventing him from removing the whole drawer. He fiddled about and his fingers touched glass and paper. There was a small brown glass bottle with a dropper, which he managed to winkle out. He looked at it and frowned. Mark opened it up and put his nose to it, and sniffed. It smelled of nothing. It didn't have a label, so he bagged it to be sent for tests. There was a notebook of sorts that didn't make any sense as the random entries were collections of words that were seemingly meaningless. He assumed they might be passwords for files and handed them to Josh who was trying to get into Mackay's PC that was password protected.

In the bottom drawer Mark found an iPad under some papers. He whistled long and low in incredulity. "Now, why would a guy like Mackay leave a tablet at work? Why not take it home?"

Josh looked up from Mackay's screen. "Where better to hide evidence but under everyone's nose at a police station? Think about it. It's the safest place there could be."

"You could be right," mused Mark. "There's something else in here, if I can just get it out." He tugged and some thick brown paper came away in his fingers. He ducked down to take a look and tried again. This time he dislodged the heavy-duty envelope with its contents and yanked them out. It held a bunch of keys. Mark studied them. One with a bright yellow tab, appeared to be for a Big Yellow Storage facility. Mark browsed through the others. There were Yale keys and mortice lock keys and more. He frowned. *What the heck were all these for?*

Allison completed his phone call as Mary stood there with her arms folded. "Don't tell me. You have to go?"

"No," Allison protested. "Nothing like that."

"Good, because if you do, I shall be filing for divorce!"

"Mary..."

"Oh, you know I don't mean it. But I shall be very, very angry."

Mary felt Amy tugging at her skirt, "You won't turn green will you, Grandma?"

"Turn green?"

"Like The Hulk?"

"What?"

Allison began to laugh, "The incredible Hulk. Don't you remember the old TV series with Bill Bixby? He played David Banner and when he got angry he turned into the hulk. I used to watch it as a kid."

"Amy can't have seen that..."

"No... In the movies..." insisted Amy.

"Yes," added Luke. "And we went on the Incredible Hulk ride at a theme park in Florida."

"I didn't," said Amy.

"No. You were too young. But, we've both seen the movie from Marvel Comics."

"Now you've lost me," said Mary.

"No, Grandma. You're here with us!" said Amy.

"What was the call about?" asked Mary fixing him with a steely stare.

"One of our witnesses has been found dead on the border of Haiti and the Dominican Republic. I won't talk about it now," Allison indicated the children with eyes.

"Of course. Come on, Luke and you, Amy. Don't hang on to Grandpa's trousers like that. He won't be able to walk."

"All right if I make a call?"

Mary nodded. "Just don't forget tea is made in the kitchen and you have to sample the children's baking."

"I'll be there in a tick."

Allison picked up the phone and dialled Mark's number. "Mark, bad news. Our star witness against Mackay against all instructions left the country and went to join Kelland in The Dominican Republic. Damn border controls didn't pick it up … It's worse that that I'm afraid. She was robbed, raped and murdered. The police are looking for two Haitian men and Kelland is in hospital, badly beaten with a crushed windpipe."

Allison exchanged a few more words with his sergeant before joining the children in the kitchen. 'Right don't eat all the biscuits, leave a few for me, please. I need to get my strength up if I am looking after you two maggots this afternoon."

"What are we going to do, Grandpa?"

"What aren't we going to do? You'll have to wait and see. I think we are going to have fun!"

Mary smiled affectionately as she watched the exchange. She hadn't seen Greg like this, not since their girls were growing up. It made her feel comfortably warm inside like melting honey on hot buttered toast.


Bill Rennie had liked the brash detective from the Met and felt quite sorry for his demise. He went to the Queen Elizabeth hospital to visit. A uniformed constable, fresh-faced Stuart Wilson was on bed-watch duty sitting outside, reading a book. "Hello, Stu. Any chance I could just pop in to see how Angus is doing?"

"You can go in, but I don't think you'll get much out of him. He's in a coma. It's touch and go."

"I just want to talk to him. They say chatting to comatose patients can help them come around. Thought I'd try. We need to know who did this. Whatever he's done he didn't deserve this."

Stuart shrugged, "You're more amenable than most. I don't think any of us want anything to do with him, now. Bent coppers should be rooted out. Puts us all in a bad light."

"Can't say you're wrong because I agree. But, he wasn't all bad. Misguided maybe."

"Yeah, maybe but didn't he try to off a prisoner?"

"Not proven, yet. I still want to talk to him."

Stuart shrugged again, "Be my guest."

Bill walked in and stared at Mackay. He had wires and tubes snaking around his body and the clunk of the oxygen machine had such a repetitive beat as if it was ticking his life away.

"Hello, mate. It's Bill. Thought I'd pop and see you on my day off and have a bit of a chat. They're saying all sorts about you that I find difficult to believe. Just wish there was something I could do to help. God, if only you'd come around... you could tell us what happened and maybe get your own back. Point the finger at the bastard who ordered this."

Bill sighed. He was finding it difficult to monologue to someone who was unresponsive. Hard work to talk without any interaction. Bill dragged up a chair and sat. He changed his voice trying to sound brighter. "You've had some good collars in your time. Got a drug dealer off the streets in London who was killing people with his product. Had some real sympathy there. We've got addicts here in Brum. I remember once I was doing some liaison work at a drug addiction centre and we had one girl, only a youngster, Maria was her name, she had beautiful hair. Long and lustrous, a real pretty lass..." He paused as remembered the girl. "The centre worked hard with her to get her off the drugs, heroin it was. It took a while and eventually she was clean. Do you know what she did when she got out?" Bill's eyes misted up at the memory. She went back to the fountain in the square, in town and sat there waiting to see her usual dealer to get a fix. I couldn't understand it. All that time and effort had gone into her, she'd got off and went straight back out to get high again. Problem was there was no follow up support. The girl was homeless, parents had kicked her out. No one had bothered to help her after her treatment. She probably felt she had nothing to live for...I don't know."

Stuart Wilson had been listening outside and turned his chair into the room. "What happened to her?"

"We got a call out to a squat in Aston. Squalid place, a condemned building all boarded up that a gang had broken into. I found Maria on a filthy, urine-soaked mattress, lying in her own excrement. She was painfully thin, skeletal, covered in track marks and sores. Her beautiful hair matted and greasy. She had sores around her mouth an absolute mess." Tears began to roll down Bill's cheek. "I don't think I've ever got over it.

"Sounds terrible."

"It was worse than that. She was dead. I've never forgotten it and Angus here had a similar experience; a thirteen-year-old on his patch died because of bad smack. He managed to collar the shit-head who'd dealt it. Think that's why I made friends with him, a shared experience. He's not all bad. He got the bastard."

Stuart sat silently, imagining the scenes that Bill had described. Bill was now choked up with emotion and finding it hard to speak; he gulped hard trying to dislodge the lump in his throat, when Stuart alerted him.

"Bill! His hand... Mackay's hand. Look!"

The index finger on his right hand that held the pulse oximeter had begun to twitch. Bill stood up and took a closer look. Now the whole hand was moving.

"Angus! Mackay! Come on... talk to me. I've been jawing on my own long enough. Angus?"

Mackay's eyelids fluttered and Bill went to the door and shouted, "Nurse! Nurse! He's coming round." He turned back to Angus. "Open your eyes... Come on!"

A nurse skidded into the room and shooed Bill out who stood at the doorway. Angus Mackay opened his eyes and scanned the room. He saw Bill and squeaked, "Bill..." His speech was slow and hesitant. "Warn Nesbitt. Warn him... he's next." Then his body began to judder and shake, convulsing erratically. His eyes closed again, and he fell still.

"What's happened?"

The nurse called out, "Ring the bell. Get the crash cart." Bill pressed the emergency button and an alarm sounded while Stuart ran down the corridor looking for help.

The nurse began administering CPR as Bill watched. A team arrived with Stuart, and they gathered around Mackay's bed. Bill was told to leave, and he stood anxiously with Stuart watching the proceedings. The electric pads whined as they charged, and Mackay's pyjama top was opened. The doctor ordered everyone to clear as he placed them on Mackay's chest and delivered a shock… Nothing… He tried again and then, again with the same result.

The doctor recorded the time of death and Bill hung his head. Stuart nudged him, "You've got nothing to beat yourself up over. At least, you were there when he died. He didn't die alone."

# 1 7

BILL RETURNED TO LLOYD HOUSE to look for Mark. He was greeted by a wave of dubious comments as to why he had come in on his day off. Pooley called, "Trouble with the missus? She kicked you out?" The banter and ribbing continued. When they didn't get the expected retort from Bill, Pooley noticed his demeanour and asked gently, "What is it? What's up?"

He lifted his head, "Mackay's dead. It's murder now." The squad room went quiet. "I need to see Stringer, is he in?"

"Chief's office," said Pooley.

Bill went into the outer office with Maddie, he knocked on the door and entered. Mark was on the phone and gestured Bill to sit. "Speak to you later." He rounded off his call, "What can I do for you?"

Bill relayed the events from the hospital and Mackay's dying words to warn Nesbitt. Mark stood up, "I better get over there. Check things out. This isn't good. If the OCG has found out about Stone Haven what else do they know? Are they aware of our other safe houses?" Bill shrugged and Mark continued. "I know you were friends with Mackay. How would you like to be the lead on his murder investigation? I think you will probably be keener than anyone else to find his killer. He wasn't a wholly popular man in the light of his criminal dealings. You can get him, Bill."

Bill perked up. "Whose on the case, now?"

"David Taylor and Josh Linton. I've sent Taylor to get front door footage from cameras in the area where Mackay was hit. He should be back soon. I wish the chief was back. He has a canny knack of knowing exactly what to do."

Bill nodded, "I'll do it. Can't let them get away with it. Otherwise who knows where it will lead. It could be open season on cops."

"Good man. Keep me informed."

Bill left Mark with a more purposeful step in his stride.

"Right!" said Mark to no one in particular. "Better get something sorted for our witness." He sat there a moment or two thinking and then snapped his fingers. He thought, *'I've got it. I wonder if our old friend Hilda Goldblum can help us again?'*

He took his mobile disappeared from the squad room and went outside to make his call.


Alex leaned back in his seat. "What do you think?"

Roy crumpled his mouth in that way he had when he was thinking. "I don't know. Nathan Murch seems to be genuine. Intel has come back that there's nothing on him, not that, that means anything. No flags, nothing apart from the fact that he's Jacob's brother."

"What about Jane?"

"What about her?"

"Do you think she'll still be targeted. This OCG seems to have a policy of no loose ends and they think Jane is a loose end."

"I hear you. From what we have overheard from conversations in the office, she may be okay, but I am not a hundred percent certain.'

"Then what?"

"We need to keep an eye on her, in work and out. Is she going to move in with you? That will help and have you put a tracker on her phone?"

Alex nodded, "And she has a pen in her handbag in case she loses her phone. We will know where she is at all times."

"What does your cop friend say?"

"He's not come back to me yet, but he has enough information to raid the agency and Matt Guard's Offices at Beech Tree Law."

"Perhaps give him a prod. It can't hurt. We have to get to work on tracking

The Ghost. According to one of our operatives he was in the Dominican Republic. I'll check and see if he's returned to this country. He could be crucial in bringing down this OCG."

"Good luck with that. He's a master of going off grid." Alex paused he was getting more and more concerned for Jane's safety. "I'll get onto Mark now."

Mark was on his way to Stone Haven. He was constantly checking his rear-view mirror as he drove towards Clent. He thought he'd check in on his fiancée, Beth, while he drove using his hands free. The conversation was light and frivolous, which gave Mark some respite from everything that was happening. Beth was now studying Law at the Open University, after qualifying as a counsellor. She had decided she enjoyed the challenge of learning and believed she could do a lot of good in society, after all she could afford it. Lately, she had been entertaining Mark with old laws that had never been repealed. "We heard about another one today," she said with a laugh. "Did you know that if you fall off a wagon, you mustn't land on a cow, or you'll be fined forty shillings?"

"What?" Mark said with a chuckle. "Good job there's not many cows wandering the streets of Birmingham."

"Or wagons!" said Beth.

"Although it could be argued that falling off the wagon could mean not staying sober…"

"Oh, yes. That reminds me …" she giggled. "It's against the law to be drunk in a pub!"

Mark laughed again. "I'll see you at home, when I'm finished."

"Bad day?"

"No day is bad if I'm coming home to you."

"Ooooh, brownie points. Any idea of the time?"

"Don't think I'll be late, book a table for us, say seven-thirty?"

"Where?"

"If you can get in, try Turtle Bay, Brindley Place. We can have a tropical cocktail and a meal, and then afterwards pop into Kelly's for a late drink."

"And watch Connie and Josh making eyes at each other?"

"That, too."

"What if I can't get in?"

"You choose. Gotta run; traffic is busy. See you later. Love you."

"Love you, too."

Mark ended the call as he needed to negotiate the tricky roundabout, ahead.

He turned off and followed the road to Stone Haven. Since he'd chatted to Beth he hadn't noticed a black Range Rover sitting in the traffic two cars behind him. He glanced behind him as the traffic had thinned out and became aware of the black four-by-four moving steadily behind him. Ever wary he drove past Stone Haven and moved on towards The Fountain. He parked outside and ran up the steps to the public house and slipped inside. He went inside and walked up to the bar. There were three staff on duty. The landlord was a large bluff man with a genial expression.

"What can I get you?"

"A coffee, please, Americano with cold milk. And do you have room for two for Sunday lunch?"

The landlord turned to a barman, "Take his money, Mick." He looked up at Mark, "I'll take a look in the book. What time?"

"One o'clock?"

The barrel-chested man flicked through the pages and studied the bookings. "Sorry, we can't do one. Can you make it at one-thirty?"

"Yes, that will be fine."

The pub door opened, and a silver haired, bearded man walked in. He was powerfully built with the air of the military about him. He scanned the bar and saw Mark standing there. He glanced sideways at him as Mark paid the bartender hovering at the landlord's side..

"Name?" asked the landlord.

"Stringer."

"And it's for two?"

"That's right."

"All booked. Pauline will get your coffee." He nodded at a girl with short blonde hair and copper streaks. "Americano with cold milk for the gent please." He turned to the man, "What can I get you?"

The man had a distinct Eastern European accent that Mark was trying to place. "Expresso, please. Double shot."

Mark retreated to a table close to the door and waited for Pauline to bring his beverage across and studied the man. He felt sure this was the chap that had been following him in the Range Rover. Two more locals came in and settled at the bar.

"Morning, Trevor. Usual?"

"Please."

"Brian?"

"Pint of Thatcher's Haze." Brian picked up a paper from the bar and began studying the sporting section. "Are you doing a sweepstake for the National, Ron?"

"Don't I always, Bri?"

"Just asking. Pound a punt?"

"Aye. I'll get the board and the names."

"I'll have a tenner's worth."

"Thirty-nine runners. Leave some for someone else."

"Okay. Make it a fiver."

Mark kept his eye on the Eastern European and wondered how he was going to get out and get to Stone Haven without him following. He knew it wouldn't be easy.


Roy and Alex had been gathering everything they could on Jeremy Patterson. He moved in the world of business and had gained public accolades for his property developments. He used charities to further his prominence in the business world and there was little to discredit him apart from his dealings with Jacob Murch. But was he the main man in charge of the OCG? Roy didn't think so. "If we can get your mate, Stringer to pursue him and the solicitor, Matt Guard it will go a long way to disrupt their organisation."

"But who is it? Who is at the top?"

Alex shook his head, "I've no idea. If only someone would talk! So, what's our next move?"

"Keep Jane safe. We must be missing something. Talk to your copper friend. See how he's progressing with the information we've already given him."

"I'll give him a call. Take a look at the office. See what's happening there."

Alex picked up his phone to call Mark as Roy continued to check the monitoring equipment. He watched on the screen. Nathan was on the phone. He couldn't hear what was being said so he turned up the volume.

"…I believe her… Not a problem… You do what you have to do… What have you found out about him? … Strange… okay, I'll leave you with it."

Roy frowned. Nathan's easy tone had changed. Maybe, he needed to dig a bit more into the man after all.


Mark sat drinking his coffee and genially chatting about the runners in the Grand National to the local called Brian. Mark claimed ignorance about the horses' form and was soaking up the tips from horse racing expert, Brian, who seemed to know his stuff.

Mark's phone rang. It vibrated in his pocket, and he excused himself from Brian and walked towards the door. The Eastern European looked up to watch and listen, "Stringer… yes?... What? No, I'm at the Fountain, just booked a table for Sunday Lunch., Thinking of having a flutter on the Grand National… Yes. Okay, I'll put one on for you, too. How much?"

The person on the other end of the line was Alex who couldn't make head nor tail of the conversation. He said, "You in trouble, mate?"

"Could say."

"Can I help?"

"Don't know. How about two quid on the pub's sweepstake?"

"Do you need to talk?"

"Yep. Defo…

"Great. I'll keep going."

"Please. Why don't you and Jane join us on Sunday?"

"I'd love to, but we have a bit of bother ourselves."

"Oh?"

"Call me when you're free to talk."

"Will do." Mark swung around and walked back to the bar. "Yes, that's great. You can either come to the Fountain now and we'll have a chat or… Yes, that's good. I just have to pick up some fresh eggs as I promised for Beth and then I'm free. Great… Okay, I'll wait here for you. We can grab some lunch… Yes… See you soon."

Mark was hoping he'd deflected the interest the man had in him, whoever he was. But he still had to get out unnoticed. He turned to the landlord, "Four names, please. Two for my friend and two for me."

"I'll get them. He picked up the jar of folded up paper names and put the board out. Mark signed his name and picked two. He drew The Big Dog and Noble Yeats."

"You got the favourite, you have," said Brian.

"Which one's that, then?"

"Noble Yeats. He won it last year."

The Eastern European drank down his coffee and went out from the pub. Mark picked another two names, drawing Minella Trump and Mr Coffey. Brian launched into a dissertation about the chosen horses. Mark wandered to the window and saw the man get into his vehicle, but he didn't drive off. He just sat there, and Mark swore under his breath. *'What could he do now? He was stuck.'* Then he had an idea. He called Allison.


Allison was painting in the kitchen with the children and although aproned there was more paint on him than on the paper. The landline rang and he excused himself to answer the phone.

"Allison… Mark?" He listened to what his sergeant told him. "Yes, that could work. Do you want me to ring? I have the number somewhere. Hold on…" he went to fetch his mobile phone and scrolled through the numbers. "Got it. I'll text it to you for the future. I'll ring off now and call. Then, ring you back. You let me know how you get on." Allison checked the number and dialled. He had to wait a while before it was answered.

"Clive Cooper."

"Clive. My sergeant's in a bit of a sticky situation." Allison explained what had happened. "I see. Yes. I'll tell him. Good luck."

Allison rang Mark back, "Clive will pick you up. You leave your vehicle there. Go out the back door. You'll need to scramble through the trees to get to the road. Clive will be waiting. Give him ten minutes. Make sure you duck down when he drives back around the front of the pub… yes, okay." Plaintive shouts of 'Grandpa!' hurried him up. "Gotta go."

Mark watched the clock. He paid for a round of drinks for Brian and Trevor as more locals flooded into the bar. Taking this as a good sign, he left his pint of Kaliber on the counter, slipped out to the back, went through the side door, down the alley and scrambled through the vegetation where he watched and waited.

Clive Cooper arrived in his battered Land Rover Defender and turned his vehicle around in the road at the side. Mark dashed out and scrambled in. He ducked down out of sight and drove past the pub where people we now grabbing tables at the outside seating. He noted the Range Rover with a sallow complexioned man sitting in the driver's seat watching the front door of the pub.

Clive breezed past and the Eastern European man didn't even acknowledge that he'd seen the vehicle. Once down the road when it was safe to sit up Mark did so and thanked Clive.

"No worries. Your car will be fine in the car park. It will be a picture to see his face when I drop you off."

"Don't think we'll taunt him. He might decide to follow you."

"True, true."

"You can bring me back and I'll get back in and walk out the front door and drive home."

"And hope he doesn't follow you home."

# 18

MARK WALKED INTO THE KITCHEN at Stone Haven where Nesbitt was having a cup of tea. Mark could hardly recognise him. His hair was clean, cut short, which had completely changed his look. He now had a neat, close-cropped beard and appeared vastly different from the unkempt person he was before. His style of clothing had changed, no longer jeans, sweatshirt and trainers but a pair of smart chinos with an open necked shirt and jacket. He had lifts inside his shoes making him appear taller. The change in footwear altered his gait, so he didn't walk in the same slouching fashion. What he had not yet conquered was his habit of sniffing when engaged in conversation. That habit would be more difficult to break. But he had been provided with a large white handkerchief, so that every time he felt the need to sniff he would blow his nose but as of yet it wasn't happening. Even so, Mark was impressed.

Mark accepted the offer of a coffee and sat at the kitchen table with him. His name had been changed to Tim Arnold. As a qualified electrician he was being relocated to Worthing and had a job organised for him at The Connaught Theatre to join the backstage crew working on lighting and sound, get-ins and get-outs and tech runs. In truth, he was really looking forward to it. He had theatrical digs organised with a family called the Dukes, who lived close to the theatre in Brougham Road until more suitable accommodation had been found for him.

Mark listened carefully to all a very enthusiastic Tim was saying. "So, what brings you to chase me up here?"

Mark hesitated, "We may have to move you to another part of the country for your training."

"But why? I like it here."

"Yes, they are one of the best, but the OCG has gone after Mackay. He ended up in a coma and before he died he said to warn you that you were next."

Tim digested this information. "Do they know where I am?"

"I don't think so. Not yet. But they are doing the damnedest to find out. I was followed all the way to Clent. I shook them off by getting Clive to rescue me from the pub. But, if they're determined enough they will find this place."

"So, what do I do?" Tim had turned pale. His hand began trembling and the nervous sniff had manifested itself again.

"I have to run though everything with you. You are still game to testify? Corroborate all you've told us so far?"

"Yes. No backing out now. They are only too quick to do away with me. I will get in first. I'll be behind a screen, won't I?"

"Yes, it will be a video link. We can't have them knowing what you look like now. Your face will be pixelated. No one will see you."

"So, what happens now?"

Clive interrupted, "We haven't finished with you yet. You're not ready. Mark?"

"I have instructions to get him to another safehouse initially until we can decide where he can finish his training."

"How safe is this place?"

"Very safe. It has been used before. It's unofficial, not on police records so no danger of anyone discovering the location unless they follow us and that's not going to happen. I will sit it out here with you until all is confirmed. Shouldn't be long."

Allison was more than relieved when Andrew stopped by to help with the children, and they decided to take them to the local McDonald's for lunch.

Allison did his best to clean himself and the children up; hands were washed, and paint removed from faces, pictures pegged out to dry ready to pop on the fridge for Mary when she got back.

The children piled out of the house and into their dad's car as Allison called out, "Just one quick call to make and I'm all yours." He picked up the phone and hunted through the address book until he found what he was looking for and dialled, "Ah, Hilda, DCI Allison here."

"Inspector," the pleasure was apparent in her voice. "How can I help?"

"Well, Hilda, it's like this… you've helped me out before and I'm hoping you will again."

"Try me."

Allison explained the situation with Nesbitt and Hilda listened carefully, "Well, Inspector, to tell you the truth, things have been rather quiet around here. I could do with a bit of excitement."

"Not too much excitement, I hope, and the right sort of excitement."

"Jessica and I will be pleased to have him. It will be lovely to have some male company. Besides, from what you have told me he just seems to be a bit of a rascal. He's not dangerous, is he? Otherwise I would have to say, no."

"No. Not dangerous, misguided maybe," and he went on to explain how he had come to Meredith's rescue.

"Then of course we will help. When can we expect him?"

"As soon as we can safely move him. I will let you know when that will be."

"And in the mean time we will get a room ready."


Mark was still talking things through with Nesbitt, now Tim Arnold who was trying to get used to the new form of address. "What if someone recognises me? Calls my old name?"

"You have to learn to ignore it."

"Now are you absolutely sure about what you've already told me?"

"Absolutely. It's a massive organisation and the ones at the top try to stay clean. I don't know everyone, but I do know the man at the top hides behind everyone else."

"What's his name? What does he look like?"

"I don't know. I've given you the names of the ones I am aware of, Paulson, Kelland, Carter, the Doc and so on. What I can tell you is, the guy at the very top is a Freemason. I heard that it has kept him out of trouble and off the books for a long time… two of them."

"No names?"

Tim thought hard. "I overheard Kelland once, talking to someone…" He screwed up his face… "I think he said Mr P. would have to be informed as would … it sounded like the tarts. I didn't think much of it at the time. Thought it was referring to the women they trafficked."

Mark nodded, "Did you ever come across Matt Guard of Beech Tree Law?"

"Only by reputation. He could get anyone off that he tried. Bet he is a Mason, too."

"What about Jacob Murch?"

Tim shook his head, "Not that I can recall."

"Nathan Murch?"

Tim thought some more and murmured, "I heard Kelland talking about Nate… could be short for Nathan… maybe."

"Maybe, indeed."

"Keep thinking. I can't risk moving you today. I'll get out again tomorrow and pick you up then… with a better plan. Some sort of distraction to ensure we get you to safety. Sit tight and stay out of sight. If the OCG discovers Stone Haven we will really be in trouble."


Gurdip was busy in the kitchen preparing a feast of dishes for the evening meal. He was feeling nervous. Dilly was expected and Siri had been teasing him all day. She flapped around him, "Need some help, brother?" she said with a wink. "Or is it to be your masterpiece of all your own work?"

Gurdip suppressed a smile, "You can make the parathas. Leave the rest to me."

"Are you sure?" she asked with a twinkle in her eye. "What about setting the table?"

"Ayesha can do that. She wants to be involved. Let her get the table ready."

"And Ronnie?"

"He's gone shopping."

"What for?"

"Wine and cheese."

"You don't drink wine."

"No, but Ronnie does, and I don't know…"

"You don't know if Dilly does."

"No…"

"Ha! You like her… my big brother is going to have a girlfriend…" This came out as a sing-song tone reminiscent of the playground.

"Stop! You don't know anything. You don't know if she likes me or…"

"She wouldn't have accepted dinner here if she didn't…" Siri interrupted.

"No… Ronnie asked her, not me…"

"Yes, for you, because you wouldn't have asked… But you made the time and date with her, the final details, the important details…"

"All right! I like her. Let's leave it at that."

"Okay, okay brother, keep your turban on! Now, let me help and I don't just mean with making parathas. You need to dress for the occasion."

Gurdip groaned. Siri wasn't making this easy. So he sighed and nodded. "I am in your hands, Siri."

Siri clapped her hands in delight and hunted for an apron as Gurdip rolled his eyes.


Mark called Clive Cooper across, "Better get me back to the Fountain."

Clive nodded and asked as they walked to his vehicle. "What about Tim?"

"With that man on the loose? It's too risky. I am going to get some help and will swing by tomorrow. In the meantime, keep him safe and I'll call you to let you know what we can do."

"Fair enough. Hop in and keep your head down until we reach where I picked you up. I'll set someone to watch the cottages in case of intruders."

"Good idea." Mark ducked down as a plan began to form in his mind.

Clive drove towards Clent and the Fountain. He passed the pub and noted the vehicle with the Eastern European was still there. "Okay, Mark, get ready. He's still there. It doesn't look like he's alone."

"I'll call you later," whispered Mark.

Clive pulled in at the kerb and Mark slipped out, went through the undergrowth and into the back of the pub. He came out into the bar and went to pick up his drink.

"You've been a while," said Brian with an odd glint in his eye.

Mark rubbed his stomach, "Bit of tummy trouble." He raised his glass. "This should help loosen me up."

"Not too loose I hope," said Brian chortling.

The pub had filled up with a few more locals since he left. Mark looked around. At a table by the door a hand went up calling him across. Mark excused himself from Brian and strode across, "Alex! What brings you here?"

"A bet on the sweepstake and to help you out of a bit of bother. What's up?"

Mark made the pretence of engaging with an old friend, shaking hands and then asked, "On your own?"

"Roy's at the bar getting drinks." Mark looked back and saw Chapman. "So, what's up?"

"I'll wait till Roy gets back, don't want to repeat myself."

The sunlight streamed through the window and pooled on their table sending rainbows of light dancing on the glass. Roy returned and set down the drinks. He straddled a chair and looked questioningly at Mark.

Mark was just about to launch into an explanation when the door opened, and two Eastern European men entered and scanned the room. They spotted Mark and seeing him with two others seemed to confirm what the first man had overheard earlier, at least that's what Mark hoped. They waited at the bar surveying the restaurant and whole area.

"Those the bozos you're worried about?" asked Chapman.

Mark assented. "Initially there was only one. Now another has appeared. He was following me. I'm trying to keep the location of our safe house secret and they are after one of our star witnesses."

"I'm sure I've seen one of them before," said Alex.

"Quite likely. They are Bulgarian. The tall lean one with thick dark curly hair is Bogdan, instrumental in trafficking women, his side kick is Penko. They are both on a watch list. Didn't know they were back in the country. Someone has slipped up there."

"So, what's your plan?" asked Roy.

"I haven't got one, yet. But three heads are better than one," said Mark cheekily. "Let's talk."

Mark glanced at his watch, time was marching on, and he needed to get home. They had all nearly finished their bar snacks and drinks. He hoped that their plan would work. He called Clive Cooper and explained.

"No problem, Mark. Two of the cottages are free. They can stay there. I don't have any more clients expected until next month after a big murder trial in London."

"Great. Thank you." Mark ended the call. He turned to Alex and Roy. "It's all arranged. You can stay there for as long as you need."

"Now we have a more pressing problem, getting you out of here," said Alex.

"What do you suggest?"

"We all leave together. We will follow you. We'll see if those men follow us. If they don't, then all's well and good."

"And if they do?"

"We can manufacture a bit of car trouble, swing the car around and block the road so they can't get through."

"Where?"

"At the underpass bridge at the roundabout. It's generally quiet and we can hold them up for as long as you need, give you time to get onto the bypass and back to Brum."

"Sounds like a plan. Let's go." Mark drained the rest of his Kaliber and stood up. He fished for his keys in his pocket. Alex and Roy did the same and they left the Fountain.

Bogdan and Penko, standing at the bar, hurriedly drunk down the remains of their drinks and started to follow them just as Brian rose from his seat and barred their way. "Sorry, gents. Are you not going to have a flutter on the National? There's only a few names left."

Bogdan cursed and rudely shoved Brian out of the way; he staggered and steadied himself at the bar. Penko followed Bogdan, knocking into Brian again. The landlord shouted, "Get out of my pub. I don't tolerate rudeness or that type of behaviour. Don't come back. You're barred."

Penko snorted and lurched after Bogdan. As they emerged from the pub they saw Mark driving away with Alex and Roy behind. They raced to their own vehicles and hurtled after them.

A car moving along the road by the pub, blared its horn and slammed on its brakes as Bogdan and Penko exited the car park. They could just see where Mark and the others had turned and sped after them.

Mark moved as quickly as he dared, and Roy and Alex kept on his tail. They could see two cars in their rear-view mirror closing up behind them. Mark negotiated the roundabout leading to the bridge underpass and then put his foot down. Roy and Alex put their car into a spin and turned blocking the way of the pursuing vehicles, which skidded to a halt behind them. The Bulgarians leaned heavily on their horns and Roy got out of his car to apologise for holding them up, much to their irritation. Just then another two cars came up behind them and stopped. The Bulgarians were stuck.

Mark hit the steering wheel in glee. It had worked. He laughed aloud. Good old Alex, he had come up trumps again.

# 19

THE SUN HAD DISAPPEARED RAPIDLY as it bled towards the horizon, sucking the day into a misty twilight that waited patiently to become the enveloping dark where only the waning moon would sneak out from the shadowy clouds to brighten the sky.

Two men in army fatigues and sporting balaclavas and night vision googles armed with AR-M1 assault rifles and Sig Pro hand guns and 9 X 19mm Parabellum ammunition jumped out of a black Range Rover that was parked and hidden from view amongst a group of trees. They crept sideways along the lane leading to Stone Haven Farm. They darted between the trees when the crescent moon dared to bare its smile in the night sky.

Cattle could be heard lowing in the fields adjacent to the milking parlour, and hay barns. A few ewes bleated plaintively calling their lambs to their side. Otherwise, there was little to disturb the night air apart from the odd owl hooting and ruffling its feathers preparing for its nightly hunt for small nocturnal rodents foraging in the dark.

The men were silent. No words were exchanged. They moved together carefully, touching each other's shoulders periodically as they swapped places in taking the lead towards the farmhouse whose lights steadily burned upstairs in the distance.

The five-bar wooden gate was opened carefully and closed so it didn't swing in the spasmodic gusts of wind that rustled the leaves on the trees lining the track. The taller man signalled to the other as they skirted around the outside of the house avoiding the cameras and light sensors. They moved into the cobbled courtyard and paused. The taller man pointed at the small cottages and converted barns encircling the square. They were in darkness except for one, where the flickering light of a television could be seen through the curtains.

The masked men moved stealthily towards it keeping close to the buildings and avoiding the central open space. They stopped either side of the window and peered inside. They could see what appeared to be the back of a man's head with long lank hair. He was watching some celebrity comedy quiz show. The tinny sound of manufactured laughter and applause resounded around the room.

The larger man pointed towards the door and the two miscreants sidled up beside it. He nodded at his partner who stopped down removed a tool kit, and began working at the door lock. There was a soft click and the door opened. They tiptoed inside, the sound covered by the waves of laughter and closed the door softly behind them.

Penko attempted to open the sitting room door, which squeaked in complaint, and he froze and waited. The man didn't turn, he didn't look. Bogdan signalled and Penko removed his gun, now fitted with a silencer, and aimed it at the back of the man's head. There was a muted pfft sound as he pulled the trigger.

Penko and Bogdan exchanged a look of disbelief as the long-haired man fell forward, and the hair fell off. Penko moved around to the front and swore, "It's a fucking mannikin in a wig. It's a trap."

An icy voice came from behind, "Freeze. Raise your hands."

Alex suitably masked, and in body armour walked around the settee to face the intruders. He removed their weapons.

Roy continued in a tone that brooked no dissent, "Down on your knees, now. Both of you. Hands behind your head."

Alex cable-tied the men's hands behind their backs before pulling off their balaclavas.

Bogdan spat out, "You won't get away with this."

"Really?" said Alex "I'm not the one cable-tied."

Bogdan swore again angrily, spittle hanging on his lips. His eyes flashed dangerously, and his muscles tensed. "You can't do this."

"Oh, but we can," said Roy.

Roy collared Penko as Alex propelled Bogdan out of the door. They forcibly pushed the pair into the cobbled yard and towards a vehicle, waiting with its engine running. The driver got out. It was Mark Stringer. From the passenger side stepped Josh Linton who arrested them both and they were placed in the car.

"That seems to have done it," quipped Alex.

"And I'll have done it if I don't get back to Beth at Kelly's."

"Where she's waiting with Connie," added Josh. "Let's get these two into custody."

"I'll be in touch," said Mark with a salute of his hand.

Clive Cooper came out and joined them. "All well, gentlemen?"

"All well. Good job Nesbitt wasn't here."

"Yes, well that's down to you," said Clive. "Good detective work."

"Maybe. More of a fluke really, but I'll take it." Mark got back in the driver's seat and the car took off down the lane.

Roy looked at Alex. "I think after that lot I need a beer."

"Agreed," said Alex. "Let's get back to my house, unless you have to get home?"

"No, wife's away at her sister's. I'll be glad to unwind, and we can check through the latest footage from Tarts."

"And I can call Jane at Tontine's where she's staying just for a couple of nights. She's safer there until I get back."


Mark and Josh had handed over the two Bulgarians and notified Interpol and Europol. They were to expect a visit in the morning, and they were to keep them separated. Mark had left a message for Allison keeping him up to date with events. If Allison had any sense he'd be in bed and that's where he would be heading once he'd picked Beth up from Kelly's.

Josh was excited, "That was a hell of a rush. Been a bit quiet of late."

"Quiet? Where have you been?"

"Trying to clear Mackay's cases with my own."

"How's that going?"

"He didn't clear anything. Too busy keeping us off his back!"

"Well, I hope you have enough energy for Connie tonight?"

"I always have energy for Connie."

"Well, better perk up, we're here. You get inside while I park up."

Josh alighted and whistled as he ran up the steps towards the concourse to the club. Mark laughed and said to himself, "Young love."

Mark found a space in Kelly's car park and slipped in through the back door. He walked to the back bar and studied the dance floor. There was Jody, dancing with Barney, doing her thing of making him feel special. Zelda was sitting at a table with champagne and someone he recognised from a few years ago. Then he remembered Chris… Janna's brother. His sister had gone missing, and Mark was instrumental in helping get her back from gangland boss, Billy Boyle. Chris always had a connection with Zelda and he it looked like he had returned. That was good. It would do Zelda good. They made a great couple, if only she could give up gambling.

He could see Josh at the top bar chatting with Connie, while Beth was having a drink with Pete, the owner of Kelly's, who at one time had managed Chaplins. He noted some new faces amongst the hostesses and spotted mother hen, Marie, engaged in flirtatious banter with another customer.

Mark moved across the dance floor and arrived at Beth's side. "Pete," he acknowledged his old friend.

"Mark good to see you. Just trying to persuade Beth to return. We miss her. She was one of my best girls."

"Well, she's my best girl now."

Beth laughed and stroked Mark's arm. "Don't worry, I'd rather be this side of the tables than on duty. Anyway, I'm actually enjoying my studies."

Mark stiffened, he thought he saw Jeremy Patterson entering the bistro by the bar, with Nathan Murch and two other men. In fact, he was sure of it."

Siri had put Ayesha to bed, after supper, and was sitting in the living room with Ronnie, Gurdip and Dilly. "That was some feast," murmured Dilly patting her tummy. "I won't be able to move for a week."

"The best way to eat," said Gurdip with a smile. "Take your time, sample all the dishes and enjoy good company."

"I second that," said Ronnie. "Gurdip is a master when it comes to Indian cuisine."

"Gosh!" said Dilly. "Is that the time? I really have to dash." She stood up and swayed, "Oopsie a little too much wine methinks," and promptly sat down again. "Just let me get my legs back!"

Gurdip wiggled his eyebrows. "Let me run you home. I haven't had a drink. You can't drive if you feel dizzy."

"I won't say, no. Is it all right to leave my car here?"

"Course. You'll be going home in style, in a cop car… at least no one will stop us if we run a red light."

"I feel bad not helping you to clear up."

Siri jumped up. "Ronnie and I will see to that. You are our guest, and we can't let the cook do it. That wouldn't be fair. Go on, Gurdip, take Dilly home. We'll say goodbye now."

The two women hugged, and Ronnie shook Dilly's hand as Dilly turned to Gurdip he blushed, his skin turning purple, but Ronnie resisted the urge to tease after a warning look from Siri. He picked up a number of plates and retreated to the kitchen, while Gurdip helped Dilly on with her coat.

Once in the kitchen, he heard the front door open and close and turned to Siri, "Well what do you think?"

"The evening went really well. I think she's lovely. She will be good for him. I can see he's smitten. And you, leave off the teasing!"

"That works both ways. You are worse than me."

"Ah, but he's my brother," she said with a twinkle. Ronnie put his arms around her and kissed her tenderly before Siri broke away. "Come on. We've got this lot to clear up. Let's get it done and we can have a warm drink before bed."

"Unless we flake out first. It's really late."

"One more kiss and then we'll start."

She gave him a quick peck on the cheek and Ronnie laughed. "Not quite what I meant." He went to the sink and began filling it up with hot water and put in the dishes to soak.

Josh and Mark tried to covertly observe Nathan Murch and Jeremy Patterson. They clearly didn't know each other very well. Who the other men were they didn't know. Josh assumed they must be minders of some sort. In fact, Nathan looked somewhat out of his depth. He seemed to look as if he was being pressurised. He didn't appear comfortable at all. In fact, when one of the other men made a sudden movement, Nathan visibly flinched.

Mark turned to Connie, "Have you seen any of those men in here before?"

Connie screwed up her face, "The tall one, yes. He comes in about once a month. He a good tipper. You should ask Ros, he always chat to her on reception."

"What about the others?"

"No. Not seen him before," she indicated Nathan with a toss of her head. "Others… Not sure, maybe. But they not regular."

"Thanks, Connie."

"You want me hover and listen like before?"

Josh leapt in, "No. Not risking that. Perhaps, Beth could speak to Ros. It may look suspicious if we do."

"Agreed." Mark looked around, "Where is Beth?"

"Talking to Pete."

"Ah, yes, I see her. Don't want her going missing again. Won't be a mo." Mark crossed to the band area, and they began to talk. Minutes later he was back."

"Beth will go and have a word with Ros. I've told her to be careful. Pete says, Patterson is a property developer. He doesn't know much else, but has never seen Murch before. He says the other two have been in a few times this month. Come from London. He says he'll look up their names in the register for us."

Mark and Josh watched as they saw Beth and Pete move off towards Reception.

Mark's phone rang, "Stringer."

"Hi Mark, Clive here. Thought you'd like to know, we've located the vehicle used by those two perps. It was hidden amongst the trees. You will need to get someone out to look at it."

"Yes, I'll do that in the morning. I'm about to go home."

"You haven't heard the best bit…"

"What's that?"

"There's evidence that the car has been involved in a hit and run."

Mark came to full attention, "Has it now?"

"What's the evidence?"

"Dented front bumper and right wing. There are some threads of material caught in the front and some blood."

"Don't let anyone near it. This could be vitally important."

"That's what I thought. See you tomorrow, then."

"You will." Mark ended the call. He turned to Josh. "That was a stroke of luck. Those bozos you arrested …"

"Yes?"

"Seems their vehicle could be the one that ran over Mackay. I'll get a team of SOCOS out there. They'll be able to tell us and then Bogdan and Penko will have more than attempted murder on their charge sheet. Pass all the info onto Bill… I'll tell Allison. Right, I'm off. I'll go out and collect Beth. I'll see you tomorrow. You okay to get home?"

"Yes, no problem. I'll get a cab for Connie and me."

Mark left Josh in the bar and walked through to Reception where Pete and Beth were still talking to Ros.

"Okay?" asked Mark.

"Indeedy, yes. Come on, I'll tell all on the way home," said Beth catching hold of Mark's hand. "Catch you later, Pete. We'll stop by again, soon."

"Do that. I miss seeing you both."

Mark snorted in fun, "In the words of the Terminator…I'll be back."

Beth and Mark dashed out and down the steps. They walked down the alley to the car park and set off home.

"So, what did you learn?"

"Some of it, you knew. Jeremy Patterson is a high flier, big portfolio of properties and develops brown field sites. Keeps himself to himself and has a few trusted friends. Nathan Murch is a first timer, not been in the club before. Don't know anything about him. The other two are from London. We know nothing about them, but..." she said teasingly. "We do have their names. You can check them out."

"Don't keep me in suspense. Who are they?"

"Mike Warner and Ricky Furness. Ring any bells?"

"Not sure... Think I've heard the name Furness before."

"Well, you'll have to think where from. It must be a lead of some sort."


In Cornflowers Holly was awake. She lay on her back staring at the ceiling trying to make sense of everything that had happened to her. If she hadn't seen the videos Paul had taken of her she would never have believed it. She glanced across at Paul sleeping peacefully. Poor Paul. He had slept little these past few months with her fits of rising early and cleaning. She knew he'd been worried about her.

It was no good, she couldn't sleep and had to get up otherwise she would begin tossing and turning and ruining his night's slumber. Holly slipped out of bed and tiptoed across the floor, opening the door as carefully as possible so it didn't squeak and lightly stepped down the stairs. She waltzed to the kitchen humming a song from The Jersey Boys, one of her favourite musicals.

She made herself a cup of tea and foraged in the cupboard for some biscuits. She could only find Jaffa cakes. "Why on earth would I have bought Jaffa cakes?" she said aloud. "Oh no... I bet that's what Grace Clifton liked. Think I better go through these cupboards in the morning and toss out anything reminiscent of her." She shuddered. "Horrible woman."

She took a sip of her tea and paused. "I really need to get back to work. Get focused and..." The temperature suddenly dropped in the room. Holly shivered and groaned, "Oh no, please no." She fingered the crucifix at her neck and held it forward and rose. She spun around in the room, went to the fridge and took out a phial of Holy water. She sprinkled some over her head, returned to her seat, still holding the Holy water and prayed aloud under her breath.

The kitchen curtains fluttered briefly and fell still. The room returned to room temperature, and she heaved a sigh of relief. Holly sipped her tea and a wave of nausea spread through her. She jumped up and rushed to the sink and heaved. But nothing came up. She waited there a moment feeling clammy. Something in her stomach was rising, as if awakening and slithering up to her oesophagus. It felt like something alive, a twisting parasite devouring her insides as it travelled up to her mouth. She raised the small bottle to her lips and drank down some of the precious Holy water. She paused as there seemed to be a frantic scrabbling and scratching in her chest and she coughed loudly and hard, feeling a physical lump in her throat. She gagged and coughed again spitting out a large black slug-like blob that stretched and writhed in the sink. Holly reeled back in shock and poured more from the small bottle onto this creature, which began to screech from a tiny mouth lined with razor sharp teeth. The sound began to penetrate her brain until she could bear it no longer and she picked up a heavy cast iron saucepan and brought it down hard on the thing, which screamed and fell quiet. She lifted the pan, and the sink was splattered in blood, which had been squashed out of the creature. She ran the tap and washed away all the fleshy debris and cleaned the bottom of the pan. Just to be sure she poured bleach on the base of and down the sink and stuck the pan into the empty dishwasher, which she set going.

Holly's mind began to rove, and she was feeling decidedly better and much more like her old self. She sat down and finished her tea, feeling pleasantly tired. It was as if her soul had been reborn, and all of the sinister happenings had been eradicated. She wandered into the sitting room and lay on the settee and flicked on the television. She switched programmes to the news channel and listened to the latest news about the war in Ukraine and now in Sudan. A minister from the Immigration department was talking about methods to stop the small boats crossing the channel and the picture disintegrated into white noise with a snow screen and voices could be heard behind the static.

Holly sat up and tried to clear her head. She began to employ strategies she had learned at the psychic school to help her focus and concentrate on what was being said. One voice was a distinctive, nasal whine with a strong Birmingham accent. Holly breathed in sharply hardly daring to breathe. She pondered on the words she heard interspersed with agonised groans.

Holly drew a ball of white protective light around her and called on God, the angels and the spirit world to guide her, to forgive the woman in torment that had invaded her body and lead the troubled soul to the light in order to pass on to the next world. Holly stared ahead out into the room and watched the figure of her biological grandmother who began to walk towards the tunnel of light when two dark shadows came out from the impenetrable black following her and with a rasping cry caught her by the arms and almost devoured her dragging her down, down until she could be seen no more.

Holly felt uplifted, released and overflowing with love. She wanted to wake Paul and tell him. But decided that wouldn't be fair. It could wait until morning. She decided to grab herself a chilled glass of wine instead, then returned to the sitting room where the television was still playing. The screen appeared to turn jelly-like and filmy when she experienced a surge of electricity through her body. A word began to form amongst the dense snow–like white dots in red accompanying the hissing noise coming from the screen. It said 'Gardener'. What on earth did that mean? But she had the pressing feeling that it was something she had to tell Allison.

# 20

ALLISON WAS SITTING READING TO Amy and engaging with her by answering her questions and asking her about the pictures in the story. He was actually enjoying himself as much as Amy. Her chirpy enthusiasm was infectious, and Allison found himself putting on crazy voices for all the characters, which delighted her.

Mary and her daughters had arrived home and she was quite enchanted with Allison's efforts at entertaining his granddaughter while Luke was engrossed in building a model plane with his father, Andrew. The house remained tidy; the children were calm. Mary stood at the doorway looking affectionately at her husband.

"Well, you continue to surprise me Greg Allison."

"Who's Greg Allison?" asked Amy with a giggle.

"Meeee!" said Allison pulling a funny face, by sticking out his bulldog chin and slapping his jowls together.

"You're grandpa!" said Amy with a giggle. "Not Gweg. I could call you Grandpa Gweg."

"Grandpa is just fine," said Allison giving Amy a cuddle.

The telephone in the hall began to ring. "Oh no," groaned Mary. "What now?" She went to answer it and called back, "It's for you!"

Allison lifted Amy off his lap amid her protests and went to the phone. "Allison." He listened carefully. "Okay. I'll see what I can do. I'll get back to you." He replaced the receiver and looked pleadingly at Mary. "Is it all right if I pop out for an hour or two?"

Mary put on her most stoic expression, shook her head as if in despair. "Off you go. But don't be late for dinner."

Allison grinned, gave her a swift peck on her cheek, grabbed his coat and car keys and dashed out before Mary could change her mind.

En route to Cornflowers Allison thought he'd make a few calls. He needed to catch up with his sergeant and felt he should check in on Nesbitt at Hilda's. He rang Hilda first.

"Hello, Hilda, Allison, here. No cause for alarm just a welfare check on how our man is doing?"

"Tim? Actually, he's a pleasure to have around. We'll miss him when he goes."

"That's good. As soon as we can safely get him back in training I'll give you a call. So, you've not noticed any strangers in the area or anything untoward?"

"No, nothing like that. It's all been quiet."

"Good, good. Any problems, anything at all, you've got my number."

"I have, indeed."

After a few more pleasantries he ended the call and then rang Mark who bought him up to speed with events and the arrest of the two Bulgarians, Bogdan Draganov and Penko Bakalov and seeing Nathan Murch in the company of Jeremy Patterson in Kelly's.

"The thing is, Greg, I know I wasn't followed to Stone Haven. I took really great care. I know it wasn't me that led them there. The information has to have come from elsewhere, but I can't see how."

Allison grunted as he listened. It certainly seemed as if Mark was onto something there. He was hoping Holly may be able to shed some light on it. That is, if Holly was Holly.

Forty minutes later, Allison was approaching the entrance to Cornflowers. He drove down their long drive and parked outside the garage. He hurried more nimbly than usual to the front door and rang the bell. Maybe his reduced intake of Mars Bars was helping after all.

Holly answered the door and beckoned him inside. She certainly looked better than the last time he saw her. He followed her into the kitchen, where she set about making a pot of tea. Allison sat at the kitchen table.

"Sorry I haven't any home-baked cakes to offer you. You'll have to make do with biscuits," she said with a wink. "Think my baking days are over as is my passion for housework."

"I'm very glad to hear it. If you start baking again I will get worried!"

Holly placed a plate of chocolate digestives on the table and set the pot on a trivet with two mugs. She placed a carton of milk next to them. "Don't stand on ceremony here. You don't mind it's not in a jug?" she asked.

"Not at all. It's quite comforting to see you being you," said Allison.

"Whatever being me means," said Holly chirpily with a quizzical expression on her face.

Paul breezed into the kitchen, "Got a cup for me?"

"Sure. Help yourself."

He went and fetched one from the mug tree, "Good to see Holly getting back to normal. She used to fuss around me like I was a chick in a nest. It was quite claustrophobic at times."

"Well, not anymore. If you want something you can get it yourself!"

"That's my girl," said Paul with a grin to Allison.

"Anyway, what's all this about?" asked Allison. "You haven't asked me over to mediate in a domestic."

"No," said Holly her face turning serious. "Last night I had... well I don't know what it was... a premonition ... a vision... a happening. I just knew it concerned you and I had to tell you." Holly moved her chair next to Allison and asked, "Do you mind if I hold your hand?"

Allison thrust out his hands and Holly took one in her grasp and held it with both of hers. "My, you have huge hands. Strong, capable hands and..." Holly seemed to drift away, and her eyes began moving rapidly as if travelling by an express train and looking out of a window. She began to talk rapidly, words bubbled from her mouth as if she couldn't say things fast enough. "So much going on with you, wonderful celebrations at home, trying to please everyone when really you want to ... get back to it. Worry... Worry about work and solving problems. Mistrust and death... people have died... if you don't act there will be more. This is important... a hierarchy... a man... blocking you, preventing you from moving on. A secret organisation, an order, involved with others in the same clan. They want to deny you success... working in the background behind you. Wait! There it is again... something to do with ... it looks like a green space, a meadow and a gardener... Yes, definitely a gardener. I can see the word spelled in meadow flowers. He's behind the leaks." Holly squeezed Allison's hands tighter and tighter and gasped loudly. "Did you get that?"

Allison retrieved his hand that was tingling like fizzy pop. He shook it to get the circulation going she had held it so tightly. "I'm not sure I understand," he murmured.

Holly's huge dark eyes blazed with a fiery light. "You must think... do you know a gardener?"

Allison shook his head, "No. Mary does the gardening, not me. I just cut the lawn. I don't know any gardeners."

"Maybe you're being too literal. What does gardener mean to you?"

"Is it a man's name?" interjected Paul.

"Yes!" said Holly. Do you know anyone called Gardener?"

Allison slowly shook his head and then burst out, "Yes! ... but that's no good he's the deputy chief constable."

"Give me your hand again. Think of this man and picture him in your mind... Come on, focus." Allison shut his eyes and tried to conjure up an image of the deputy chief. "Keep going... Yes... Yes... That's it ... I can see his name plate, Deputy Chief Constable Nigel Gardener." Holly let go of his hands.

Allison sighed, "So what you are saying is that Nigel Gardener is somehow involved in something?"

Holly nodded and pursed her lips, "Yes. He's ... in some sort of clan... a club..."

Allison thought more carefully. "I believe he's a Mason."

"That would explain the bricks I am seeing... a mason. And are any of your suspects Masons?"

"I'm not sure."

"This man is involved. He is involved in shielding others from this group and informing those on the wrong side of the tracks."

"No... he can't be."

Holly was insistent, "Yes, he is. Has anything happened you can't explain? Anything at all."

"Ha! Many things, but we got our bent copper Angus Mackay. He was reporting sensitive information to the OCG, but he's dead now."

"He was murdered."

"Yes," said Allison incredulously. "A hit and run."

"He's trying to find out where a witness is..."

"He won't have any luck with that. There's only a few of us who know where he is and they're all good blokes that I know and trust implicitly."

"I hope you're right."

"I am... but maybe you should pay the station a visit and test them out yourself?"

"You're on. God, I have missed this. It's great to be back."


Meredith stared at the Indian Scout bikes in bits with the gold missing in Stan's garage. '*What am I going to do with them?*' she thought. '*They weren't going to be worth much in bits like this.*' She made up her mind that she'd call Dilly and maybe those two very pleasant detectives who knew so much about the bikes. '*They would know what to do.*'

She decided there was no time like the present and pulled out the card that Ronnie had left and dialled his number before ringing Dilly.


Alex and Roy were watching activities and listening to a one-sided phone conversation in the estate agent's office. Nathan looked agitated and was turning red in the face. He was on the phone. "I've already told you, I know nothing about the business my brother was conducting with you. I only met you the other evening out of courtesy... Your insinuation that Jane is something of a danger to you and whatever you're involved in is nonsense. She is a sweet girl who is good at her job... No, I've told you before... I am not my brother. As soon as I can get someone to take over this business the better. You will have to find someone else… Are you threatening me?" Nathan cut off the call angrily. He stood up and paced around the office before coming to a decision.

Nathan opened the door to the outer office and spoke to Jane, "Sorry to interrupt. I think we need to talk."

Jane stopped typing out the advertising material she was working on and looked up. She noticed Nathan's manner was harassed but his facial expression was an enigma. "Of course." Jane rose and went into Nathan's office.

"Jane, please sit. I don't know what to say. Oh dear, this is most awkward." Jane just looked at him expectantly and didn't speak. "Jane, I think both you and I are in grave danger."

"What?"

"That man Patterson is involved in some very bad business, and I am sorry to say, so was my brother." There was a pause while Jane took this in, and Nathan continued. "I don't know what to do."

"What sort of bad business, sir?"

"I am not sure of all of it but definitely he has been using our estate agency for dishonest dealings and I believe the less you know the better. I feel I should get someone in to run the agency. I can get back to my own work… I'm not very good at this anyway and I want you to take some time off. Until I can find a buyer or someone with the talent to take over."

"But, sir. I need this job. I can't afford not to work."

"No… no… of course. I understand. I will pay you until something is sorted out. In fact, I may have an opening in my company. Let me see what I can do. But… And I hesitate to say this… I don't think either of us is very safe right now. I have enough problems with my sister, who thinks her husband is having an affair. I even got a P.I. to investigate. And now, this. This is frightening."

Jane looked visibly shaken.

Alex and Roy were watching the whole proceedings and Alex's knuckles turned white as he saw Jane's fear.

"Listen, Jane..." He scribbled something on a piece of paper and passed it to her. "This is my personal number. You can always call me on that. I want you to go home, now. I am going to shut up shop. I'll make an excuse about family illness or something until I can figure out exactly what to do."

"Can't you go to the police?"

Nathan shuddered, "No, I think that would bring a ton of trouble on our heads."

"I may have someone you could talk to, someone who can help."

"Who?"

"Let me check in with him first and I'll call you."

"Jane... you must take this seriously. These men... they are... dangerous. I think they are planning something to take us both out. He described us as 'loose ends'. Jane, take the time off, get away somewhere, anywhere. Now," he raised his hand to silence her. "Leave now and I will be in touch as soon as I can. I have your number. Go now, go."

Jane looked really frightened now and rose. She left his office, got her coat and walked out. Tears had begun filling her eyes and started to spill out.

Alex and Roy looked on the scene in disbelief.

"We have to do something," said Alex.

"Yes, but what?"

Allison had managed to escape the house that had dissolved into babbling female chatter; the children were running around playing hide and seek and he needed to escape the bedlam. He managed to get Mary's approval and gratefully slipped away to town. He had arranged to meet Mark in the wine bar, Vinoteca's in the library complex. The day was gloomy and suggestive of impending doom with its dull blanket grey skies without any cloud definition.

Allison sat with his latte and watched folk go about their business marvelling at the different shapes and sizes of people; female students scantily clad with bared midriffs sporting belly button rings, wearing short shorts, some with tattooed legs. One leggy redhead whose hair was artificially coloured and styled to resemble that of an exploding volcano spun with gold, had a tattoo in the shape of a vine that travelled all the way up one leg. Allison couldn't understand it. He just wasn't into this fashionable craze of body art. Besides, some of it must hurt and although no stranger to pain he didn't feel like he would enjoy self-inflicted discomfort for something that he might regret years later. How many of his friends had emblazoned their girlfriend's name on their arms and then been stuck with it after they had broken up? It often caused problems for them when a new lady came on the scene. No, he thought. He'd rather be stuck in his so called fuddy duddy ways than experience such discomfort either physically or emotionally.

Allison had just begun eavesdropping on a conversation at the next table where two women were discussing their husbands. He was fascinated with how the human brain worked and how men and women were so very different in their perceptions of each other. It was just getting to an interesting part in the conversation when Mark arrived with his coffee and sat with him, so he was forced to tune the two women out.

"Chief."

"Mark."

"What's happened?"

Allison looked around him to ensure no one was listening, "It's a bit tricky, delicate, you might say."

Mark was curious. It was unlike Allison to be coy. "Tell me."

"I went to see Holly."

"Is she all right?"

"Seems to be and appears to be back on form, thank goodness... No... this isn't about Holly. Well, it is, and it isn't."

"Now you've really got me interested."

Allison lowered his voice further, "It's about our deputy chief constable. What do you know about him?"

"What, Gardener?" he said too loudly.

Allison tried to shush him and in a conspiratorial huddle he explained what had happened at Cornflowers and what Holly had told him.

"I've got her coming in to the station tomorrow but it's not great news. Someone has been feeding information to the OCG."

"I thought that was Mackay."

"It was. But, he's not alone. Holly thinks Gardener's implicated."

"What are you going to do?"

"I don't know, yet. We will have to do some subtle digging. But, how do we set about it? That is the question."

"Won't you have to get Internal Affairs involved?"

"Not yet."

"What about the Independent Office for Police Conduct?"

"The IOPC will have to be involved, eventually."

"We need to gather as much evidence as possible. It's likely that the Masons are involved."

"How?"

"Friends in high places doing favours for others."

"Like getting villains off?" asked Mark.

Allison assented and repeated, "Like getting villains off."

"Strange we've not had a whisper of this before."

"No," said Allison thoughtfully. "But now we know..."

"We can look for it."

"Exactly."

"Who else knows about this?"

"No one, just you."

"Are you bringing anyone else into this?"

"Not yet. We'll keep it between the two of us for the moment. Holly is coming in. She will be able to see if there's anyone else implicated. We'll see how far we can get and then judge who it is safe to involve. God, I could murder a Mars Bar." Allison rubbed his grizzled chin before finishing his coffee. "Right, I should get on. I must say, I'll be glad when I can get back to work properly."


Ronnie scratched his head as he stared at the remnants of the Indian Scout bikes. "Such a pity. They were beautiful."

"But too heavy to use," prompted Gurdip.

"Look," said Meredith. "Is it possible to get replacement parts in aluminium?"

"I expect so, if you know where to go."

"They're no use to me like this and I will have more than enough with the reward money and everything else. Why don't you take them? You and your friend here and put them back together. You might get something for them, even if it's only for spare parts."

"I couldn't do that," said Ronnie looking shocked.

"Yes, you can. They're no use to me and they're better off with a young lad like you who appreciates them."

"It's not ethical. It would be like taking a bribe."

"Well, it's not. I am gifting them to you. If you say no, then I shall bequeath them to you in my will. I've no one else I would rather give them to."

Gurdip wiggled his eyebrows at Ronnie, "What do you say?"

"Well, I think you should take them," said Dilly who stood there with them.

"Think I'll just ring the chief. Give me five." Ronnie stepped outside and made a call.

He soon returned and said, "The chief says it is a grey area as Meredith is a victim of crime and not a perpetrator."

"I should hope not," said Meredith.

"If you were, it could be considered as bribery. But this needs to be reported and recorded. We are not allowed to accept anything that might question the police's integrity."

"That's crazy," said Meredith. "Let me speak to your chief and explain."

"No need. I have thought of a solution."

"What?"

"I'll organise getting the bits, work on the bikes and put them back together. You can sell them for your charity or whatever you want to do with them and just recompense me with the cost of the parts. I'll do it for you."

"But what about all your labour? ... All your hard work? It means you'll get nothing out of it."

"Ah but I will. I'd just like to be able to ride them a few times before they go. Remember, it will take me a long time to get them back into tip-top condition and I'll enjoy doing it. That way I won't compromise my job or the reputation of the force. What do you say?"

"Well, I think it's a silly rule," said Meredith.

"Not really," said Gurdip. "It's to safeguard our honesty. There is always someone who wants to do something for their own benefit. The force is trying to eliminate that type of corruption."

"But it's not corruption. It's in appreciation of all you have done for me."

"Just think," said Dilly. "You'll have someone working on them opposite you in Stan's garage until the house is sold. You will feel much safer."

"There is that." Meredith sighed. "Very well. But I still think it's barmy. And I might still ring your boss and see what I can do. Surely, if it's all reported and recorded..." she trailed off. "Okay, for the moment that's a solution."

Ronnie beamed and rubbed his hands. It will be fun to do. I mean it could take me more than a year."

"Oh dear, I hope the house sells before then."

"We'll deal with that when it happens. I'll need help to move the bits to our place."

"No," said Meredith. "You can move the bits into my garage and work on them there. I don't drive anymore, not with the price of fuel these days. You can work in my garage."

"Perfect," said Dilly. "We'll move these bits across to your garage now. Won't we, Gurdip?"

"Er... yes."

Ronnie grabbed the tarp sheet that had covered them. "Don't get the parts mixed up. We'll do one bike at a time."

# 21

THE MORNING SUN PEEPED FROM behind a small soft bubbly cloud, which was floating happily towards the east on the soft breeze. The day was comfortably warm with young men in T Shirts and women in warm weather gear, all minus their coats. It was really beginning to feel like summer at long last.

Golden beams of sunlight forged through the window in Allison's office and danced on the floor. It caught the stone in Holly's ring and sent a myriad of small lights to smatter and dance on the ceiling, which moved as she moved her hand.

Holly sat primly in Allison's office as Allison looked her over, "How are you feeling now?"

"Fine and raring to go," she replied.

"Are you sure?"

"Absolutely."

"Good. Here's what we'll do. I'll walk with you into the squad room, and we'll stop at each desk and work station, and you can see what you can pick up before we move along the corridor towards some of the other offices. How we can get you to encounter the DCC I don't know."

"We might not have to as long as I can touch or hold something of his. Anything will do and I should get an idea then of what the man is like."

"I'll see what I can do."

Allison rose and opened his door into Maddie's office who smiled brightly at Holly. "Holly, lovely to see you, again."

Holly returned her smile and said, "Don't worry about John. He's going to be fine, and he will get the job."

Maddie's mouth dropped open in awe. "How did you... never mind. Thank you. That's great to know."

Allison gave one of his rare smiles at Maddie and winked, before they moved out into the squad room. They paused at each desk and Allison exchanged pleasantries with each member of his team, checking on progress with the different cases they were working on. Holly stiffened and paused at an empty desk and shuddered before moving on. They covered the squad room and a couple of outer offices and progressed along the corridor.

"Well?" asked Allison. "What happened in there?"

"Your men are all fine. You have a good team."

"What about the empty desk?"

"Not a good feel... duplicitous, a liar and then I realised this must have been Mackay's desk."

"You're absolutely right," said Allison marvelling at Holly's ability.

They reached the stairwell and lifts where people were coming and going. Holly exclaimed, "It's a little busy here, too many energies. Can we go back to your office and maybe you can try and get something belonging to this man?"

Allison nodded. "Yes, I'll get Maddie to put the kettle on. We can talk there. I'm sure she'd like to hear some more from you about John," he said with a laugh.


Jane took off her jacket. It was getting uncomfortably warm in Riverside Cottage. She looked up expectantly at Alex, "There must be something you and Roy can do? Talk to Mr Murch. Or do I get him to talk to Mark Stringer?"

Roy stared at Alex who was silent, so he jumped in. "This is really difficult, Jane. We shouldn't get involved. We were selected and ordered to getting Kelland out to face justice by any means possible and break up the people trafficking ring, by going for the major players. But this is even bigger than we anticipated. We need to pass our information on to the police. I can't tell you anymore and you shouldn't ask. I've already said too much."

"What about my job?"

"You said he's going to pay you as usual?"

"Yes. He's a good man. He said he might find an opening for me in his business."

"What does he do?"

"I've no idea. What if it's something I don't like. My skills are in property, advertising and selling."

Alex picked up Snooks who was wrapping herself around his legs and began to pet her. She jutted her chin out forcing him to tickle her under it. "I'll call Mark. Tell him what we have. You can call Nathan and fix up a meeting somewhere neutral, once we've spoken to Mark."

Allison led Holly into his office and left to try and get something from the deputy chief constable's desk; what that would be, he had no idea. He stuck out his chin and lumbered down the corridor to the lifts and took one to the top floor. He moved along the corridor past the offices until he reached Gardener's door. He could see through the glass window that he wasn't present. There was no sign of his secretary, June either. He hesitated but knocked anyway and entered. He looked around the office. He needed something the man used that wouldn't be missed immediately, but what? And what excuse could he give for 'borrowing' something? There were the usual stationery items, hole punch, pens, stapler, paper clips, letter opener and so on.

There was a navy-blue raincoat hanging on the back of the door. Allison felt in the pockets. In one was a small mini calculator and a man's white cotton handkerchief. He quickly pocketed both of them and turned to the door, which opened and DCC Nigel Gardener walked in. He was a tall lean man with a chiselled chin. He clearly looked after himself. He had clean cropped auburn hair that was just turning grey, and Allison noticed he wore a heavy gold signet ring, embossed with his initials. He stared with limpid blue eyes at Allison in surprise. "What are you doing in my office?"

"So sorry, I was going to leave you a note but couldn't find anything to write on." Allison felt his face turning red. "Your secretary June wasn't here either."

"No, she's on annual leave. Well, I am here now. You can tell me. What's so important that you had to come up to this floor to see me?"

Allison pretended to look around him and dropped his voice, "You know that we fingered Angus Mackay as an informant to the OCG?"

"I heard. Yes. What about it?"

"Well, we believe we've found the perps who ran him over and the evidence to corroborate the allegations." Allison knew he was winging it. He had to reveal something of substance to appear innocent.

"Yes?"

"Apparently," Allison swallowed hard and jutted his chin forward. "He's not the only one. I was going to leave a note to ask to speak to you in private."

"Go on." Gardener's voice had taken on a brittle tone, although his face was impassive.

"It seems one of the accused Bulgarian men let slip in interview that they would soon be helped by someone inside this building."

Gardener's eyes narrowed, "What's that got to do with me?"

"It was implied that one of the uniformed branch would take over from where Mackay left off."

"Really?"

"I just needed to give you a heads up that someone under you, in your department, is possibly an informant, unless they were trying to cloud issues for us. It would be very handy for them to send us on a wild goose chase that brings us nothing."

"I see." If Gardener was rattled he didn't show it. "Is anyone else aware of this?"

"Just my sergeant and the detective with him," Allison lied.

"Good. Best to keep it that way. Don't want to alarm anyone. I'll do some subtle investigating and see if anyone springs to mind. You were right to come to me with this. The less people know the better. You'll keep me informed if you discover anymore?"

"Of course, sir."

"Good. Similarly, I'll let you know if I learn anything."

"Do we need to involve Internal Affairs?"

"Not yet. We'll wait until we have something of substance. Thank you, Allison."

Allison nodded at Gardener and left. His heart was thumping like it wanted to escape his chest. It had pounded loudly in his ears. He almost thought it was so loud that Gardener would hear it.

Allison made his way back along the corridor to the lifts. He thought about taking one down and then decided to take the stairs. Going down would not be such an effort and he was then doing something to help his activity levels and diet. Although, he did think that if the grandchildren were around all the time, he would be much fitter than he was; he had been quite exhausted kicking a ball around with Luke the other day.

Allison passed a few coppers on the way down and grunted his usual greeting. He reached his floor and crossed the squad room and studied his men. He was delighted that he had a good batch. He knew he was lucky with his department. They were all good men.

Allison entered his office to find Maddie engrossed in what Holly was telling her. She sat up straight and offered, "I'll get out of your hair now. Holly, thank you for that. You don't know how much you have eased my mind. I believe I will sleep tonight. Thank you."

Allison studied Maddie's face. In truth, he hadn't noticed how drawn she had looked of late. Now, he could see the dark circles under her eyes. He remonstrated with himself and decided he would make a point of seeing if she was okay in the future. Maddie said her goodbyes and retreated to her office.

Holly looked up expectantly, "Well? What did you get?"

"I almost got caught, that's what. But, I managed to snaffle these." He removed the mini calculator and gent's white hankie and passed them to her. "Don't know how I'm going to get them back."

But Holly wasn't listening she was focused on holding the two items and she gasped loudly. "He's a powerful personality and he's ambitious. I see he's a member of a sect of some sort and it is from his contacts there that he has become embroiled in criminal activities with cover-ups and more. This man is the leak, the informant you have been worried about." Allison went to speak but Holly silenced him with, "There's more. He's got an expensive habit and needs to maintain his lavish lifestyle. He's on their payroll... masquerading as a legitimate consultant in security for a few businesses."

"What's his habit? Drugs?"

"No, not drugs. I've seen it before. He's a compulsive gambler. Run up some debts, which he's still paying off. Will that be of any use?"

"It maybe if he hasn't declared it or he's associated with a business that could be construed as a conflict of interest. It's a starting point. Thanks, Holly."

"I'm afraid I can't tell you anymore. You will have to do some digging. Or..."

"Yes?"

"If I could meet him, somehow... I could tell you more then."

"No. I don't think that's feasible, and it could be dangerous."

"Huh! After what I've been through it would be..."

"An easy ride?"

"Something like that."

"What if..."

"Hold on, I'm not doing anything that could put you in danger. Paul would never forgive me."

"Let me worry about that. Just listen. I have an idea..."

Allison groaned.


That afternoon, Mark and Josh accompanied two teams of uniformed coppers to execute a search warrant that had finally come through on the solicitor, Matt Guard of Beech Tree Law in Birmingham who had been dealing with Jeremy Patterson. With the information Alex had passed Mark anonymously on the memory stick and the photos Jane had taken of some of the estate agent accounts the judge had finally agreed to a search warrant of Matt Guard's premises and his home. A further file had come through from Alex tracing Guard's financials. It was all beginning to stack up.

Matt Guard lived in a select part of Solihull and Mark wondered how the six bedroomed property compete with pool could be afforded, even on a solicitor's fabulous salary. Mark supervised Stuart Wilson and the other constables conducting the search. It was in the attic some boxes were found relating to conveyancing and other cases. Josh Linton had gone to the law practice's address and managed to stop Matt Guard, himself shredding a number of documents, which were also taken away for Forensics to study and try and piece together.

Matt Guard himself was complacent, one might say cocky in insisting that the case would be dropped, and that Josh and the team would be in for a roasting from above. It didn't deter them, and they came away with a number of valuable files and documents relating to Jeremy Patterson and his various firms that he had used in the innumerable transactions. Mark felt sure that there would be enough to bring a case against the solicitor for money laundering and he was anxious to get back to the station to see what else he could unravel from the files.


Holly had taken herself out from Allison's office and gone to the lifts. She had stepped inside one with a couple of other people and travelled to the highest floor where the top brass had their offices. She wandered out after a couple of others and waited until they had disappeared into their respective departments and the corridor was now quiet and deserted. She walked along it until she spotted Gardener's door.

There she feigned a fainting fit, and collapsed to the floor. Nigel Gardener saw her go down and dashed out from his office and helped her to her feet. As soon as he touched her a wave of electricity surged through her. He felt a strange tingling and guided her inside his office and sat her down. Holly pretended to be woozy. "Think the static gave me an electric shock," she murmured.

"Is that what it was? I thought I felt something." He went and grabbed her a cup of ice-cold water from the dispenser and handed it to her.

"Are you all right?" he asked looking concerned.

Holly shook her head, "I don't know what happened. When I got in the lift

I felt dizzy and didn't press a button. I ended up soaring up to the top floor with the other people in the lift and followed someone else out. I'm so sorry, I don't know where I am…"

"I see you are wearing a visitor lanyard. Who are you supposed to meet?"

"Um… DCI Allison."

"Well, we'll have to get you down there, he said taking her elbow as if to lift her up."

"If I can just sit a moment while my head clears."

"Of course, of course. Do you need a doctor?"

"No… I suffer from low blood pressure and when it drops below a certain level I'm afraid I flake out. It sometimes happens going from a hot room to a cold one and vice versa."

"I'll ring down and call Allison. He can come up and collect you. That is, if you are sure you don't need medical assistance."

"No, I'll be okay in a minute. Thank you. You are very kind." Her head had begun to swim. She was picking up so much from this man. There was a lot she needed to tell Allison."

"May I take your name?" he asked as he picked up his phone.

"Holly… he'll know who it is."

Nigel Gardener dialled on the internal line and Greg Allison picked up almost immediately. "Allison," came his gruff tones.

"I have someone called Holly sitting in my office. She sort of collapsed outside my door. Says she's here to see you."

"Oh, my word. Yes. I wondered what had happened to her, she is usually so prompt. Is she okay?"

"I believe so. Something to do with low blood pressure."

"I'll be there in a moment."

"Fine." Nigel replaced his receiver. '*Allison again. Twice in one day. Was that a coincidence? And who was this female, Holly?*' Gardener decided he would find out.


Holly and Allison made their way to his office. Again, Allison had that same unnerving feeling that plagued him sometimes, when he had a hunch. He sometimes thought Holly's abilities were rubbing off on him. Once inside his office door they sat down.

"Well?" asked Allison.

Holly nodded, "He's not to be trusted. He's definitely involved in more than you know."

She stopped and paused. Allison broke in, "What aren't you telling me?"

"He's dangerous, really dangerous and I don't think he believed me. He's suspicious of you and your actions and I don't feel so safe myself either. I was reminded of a shark circling its prey. It sent shivers down my spine."

Allison pursed his lips, "I wanted your assessment, but the problem is, how on earth do I take down a deputy chief constable?"

# 2 2

ALLISON HAD RETURNED HOME AS he had promised Mary. He arrived to find her in floods of tears. He rushed to her and wrapped her in his arms. "Whatever is it? What's happened? Who's upset you?"

Mary smiled through the tears streaming down her cheek, "No one, Greg. They're tears of joy. I can't believe it." She looked up at him her eyes shining.

"What?"

"It's Rosemary and Andrew."

"What about them?"

"They didn't want to tell us, the real reason for their trip." Allison looked puzzled. Mary continued, "Andrew has been headhunted. Rosemary was getting homesick and now Andrew's parents have passed away they thought it would be good for them and the children to come across and see if they could settle here, that's if the job interview went well. And it did!"

"Well, I'm blessed…"

"Yes, we are. You know Andrew's been disappearing mornings leaving the children with me. All the time he was going into his new place of work to get a feel for it and house hunting, looking at schools, everything."

"What about Australia?"

"They'll have to go back to sell up and pack their things and Rosemary will keep her dual nationality. Oh, Greg! Isn't it wonderful?"

Allison smiled catching Mary's enthusiasm. "It is indeed. What's the job?"

"C.E.O. of National Travel in Birmingham."

"Is that in Digbeth? The coach station?"

"Not sure. You'll have to ask him. It will give you something to talk about later. It's so exciting I am thrilled for them, and they are looking at properties in Harborne, Edgbaston, and Bearwood. We will know more later. I hope they find something close to us."

"What about schools?"

"Funnily enough, they have sourced three outstanding schools. They have to interview and hopefully one of them will take the children. The thing is they are all catholic schools."

"Is that a problem?"

"No, because Andrew is catholic but non practising, although he hasn't said he isn't. Rosemary, of course is C of E."

"I expect getting a place at one of the schools will decide where they live."

"I expect so. Oh, Greg isn't it bloody marvellous?"

Allison suppressed a grin. He wasn't used to Mary swearing, even mildly. He had to agree, "Yes… bloody marvellous," and he held her close.


Matt Guard was seething. Being taken into custody for questioning in front of all his employees was humiliating. Although, he was capable of representing himself he was waiting for one of his team to come and stand alongside him. He had more than enough capital to post bail. He was due his phone call. He thought carefully about which staff member would be best. Who could he manipulate? He had an idea. He had one person in mind who would be good to groom. He also needed to get word to the DCC. He needed to get out and get out quickly.

He looked across at the uniformed copper on duty, one, who he understood, had been involved in the search of his house. Stuart Wilson. He called across. speaking in his most commanding tones. "You. Officer."

Stuart looked across at the solicitor who complained, "You know, all this is a nonsense, don't you?" Stuart said nothing. "I am allowed a phone call. I need to speak to my wife, as well as my business colleagues." There was still no response. "Can you get a message to DCC Gardener?" At Gardener's name

Stuart perked up and listened more carefully. "That made you sit up and take note. Yes, DCC Gardener is a personal friend of mine. He will see immediately that these charges are trumped up, fake. I need to speak to him. Oh, for heaven's sake, get me someone I can speak to, to sort this mess out."

Stuart didn't move or blink.

Matt Guard thumped his hands on the small table in the cell in exasperation.

Allison and Mark were deep in conversation on the phone. Allison was trying to be as discreet as possible. "I don't know how you do it, but it must be possible, surely?"

Mark paused, "Josh Linton is the best tech guy I know. He may be able to do it. Maybe…"

"Yes?"

"Yes. Perhaps we could slip a bug or two in his office?"

"That will be hard. How do you get in without being detected?"

"Gardener knocks off early. One of the perks of the job. And put some surveillance on him. He needs watching without raising his suspicions."

"Who do we get to do that?"

"Woodward. He's always been a bit of a lone wolf. He can be trusted. But none of this must get out. None of it. Understand?"

Mary called out, "Finish your call, Greg. Tea's ready."

"Gotta go. I'll call you later."

Allison rubbed his grizzled chin. It wasn't tea he wanted. It was a Mars Bar. He needed to be able to hold Matt Guard as long as possible. He would get onto that as soon as tea was over.

DCC Gardener was looking through some files when he received a call on his personal phone. It was Matt Guard's wife, Coral. She protested loudly about the police taking her husband away from his place of work and being subjected to gross humiliation. She explained what had happened at the house and finished with, "Can't you do something? He's your solicitor. Surely you can help?"

Gardener listened with anxiety growing around him like a prickly bramble patch overrun with ivy, creeping up his body and strangling his heart, which was punching his ribs, madly. He muttered that he would see what he could do and terminated the call. Gardener was feeling twitchy, first the contact with Allison, and his so-called consultant, Holly. He didn't even know her second name and hadn't been able to deduce much from that only that she was some kind of advisor to the DCI. He didn't want to, but knew he had to go down to the holding cells, see what the charges were against his friend and try and get Guard out.

Gardener left his office after a message to the switchboard to hold any calls and took the lift down to the basement. He examined the charge book and walked past the holding cells checking the inmates. There was no one he recognised or knew until he came to the last one, peered inside and saw Matt Guard sitting glumly with his head in his hands. He looked up as the cover slid open and saw Gardener. "Jeremy! Thank God. Can you tell this idiot of a copper to let me out. I know my rights."

Gardener grimaced, "Matt. I didn't expect to see you in here. What is it? A traffic violation, unpaid parking ticket?"

"No. They seem to have some crazy idea that I am a Mr Big in the criminal underworld."

Gardener laughed, "There must be some mistake. Surely?"

"That's what I said."

"Officer Wilson, it is Wilson, isn't it?" Stuart nodded. "Unlock the cell, let me talk to the prisoner."

Wilson afraid of disobeying a direct order from someone higher in command, foraged around for the keys and walked to the cell and unlocked it. Gardener entered. Stuart saw the two men shake hands, but not in an ordinary way. It was some kind of fancy handshake and Stuart closed the door. He was now very curious and wondered what the relationship was between the two men, who were now talking in hushed tones inside.

Footsteps were heard and revealed Mark Stringer with Josh Linton striding along the corridor towards him. Stuart said quietly, "Sir, the DCC is in with the prisoner now. I couldn't do anything about it."

Mark nodded, "Of course not. Have you locked them in?"

"No, sir, just closed the door."

"Protocol, Stuart. Lock it. The DCC will soon bang to be let out."

Stuart nodded and the key rattled in the lock sealing them both inside. Mark said something quietly to Josh and took full advantage of the situation and raced up the stairs to the top floor and along the corridor. Many of the staff had already left for the evening. He quickly entered the DCC's office unobserved, drew down the blinds, turned the slats so they were shut before he secreted two listening devices. One just under his desk and one behind a picture on the wall that faced the desk.

It was lucky Gardener's computer was still on. Mark quickly downloaded the software, 'AnyDesk'. There were so many apps on the desktop he hoped it wouldn't be noticed. His phone buzzed in his pocket. It was Josh, "Gardener's out. Get out now."

Mark didn't need telling twice, he hurried out and made for the stairs. Just as he disappeared behind the fire door, Gardener emerged from the lift and briskly marched to his office. He opened the door and looked around surprised. He didn't remember dropping the slatted blinds. He looked around him suspiciously until he saw a cleaner hurrying past with a duster and polish in hand, and incorrectly assumed that she must have done it in preparation for cleaning and instantly felt calmer. Gardener switched off his PC and collected his overcoat, although he hardly needed it this weather and made his way back to the lifts. He would have to speak to the judge tonight. He had a few favours to call in.

Jane sat smoothing Snooks who was sitting on her lap. She was looking miserable, and Alex tried to cheer her up, "It's not that bad. You never know, it might be more interesting and exciting for you."

"I know you're right. It's just... I love what I do, and I love this town, even more now since you and Snooks came to live here. But I can't bear looking over my shoulder all the time, wondering if a man with a gun is going to pop up."

"The Agency might take a little time to sell, so what then?"

"Nathan will pay me, and I am going to his company for the day, next week when he finally shuts the office, and the business is advertised."

"What exactly does he do?"

"It sounds a lot of fun. It's called 'Media Play' and they deal with advertising and promotion work in all mediums. He's actually asked me to shadow his PA as she is retiring soon, and he believes I could be trained to replace her."

"That's great! It sounds amazing."

"Maybe," said Jane perking up. "You could be right. It could be a wonderful opportunity. I must let go of the old and bring on the new," she said smiling. "Banish the blues and look forward as long as no one is coming after me."

"They won't. Roy and I will see to that."

"Then let's open a bottle of wine to celebrate. You'll have to get it. I can't possibly disturb Snooks."

Alex laughed as he stood up. "I swear that cat is getting fonder of you than me!"

"Alex… about what you do… it's dangerous, isn't it?"

"It can be. But I'm well trained. You have no need to worry."

"Where are you off to next?"

"Not sure. Roy will let me know but this situation with the OCG is not over yet."


Ronnie and Gurdip were in Meredith's garage, and she had been supplying them with copious amounts of tea and treats. Her wild banana cake was simply the best thing Ronnie had ever tasted and he said so, much to Meredith's delight.

They were still waiting for parts to come in, but had a few. Ronnie was working on one bike and trying to assemble what he could from all the pieces, and one was starting to take shape.

It had been all over the press, how some gold from the major heist years ago had turned up and Trevor Booth, the Birmingham Post and Mail reporter, had done a great job on the story. Meredith, however, was concerned that the article and publicity might cause problems for her. She didn't like being in the limelight.

The young men were interrupted in their endeavours by the arrival of Dilly, who after a quick cuppa had dropped in to see how the boys were getting on with the bikes. Gurdip stopped handing Ronnie various tools and took time out to chat to Dilly. Finally, Ronnie took a break and said, "For goodness sake, you two. Just accept you like each other and go on a proper date."

Gurdip looked down in embarrassment but Dilly grinned and said, "Yes. You're right, Ronnie. How about it, Gurdip?"

Gurdip swallowed hard and nodded, "Yes, okay."

"Look," added Ronnie. "Do yourselves both a favour, clear off out of it and leave me to get on with this," and he immersed himself in fitting the pedals back onto the bike.

Dilly giggled, she took Gurdip's hand, and she led him from the garage and outside like a little boy.


Woodward was parked around the corner of the cul-de-sac where DCC Gardener lived. He had followed Gardener home and was now out of the car and keeping an eye on the house. Nothing had happened and Woodward was getting tired. It was a thankless task especially on his own. He was just thinking about knocking off for the night and going home when he saw Gardener coming out of his house. He became alert and watched as Gardener opened his garage door and stepped inside. Moments later, he came out and began driving up the road. Woodward hurriedly raced back to his car and started it up. He had to turn around and hoped he would be able to catch up with the DCC and see where he was going.

It was tricky following him, he had to remain comfortably behind Gardener but remain unobserved. He followed the man out from the suburbs and into the town. He paused as he saw Gardener park in the police car park and enter Lloyd House. Woodward was unsure what to do. He decided to wait in the car park for Gardener to return. Fifteen minutes later, Gardener emerged and got back into his car.

He left Lloyd House and Woodward followed carefully. They were soon on their way to Moseley. Gardener turned into Russell Road, a quiet and pleasant residential area, close to Cannon Hill Park. Woodward slowed and continued on past the palatial house where Gardener had parked. He turned into John Rose Way, grabbed his night vision binoculars and hurried back to the £900,000 house where Gardener was waiting on the step.

Woodward tucked himself out of sight of a street lamp and watched from a driveway with adjoining trees, which he used for cover. He raised his binoculars and saw a tall distinguished looking man open the door. The two men shook hands in a somewhat unusual way, before the man peered up and down the street and admitted Gardener into his house.

Shocked, Woodward resisted the urge to whistle in disbelief. He knew the man. It was Judge Fleming and Woodward knew he had to get closer. He saw the judge admit Gardener and the door closed.

Woodward walked stealthily towards the house and noted the security lights and CCTV cameras. He noted the garden door adjacent to the garage. He could just discern a light going on garden side of the house and tiptoed carefully across the road, which was quiet. Now, could he get closer without turning on the lights or alerting anyone?

# 23

WOODWARD HAD, WITH DIFFICULTY, MANAGED to get himself over the garden gate at the side of the garage. He had crawled along the side of the house to the lit window. He was lucky that the small windows above the main windows were open.

The judge and DCC were talking together in low tones, and he only managed to catch some words.

It was enough.

Woodward crept back the way he came taking advantage of Gardener's exit from the house as the security lights were on; so no reason to raise any suspicions about someone else's presence. He slipped away carefully and hurried back to his vehicle, which he started. He checked his watch. It was getting late, and he needed to see if Gardener was going anywhere else.

He hoped he could catch up with Gardener and set off from John Rose Way into Russell Road. His eyes searched the road, and he could see car tail lights three hundred yards ahead. He kept his eye on them and followed discreetly. He could see that Gardener was headed for Solihull.

Woodward watched Gardener's vehicle turn into Lovelace Avenue known locally as Millionaires' Row. He found somewhere to park in Widney lane and hurried down the street of high-end real estate. Gardener's car drove in through expensive electric gates and went up to the house. Woodward checked out the address and returned to his car and went back to the station. He wanted to discover who lived at that address. He had a suspicion but wanted it confirmed.

After logging into his computer in the empty squad room he found the name of the owner. It was confirmed. The owner was Jeremy Patterson. Woodward logged off and sat back in his chair. He couldn't quite believe it. But, what in hell could Allison do about it?

The warm summer sunshine filtered through the windows into Allison's kitchen where his daughters and family had gathered. He intended to slink out unnoticed, but it wasn't meant to be just yet as Mary caught him by the arm and propelled him back to the table.

"Isn't it wonderful, Greg? Andrew and Rosemary have got places offered to the children for St. Gregory's Catholic Primary School in Bearwood. According to Ofsted it's rated outstanding."

"Oh, my. Congratulations. That's exciting."

"The children are spending a day there to see how they like it and how they get on before the school breaks up for the summer holidays."

"What about the other schools on the list?" asked Allison.

"Our Lady of Fatima has no spaces whatsoever. They were hoping against hope that they may do and then they could look for a house nearer to us. But it's obviously not meant to be."

"What about the C of E school in Oxford Road, Moseley? That was outstanding, too."

"They've been put on the waiting list, there. But they would have been silly to turn down a good place."

"Let's hope Amy and Luke have a good day then. So what about the house hunting?"

"We have a viewing this afternoon, Dad. In Carisbrooke Road."

Allison's ears pricked up, "Yes?"

"Apparently a house has just come on the market again because the new owner had died."

"Oh, yes?"

"The details look great and it's just a short hop to Park Road where the school is and not far to get to you. Ideal really, if we like it." Rosemary passed her father the details. Allison only had to see the image of the outside with the brick arched entrance and knew it was where Mackay had lived.

"I know the house," said Allison. "And it is a beauty. Spacious, big garden just around the corner from some local shops. And perfect for Park Road. Ideal I'd say." He didn't add that it was where his murdered detective had lived. After all, it was a lovely property. "Enjoy the viewing. Mary, are you going, too?"

"Yes, we've made the appointment for when the children come out from school. So we are all going."

Allison nodded, "Then, I'll be off. I'll see you all later," and he quickly made his escape. He had a number of missed calls. Woodward had been trying to get hold of him and he wanted to talk to him before he got to the station.

Allison stopped in the car park and called Woodward. He didn't want to risk speaking to him in the station. He listened carefully, to everything he'd been told, and thanked Woodward.

"So, what now, Chief?"

"Keep up the surveillance. A couple of bugs have been placed in his office and we'll put a tracker on his car. At the moment, I'm not sure how to move forward. Let's build up a case first." Allison left his vehicle and made his way into Lloyd House. He made straight for his office and grunted his good mornings to his colleagues and Maddie who immediately went to make him some tea.

Allison sat there pondering over the strange way all the cases were linked and led back to the OCG. He opened his drawer and reached for a Mars Bar as he had some serious thinking to do. Maddie popped in and gave him his tea and left just as quietly.

Once he'd savoured the last strand of nougat that had caught on his lips he had decided what to do next. They had Woodward's information and Nesbitt's statements. He needed Josh Linton to come and reveal what he had learnt from Gardener's computer and to hear conversations that had occurred in Gardener's office. He knew they would need to put a tap on the DCC's home phone, and any other communication devices Gardener had. It was not going to be easy. He also needed Pooley to check Gardener's financials and try to track the money trail. Unravelling the links would be a big part of his evidence. Then, he could take the proof against the DCC to the top.

Mark Stringer had picked up Nesbitt from Hilda Goldblum's house and was on his way back to Stone Haven. This was on the orders of the Commissioner, who appreciated the need for secrecy regarding the unidentified safe house because of Angus Mackay. However, now Angus Mackay was dead he saw no need for its use despite Allison's protestations. Nesbitt was to return to complete his training and resettlement and that was the directive.

Nesbitt had said a reluctant goodbye to the two old ladies that had helped him, but he was looking forward to returning to Stone Haven. The sooner he was resettled in Worthing the better. He felt he was being given another chance at a brand-new life and said so.

"This job sounds great. I can't wait. I really can turn my life around."

"Just make sure you don't waste the opportunity," said Mark, nodding. "The chief stuck his neck out for you. Don't let him down."

"I won't," said Nesbitt. "If it wasn't for him, I'd be dead."

They progressed along the main road and turned off onto a by road. A black Range Rover that had been quietly following, a number of cars back, since joining the Hagley Road came into view. Noticing it in his rear-view mirror, Mark frowned. He recognised it as the type of vehicle used by the OCG and became alarmed. This stretch of road in the countryside was notoriously quiet. Mark murmured, "Hold tight!" as he put his foot down and sped off down the narrow country lane. The Range Rover accelerated and gave chase, its more powerful engine easily bringing it right up behind Mark's car. The pursuing car was dangerously close, and Mark knew it intended to ram them and then what?

Mark increased his speed further, his foot flat on the peddle to the floor and screeched around the bends. To his horror, a tractor emerged from a gateway ahead of him and he was forced to slam on his brakes. He skidded on the road surface and the Range Rover crashed into the back of them. The rear of Mark's

BMW concertinaed pushing the front seats onward and setting off the air bags. Nesbitt was propelled forward and hit his head on the side window. Mark smacked his head on the other side and was dazed. He was aware of the front passenger door being wrenched open and Nesbitt being dragged out, before he passed out. Nesbitt was being hauled along the road to the Range Rover. Mark lay slumped in his seat bleeding profusely from his head.

The tractor had stopped at the commotion and the driver jumped down to see what was happening. One of the men holding Nesbitt shouted something to another who strode up the lane with a sawn-off shotgun and fired at the tractor driver, full in the chest, who fell to the ground. The men thrust Nesbitt into their vehicle and reversed back down the lane, spun around at the turning and raced off.

The tractor driver's mate who had been standing alongside the driver in the cab jumped down and stared in horror at the carnage. He rushed to his friend, but it was no good. He was dead. He hurried to the BMW and took out his phone and called 999.

Allison looked grim as he munched his Mars Bar. He had just received the news that Mark had been taken to hospital after being ambushed by two men in a black Range Rover. Worse still. Nesbitt was nowhere to be found and Allison knew the men who had abducted him were unlikely to let him live. He was half expecting a call to come through saying his body had been found and probably tortured. He needed to get his team to find him before it was too late. But first, he wanted to visit Mark and see if he was badly injured. He also needed to speak to Woodward again and then he would find out what Josh Linton and Pooley had discovered about Gardener. It was the usual story, too much to do and not enough man power. Dare he tie up his men with an investigation into one of their own without repercussions? All these thoughts swarmed around Allison's head. But, now, now it was time to get to the hospital and see Mark.

Mark sat up in bed. He was still dazed. He was concussed, badly bruised, with cuts and abrasions, cracked ribs and a dislocated shoulder. Beth was sitting anxiously at his side, holding his hand. She was trying to lift his spirits with more stories of outdated laws and Mark had started to laugh and groaned as he clutched his side, "Please, don't make me laugh. It hurts. It hurts to breathe and laugh."

"Sorry," said Beth flicking a strand of her blonde hair off her face. "I hate seeing you like this. What do you want to do about the weekend?"

"The weekend?"

"We have Christian and Catherine coming to stay. Remember?"

"Of course …Sorry, the concussion has made me somewhat confused. Of course the visit must go ahead. I'm sure I'll be out today they need the bed."

"Don't come out too soon," came the gravelly tones of Allison as he walked into Mark's room. "I need you fit and well."

"Chief!" Mark struggled to sit up straighter and winced and grimaced at the discomfort.

"Beth, talk some sense into him, will you?" growled Allison.

Beth turned her bright green eyes on Allison. "I will, I need him home fit and healthy. The children are coming this weekend."

"Good luck with that," said Allison. "They are lovely little monsters but hard work and a lot of fun."

"He says it as it is," said Beth with a smile. "Things are going really well with the children, and I don't want anything to scupper that." She noticed Allison's serious expression. "Look, I'll get off, I've a lecture in…" She glanced at her watch, "Yikes, I've gotta run." She stood up, and gave Mark a gentle kiss on his cheek. "I'll be back later. Bye Greg." Beth scooped up her college bag and dashed away. Allison took her seat.

He studied his sergeant, "left you in a bit of a mess, didn't they?"

"It could have been worse," said Mark making light of it. "It could have been you."

Allison let a rare grin manifest on his face, "At least, you're still alive."

"Nesbitt?"

"Not so lucky."

"Not dead?"

"We don't know. Haven't a clue where he is but I don't hold out much hope for him."

The sun poured in through the hospital window, where Kelland was being treated. The heat was aggressive leaving him hot, sticky and uncomfortable. He was also in a panic, knowing that he had been targeted, had become a liability and the men after him, would not give up. He needed to get away, needed a change of identity and start again. He had plenty of money stashed away, but needed to access it without being spotted. He knew that his transactions would be spotted and traced. He needed help. He was now regretting not only Kira's death but Paulson's, too. But first, he needed to get out of hospital before someone came to visit and finish the job. He groaned, they would do it carefully, make it look as if it was natural causes, something to stop his heart maybe or a heavy dose of insulin, maybe an injection of air. There were any number of ways to employ and how would he know? How could he tell if they were real medical personnel or not. He needed to get out now and get back to his villa without help but how?

Kelland frowned as a male nurse entered the room and studied his chart. It was no one he recognised. He started to panic. Kelland threw back the thin cover and swung his legs out of bed. The male nurse ordered him in Dominican Spanish to remain in bed, but Kelland replied that he needed to pee and pressed the button to call for assistance. The man moved around towards him just as another nurse arrived that he recognised, who spoke reasonable English. He reiterated his need to pee, and she moved to help him before noticing the other male 'nurse'. There was a rapid interchange between the two of them in Dominican Spanish that Kelland couldn't follow. The 'nurse' looked angry and menacing to Kelland until another member of staff stopped at the door of Kelland's private room. He said something else and walked out.

Kelland asked, "What was that all about?"

"I told him he had no right to be on this floor and to get back to the neo natal unit as his badge said. He said he was just checking out this area as he wanted to transfer. So I told him to go through the proper channels."

"Did you know him?"

"No. he said he'd only recently started. There was something strange about him. He was very rude."

Kelland felt more and more unsafe and knew he had to get out. He might even be forced to speak to the police. That thought did not sit easily with him.

Roy and Alex had their orders. They had received intel on Nesbitt's whereabouts and had been instructed to get him out. That's if he was still alive. The longer time went on, the more likelihood he would be dead.

They had been given an address in Northfield. A large, detached house in Norman Road with a long, curved gravel drive that led to the big house. There were three vehicles parked, all Range Rovers. The question was, how could they get to the house without being spotted, as surprise was key? If they waited until dark it could well be too late, if it wasn't already.

They had driven around the block twice and noted that an Army Cadet Corps building was at the back of the house, which could be very useful. Roy got on the phone. The conversation was short and quick. Roy affirmed various details. He took down a number and began another call.

Alex checked his watch, "Time to go," he said. "The C.O. should be at the gate now." They pulled on their balaclavas and drove around to the main gate. A military looking man marched smartly to the aluminium powder coated gates and opened them up in readiness while Roy parked on the concourse next to a red Mini Cooper. They stepped out and the man waved them through. They walked towards the low bungalow type building where they were met by the Commanding Officer. They exchanged a few words and were led around the side of the building and out to the expanse of green and trees that backed onto Norman Road. They watched from the trees and observed an Eastern European man with a dog walking around the house as if on patrol.

"That's a blow. What about the dog?"

"Difficult."

They continued to observe in silence as Alex took timings of the man taking the circular route around the house. They had been watching for just over fifteen minutes when at the next appearance it was a different man, with no dog.

Alex whispered, "Where's the dog?"

Roy shrugged, "No idea. Let's watch one more round and see if the dog reappears." They waited three minutes, the man strolled into view. Still no dog. "Let's take it as a sign. As soon as he disappears around the side we make our move. Get your gloves on."

Alex nodded as the guard went out of sight, the two MRF officers scrambled through the undergrowth and approached the tall fence. Roy used his heavy canvas gloves to deal with the barbed wire that topped it and leapt over. He darted to the shrubbery, ducked down and waited. Alex followed. "What now?"

"We're going in blind. But, we have surprise on our side. If we can get to the back gate we can restrain the watchman as he comes around and silence him. Backup is on its way. You tackle the guard, once that's done we'll find a way in." Alex nodded and threw his gloves down in the shrubbery.

They waited. The man came into view. He stopped to light a cigarette and puffed, drawing the smoke deep into his lungs. The man looked Eastern European; he began to stroll slowly towards the side of the house. Alex was quick, and silent as he left the cover of the bushes and leapt onto the man's back and floored him knocking the wind out of him. He sat on him, pushed the man's face down into the grass and held his neck, his fingers spanning the man's scrawny neck and pressed on both sides. His fingers found the carotid artery either side and he applied pressure for eight seconds and the man blacked out. He knew he didn't have long. Quickly, he cable tied the guard's hands behind his back and his feet. He taped the man's mouth and began to drag him towards the bushes as the man began to stir. The guard began to struggle but Alex was too strong. Roy darted out and helped him drag the man to the shrubbery, where they secured him to the wire fence hidden from view. It was now time to move.

With knees bent they crept towards the house and laid themselves flat against the wall before side stepping along it and ducking down under the windows. They came to a side door and tried it. It was open and they slipped inside. They heard a shriek of agony coming from below and headed warily towards the sound, through the utility and into the kitchen where there was a door leading down to a cellar.

Filled with adrenaline and trepidation, they started down the stairs to a gloomy looking basement with a single lightbulb hanging down. There was a chair underneath it and in it was Nesbitt, bound tightly. A bench was at his side with various implements laid out and two thugs, were working him over. One of them switched on a searchlight and shone it straight in his eyes, which had been taped open. Roy signalled to Alex, and they hurtled down the last three steps and each took one of the men.

Taken by surprise they were easily subdued, bound and secured. The men were bundled into a corner and their mouths taped up. Alex hurriedly dashed to Nesbitt and turned him away from the searchlight and cut his bonds. He helped him to his feet, which didn't seem to work properly. The tape was removed from his eyes, and he was at last able to blink, but his face was a mess. His chest and arms were covered in cuts and abrasions as if he'd been hauled along gravel. He was bleeding profusely.

"Come on, we need to get you out of here."

"Who are you?" mumbled Nesbitt.

"Never mind that now. How many men are there?" said Alex quickly.

"I'm not sure. Two down here, a couple of guards. Maybe more."

"Can you walk?" Nesbitt nodded. "Stick close to us."

Alex thrust Nesbitt between the two of them and gingerly they made their way up the stairs. They could hear voices in the kitchen and pressed themselves against the wall and tried to listen, but the voices were too indistinct, and they only caught odd words. Then, there was quiet. Roy signalled again and they moved to the top of the stairs.

They slipped out into the kitchen and through the side door. Alex helped Nesbitt who could only hobble and eventually said, "Get on my back. I'll carry you. I can move more quickly." There was a shout from the house and three men came running after them followed by the large dog that barked and began to chase them. As they approached the shrubbery, sirens were heard, which stopped the men in their tracks, but the dog kept coming.

Alex released Nesbitt to the ground and he and Roy stepped in front of him protectively, as the dog approached, its hackles raised, its lips curled in a snarl with a deep, threatening rumbling in its throat.

Roy raised his hand authoritatively and gestured for the dog to be still and to lie down. He said firmly "Platz!"

Alex stared in awe as the German Shepherd went quiet and lay down in front of them. "How did you do that?" he gasped.

"Dog handling course. I trained with the unit. So, I was banking on the training and instructions to be the same or similar. I wasn't sure it would work. But, we can't move. We have to stay put until the dog is called off by its handler but at least it shouldn't attack unless we make any sudden movements."

Armed Response Officers poured into the garden and house. One of them, was pushing one of the thugs before him and forced him to call off his dog, which came running back to his side. The officer had a catchpole to restrain the animal and Alex heaved a sigh of relief as the canine and his handler were marched away.

"Now what?"

Roy took out his phone and dialled a number. "An ambulance is on the way. Let's get out and back to the car."

They were met by the officer in charge. "MRF?" Roy assented. "This Nesbitt?" He nodded.

"What about the gang?"

"All rounded up and we got more than we bargained for."

"What do you mean?"

"We found twelve Eastern European women locked in a room. They are being freed and taken to the station."

"More ammunition against the owner."

The officer grunted and stared at them both uncomfortably. "I know you have to keep your identity secret. It's just a bit disconcerting seeing the balaclavas, you understand?"

Roy nodded. "We'll just make sure he gets safely into the ambulance."

The officer nodded, "Understood. This way."

Allison stared at his Mars Bar. "Not another change," he grumbled. They had messed about with them so much through the years. They had started off at just 51 grams and increased to its chunkiest at 65.5 in the 1990s. They were the most satisfying then. Of course, 2002 they made them smaller with less nougat and thinner chocolate under the excuse that they wanted people to eat healthier. What ever happened to, 'a Mars a day helps you work, rest, and play'? Although, he thought shamefully, he would never be satisfied with just one a day. They were smaller now and they had changed the logo on the paper. Allison didn't like change; but then the plastic in the wrapper was being taken out so it was better for the environment. "Bugger it," he said aloud as he tore off the wrapper and bit into his treat. He had hated when there was a shortage of Mars Bars and he'd been forced to buy a different chocolate treat. In his view nothing was as satisfying as a Mars. He munched. He was finding it tough to limit himself to three a day. However, he had to admit it was having an effect on his waistline. His trousers had dropped down a size. Things were looking good for getting into a morning suit for Cally's wedding and he was feeling fitter.

He stared at his in-tray as Pooley knocked and entered. "Chief, Nesbitt's safe. He's been checked over in hospital and we are taking him back to Hilda's until we decide what to do."

"Yes, and keep that under your hat."

"Sir," and Pooley left.

Allison rubbed his bristly chin and was left alone with his thoughts. 'What the hell was going on?' He just knew everything had been linked. For once, he was grateful for the help of the MRF, and he never thought he'd say that. They had foiled the OCG and caused them a lot of pain. They had rounded up most of the gang but more elusive was Jeremy Patterson and the deputy chief constable. That was going to be trickier than a basket of rattle snakes tipped at his feet. How were they going to get to him? He hoped his sergeant, Mark, would be well enough to come back soon and they could work on a plan together. Meanwhile, he would gather as much information as he could on Deputy Chief Constable Nigel Gardener. He was going down.

# AUTHOR THANKS

MANY THANKS FOR READING THE seventh of the *DCI Greg Allison Crime Thrillers*. If you have a little time, I would appreciate a review. I really value my readers' thoughts about a book. It often helps me craft future stories. They are vital for indie authors like me.

You are welcome to contact me at elizabeth@elizabethrevill.com or visit the website: www.elizabethrevill.com

****

I have free stories for you as well, all I'd like in exchange is your email address and you can unsubscribe at any time.

The first is called *Dead or Alive* just follow the link.

I'd like to keep in touch. Either via the newsletter, I'll send out once a month, or you can join my Facebook page: Elizabeth Revill. If you join either, there will be notifications of new stories, releases of covers and the occasional giveaway and special deals just for you. There will also be an opportunity to join my *Advanced Reader Team*.

# OTHER TITLES BY ELIZABETH REVILL

**DCI Allison Thrillers:**
Killing me Softly
Prayer for the Dying
God Only Knows
Would I Lie To You?
Windows For The Dead
Dead Eyes Opened
Mother's Not Dead

**Llewellyn Family Saga:**
Whispers on the Wind
Shadows on the Moon
Rainbows in the Clouds
Thunder in the Sun

Against the Tide
Turn of the Tide

The Electra Conspiracy Part 1
The Electra Conspiracy Part 2

**Stand Alone Novels:**

Sanjukta and the Box of Souls

The Forsaken And The Damned

Web of Fear

*The Dreamtime of the Artful Dodger* with Norman Eshley

**Children's book**

And an illustrated children's book *The Secret of Gidon*